DOUBLE

TROUBLE

{Book 2 of the Final Option Trilogy}

A
CARIBBEAN
MURDER/MYSTERY

JOHN
ANDERSEN

AUTHOR'S NOTE

Some of the events and references in this book were the subject of the first book in the series. I have attempted to give an abridged version of these events where necessary. However, I will not include any spoilers which will take away from the original book. For a more detailed version, please see Book 1 of the 'Final Option' trilogy.

OTHER BOOKS BY THE AUTHOR

The Final Option (Bahamas)
Book 1 of the Trilogy

This book is once again dedicated to my wife, Suzanne,
and also to several good friends, who for reasons of their own, wish to remain anonymous.
Thank you for the help, expertise and encouragement you gave me,
and for keeping me on track throughout this project.
My wife, as usual, did a superb job in keeping the facts straight
and the story flowing during her proofreading of the drafts of this book.
That being said, any mistakes the reader may find,
I acknowledge are mine and mine alone.

Any comments, encouragement or criticisms can be left on the author's page
at goodreads.com or the reviews page at amazon.com
I check them on a regular basis.

Present Day

It was the smell that finally woke him. On impulse, he opened his eyes and was met by a blinding, stabbing pain that caused him to close them again immediately. He lay still for a long while in the not-quite darkness of his closed eyelids before tentatively easing just one open to a slit. The pain was not quite as bad this time but it was augmented by the little elves with the big sledgehammers making small rocks out of big rocks in his brain. With that one eye open just a smidgeon he was able to see the cause of the smell which had awoken him. He was lying in a puddle of vomit. It was his own, he presumed, if for no other reason than the chorus of anvils going off in his head.

'Oh, no,' he thought. *'Not again.'* Presumably, he had tried once again, unsuccessfully, to drink someone under the table the previous night as he had tried in Key West, only to be suffering similar consequences this morning.

He rolled over to his right, away from the source of the smell, but his stomach rebelled. The final remnants remaining in his stomach of what must have been his last meal were forcibly ejected from his body to form another puddle in the sand.

'God, I hope it tasted better going down than it did coming up.'

He slowly struggled into an upright seated position, trying to ignore the merry-go-round racing through his skull. He managed to pull his feet closer to his butt, rested his forearms on his knees and gratefully lowered his throbbing head onto the back of his arms. He sat like that for a long time, eyes closed, rocking gently, letting the salt-tinged ocean breeze try its best to sober him up. When he finally regained some semblance of equilibrium, he lifted his head and cautiously opened his eyes.

He was seated on a small crescent of beach a few yards above the high water mark, between two puddles of what used to be the contents of his stomach. He slid, on his butt, a couple of yards toward the water to try to escape the smell of his own making. He noticed for the first time that the smell was not receding because it was plastered all over the front of his once-white T-shirt. With some difficulty, he managed to pull the T-shirt over his pounding head and then he threw it forcefully toward the water.

He felt better. Well enough, in fact, to try to regain his feet. It proved to be a struggle, but when he finally managed to straighten out, he slowly turned a full circle trying to ascertain his whereabouts. Apart from the ocean, he seemed to be completely encircled by house-sized granite boulders that appeared to be tumbling down upon the narrow strip of sand, even into the water at each end of the beach.

'The Baths,' he thought. 'On Virgin Gorda. This must be the beach at Devil's Bay. Now, how the hell did I get here?'

Slowly, for he did not wish to disturb the tranquil waters within his brain that might start swirling again with the slightest provocation, he looked down at himself. He saw a fairly muscular upper body with a flat stomach, a pair of tan six pocket boating shorts, no belt and no shoes. The latter didn't bother him much since he had spent years of his life walking around barefoot.

'Now how did I know that?' he thought.

Inside the waistband of the shorts, he felt underwear, slightly damp with seawater, as the salty taste on his fingertips told him. His pockets were also a little damp, as was the side of the shorts upon which he had been lying. There was, unfortunately, no wallet, no ID, no credit cards, no folding money, and not even any change.

He suddenly heard distant voices growing steadily louder, so he turned slowly and spied in the shallow water his discarded T-shirt. Feeling semi-dressed, despite the fact that he was on a beach, he was determined to reclaim his only other piece of clothing.

With infinite care and holding his head with both hands to stop it from jostling, he made his way to the waterline. He waded the few feet into the water to the sodden scrap of material, and gingerly, keeping his back straight and bending his knees, picked it up.

He was gratified to discover that the immersion into the salt water had washed most of the vomit off the front of the T-shirt. He also noticed the outline of a motor yacht printed in the upper left corner of the material right above the words 'Final Option'.

'Now why does that seem familiar?' he wondered.

Turning slowly, he walked back up the beach, feeling a little steadier now. He sought out, and found, a small shaded spot amongst the jumbled boulders. Placing his T-shirt on a piece of sunlit rock to dry, he lay down on the beach to finish the recuperation process.

As the voices were quite loud now, children's as well as adult voices, he silently wished for a magic knob to turn down the ever increasing volume. His hands involuntarily covered his ears, and his eyes screwed shut as the shrieks from half a dozen young children discovered the beach that the boulders had, until now, hidden from their view.

He curled himself into a fetal position and, hidden from the thirty or so people on the beach behind his granite boulder, tried to shake off the hangover he was fighting. Surprisingly, he fell into a deep sleep quite quickly, since the water in which the children were now playing was muffling the noise of their exuberance.

He awoke in the middle of the afternoon, opening his eyes to a tiny, blond girl who was squatting in the sand not two feet from his face, her right arm extended and one finger poking him on the nose. She was staring at him intently. Such a suddenly unexpected sight caused him to move his head backward and as he did, he cracked it on the rock behind him. He saw stars and, once again, the elves with their big sledgehammers inside his head started up their pounding.

"Are you OK, Mister?" the little imp wanted to know. "I didn't mean to startle you."

"Yes, sweetie, I'm OK. I just didn't know you were there." He reached his hand to the back of his head, and felt a sizable knot had formed there, far out of proportion to the slight blow he had just taken.

"AMY!!" The anxious call of a searching father came from behind the boulder.

"I'm here, Daddy." the little blond called back.

The man who hurried around the boulder was in his mid-to-late twenties, tall and obviously very fit. He snatched up the child with one arm and demanded, "What are you doing with my little girl?"

"Nothing, sir. I've been asleep right here since before all of you arrived. Your little girl came up to me while I was asleep."

"*Really?*"

"Daddy, I saw him from the water and he wasn't moving. I just wanted to make sure he was OK. Please put me down, you're hurting me." The little girl was squirming in his arms.

The father looked as if he wanted to kill, but he released his daughter, who muttered, "Sorry, Mister, I'm glad you're OK," before scurrying off back down to the water.

"*Are* you OK?" The father wanted to know.

"Sure, just bumped my head when your daughter startled me. I'll be all right."

The father turned and followed his daughter after the warning, "Just stay the hell away from us!"

A short while later, he collected his now dry T-shirt and put it on. He made his way out onto the beach and found the trail leading to the intricate passages and grottos in amongst the huge granite boulders, stacked one upon another, which made up the National Park known as The Baths. Squeezing his way through the small triangular openings between boulders, he slid down a slippery sand-covered slope barely aided by a rope set on pitons in the side of the rock. He waded through the knee deep pools of seawater between forty foot boulders, and agonizingly traversed the narrow uphill climb, and he finally made it to the restaurant at the top of the hill. This was where the buses from the pier dropped off the tourists who had come across the Sir Francis Drake Passage on the ferry from the cruise ships berthed in Road Town, Tortola.

'Now what,' he thought. *'No money or ID, how am I going to get to Road Town?'*

Just then, he heard a shout behind him. "Hello, wait up."

He turned and saw hurrying toward him the father from the beach, a beautiful woman whom he assumed to be the man's wife, and between them, holding their hands, was the little imp, resplendent in her bright patterned sundress.

"I'm glad I caught you," the man said. "I just wanted to apologize to you for earlier on. I came on way too strong, and I'm sorry to have given you any grief. I am just so worried these days about my little girl."

"I can understand that."

He extended his hand, "I'm Bill, this is my wife, Caroline, and you know Amy."

"Bill, Caroline, and Amy. Pleased to meet you under better circumstances. I'm Jack." He didn't know where the name had come from and he hoped that it was correct. It just seemed to him that it was the way he had always introduced himself. He extended his hand to Bill and Caroline, and then Amy tore herself loose from her mother's grip and solemnly shook his hand, too.

"Hello, Mister Jack," she said. "I'm glad to see you feeling better. Where are your shoes?"

In that charming way that children have, changing subjects in the middle of a single statement, Amy had put her finger directly on the problem facing Jack in his immediate future. He put on his brightest smile, and knelt down to her level.

"Hi again, Amy. Well, you see, I don't know where my shoes are, or my wallet," he glanced quickly in Bill's direction. "I think someone must have taken them while I was asleep."

"It wasn't me!" she cried, a little fear in her eyes.

"Of course it wasn't. It happened long before you came to the beach, and besides, take a look at how much bigger my feet are than yours. You could never fit in those shoes. You would look like one of those circus clowns with the big floppy shoes if you tried to wear them." Jack was pleased to see the fear disappear right out of her eyes, to be replaced a split second later by a huge

9

grin as her imagination supplied her with the image of herself in clown shoes.

"Your wallet is gone?" Bill seemed concerned. "I've heard that sometimes things have a tendency to disappear from places where tourists go, wallets, money, even cameras and cell phones, but shoes? That's a new one."

"I'm not really concerned about the wallet or the money in it, but my ID and credit cards and my ferry ticket were in it, and now I have no way to get back to Road Town. Unless I get lucky and can hitch a ride with someone going back for free." Jack feigned helplessness.

"Don't worry about it. Just hang around with us; you can be Amy's Uncle Jack. They don't check the tickets that closely on the way back, but if they do catch you, just explain the situation to them. What can they do? Put you off at the next port of call?" Bill smiled hugely at his own witticism, turned to Caroline for approval, which was granted by a nod of the head, and finished with, "but if necessary I'll buy you a ticket."

"Thank you. I mean that sincerely. I haven't been thinking too clearly all day." Jack was being totally honest, and was quite surprised by the man's generosity toward a stranger, especially considering that a few hours before he had almost accused Jack of child molestation. Jack suspected that the reversal had something to do with Caroline, who did not seem surprised or put off by Jack's easy going manner with Amy.

It was only a short ten minute wait for the bus which would take them to the ferry terminal. The time was spent pleasantly with Jack quizzing Amy about her vacation and her schoolwork.

Together they boarded the bus as a family group and it was only when they were on their way that Bill asked, "So, Jack, are you going back to your boat?"

Caught off guard, Jack stammered, "Yes. Yes, of course. How did you know?"

"It's there on your T-shirt, 'Final Option'. We saw her at the marina in Road Town when our cruise ship docked. You know, she is a really beautiful boat, even Caroline commented on that, and she is not into boats as much as I am. Someday I hope to have a boat like that to live on, but I don't think I could ever afford one that size. What is she, around seventy feet?"

"Yes."

"What brand?"

"Neptunus." Once more the answer sprang to his lips before he had a chance to think about it.

"I don't suppose there is a chance of taking a look at her when we dock?" Bill asked hopefully. Caroline and Amy had been listening to the conversation and both looked on with anticipation.

Jack, always the impulsive type, jumped in with both feet. "Sure, as soon as we dock, we can walk over and take a look. Sure hope I left it in decent shape; I wouldn't want to disappoint you."

The trip from Virgin Gorda to Road Town took about forty five minutes and before they knew it, the ferry was sliding into the dock next to the huge cruise ship that was Bill, Caroline and Amy's temporary home and transportation. Full of anticipation, Jack's three guests followed him past the cruise ship to the marina on the opposite side of the harbor. Jack made a show of walking up to the locked security gate, and rattling it.

"Something must be up," he said. "This gate is usually open. Obviously, since my wallet is gone, I don't have my swipe card anymore, so I'll have to walk to the office to get a new one. Why don't you guys wait here on the bench and I'll be back shortly. OK, Amy?"

"OK, Uncle Jack."

It took Jack only two minutes to get to the dockmaster's office and as he walked in, he was greeted with, "Good afternoon, Mr. Elliott, how can I help you today?"

Jack took a chance. "Unfortunately, I was mugged today and all my ID, credit cards, and money were taken, including the swipe card for the gate. Can I get a new one?"

"Of course, sir. It'll just take a second." With that he grabbed a blank card from the drawer, swiped it through the register and with a flourish, handed it to Jack. "Anything else I can do for you?"

"I've forgotten. Did I leave a spare key to my boat here in the office?"

"Yes, you must have, since it's a requirement. We might have to get into your boat while you are gone, in case of fire or sinking, you know what I mean? Or in a situation like this, since I presume they stole your keys, too, right?"

"Yes, exactly for a situation like this."

"OK, let's see. Jack Elliott, 'Final Option', that's Slip A44, aha, there you go, sir, your key and alarm fob. Anything else I can help you with?"

"No, I think you've helped me enough for now, and I thank you."

As he exited the building, Jack did not notice the dockmaster pick up the phone and dial a local number. A few seconds later, he said, "He's here."

Jack retraced his steps to the locked gate where his new-found friends waited for him. He waved the new swipe card as he approached and they joined him at the gate as Jack swiped them all inside. Jack walked confidently up to 'A' dock and led them to Slip 44. He could see their anticipation building the closer they got to the big yacht.

As he walked past the yacht toward the boarding ladder, all the details of the boat came flooding back. He knew the boat intimately, all the cabins, what was in the galley, and where every instrument and light switch was located. He led them onto the boat, back to the aft deck, disabled the alarm system, which appeared to already be disengaged, and opened the aft main salon door.

As they entered, he switched on the lights and the beauty and simplicity of the salon shone brightly. Jack remembered the time and effort that had gone into the new design of this cabin and was justifiably proud of it, and from the dropped jaws and instant smiles on the faces of his guests, he felt that he had hit the ball out of the park. The three of them walked around, touching and admiring; even Amy seemed overwhelmed.

Jack spent almost an hour with his new friends showing them the wonders of his floating home, finishing the tour with drinks for the adults and apple juice for Amy. Sooner than anyone wished, it was time for them to rejoin their cruise ship for their journey home. Bill handed Jack his business card before he left, which had a Wellington, Palm Beach address and phone number on it, and asked him to come see them when Jack returned to the States. Jack promised that he would.

Looking forward to a hot shower and a change of clothes, Jack waved to his guests as they proceeded down the dock toward the shore. Just before they reached the end, they stepped aside to allow a well-dressed gentleman to pass. Jack was about to turn away, but something about the man made him stay and watch as he walked determinately toward him. The man was tall, easily as tall as Jack, but rail thin and pasty white. His suit was immaculate, but the bow tie was somewhat incongruous. It was the look of utter seriousness on his face that made Jack wait as he approached.

"Mr. Jack Elliott?" The accent was pure English, straight out of Downton Abbey.

"That is correct."

"Please allow me to introduce myself. I am Chief Inspector Ian Cavendish of the British Virgin Islands Police Force. If I may have a moment of your time, I wish to speak to you on a matter of some urgency."

"Can this wait till I have had a shower and changed into something more comfortable? As you can see, I am somewhat filthy at the moment."

The man considered this for a few seconds, then said, "As long as I can wait comfortably inside, I don't see where that would be a problem."

"Then, welcome aboard. Make yourself at home in the salon. Help yourself to a drink, if you wish. I won't be but a few minutes."

Jack went below into the main cabin, quickly undressed and showered and changed into tan Chinos and a light blue, short sleeved shirt and slipped into a pair of well worn boat shoes. He felt a whole lot better, but wondered what the Chief Inspector would want with him.

As he climbed the stairs, Jack called out, "OK, sir, I am now clean and at your disposal. How can I help you?"

The Chief Inspector actually smiled as Jack entered the salon. "Have a seat, Mr. Elliott. We have a matter to discuss."

Jack sat in a chair across from the sofa upon which the Chief Inspector had seated himself.

"First, can you tell me where you took this boat last night when you left the marina around ten thirty, and when did you return?"

Jack was stunned. He had no idea that the boat had been out the previous night. "I don't know, Inspector, I don't remember anything about last night. All I can remember is that this morning, I woke up with a terrible hangover on the beach at Devil's Bay on Virgin Gorda, and it has taken me all day to get back here."

"Chief Inspector, if you please. Can you tell me where your wallet and ID are?"

"I have no idea. All I know is that they are missing, along with my shoes. I have to assume that sometime last night I was mugged."

"And you have no idea where or by whom?"

"No. I have no recollection of anything that happened last night. I must have been so drunk that I passed out."

"Is there anyone who can verify that you were on Virgin Gorda this morning?"

"Yes, the couple and their child who passed you when you were on the dock were the ones who found me on the beach and helped me back here to the boat."

"Do you have their names and address?"

"Sure, that is his business card there on the table. After I finished showing them my boat, he asked me to come see them when I get back to the States."

"And where are they staying here in Tortola?"

"They are not. They are on that cruise ship just leaving now." Jack pointed out the salon window.

"Well, that *is* regrettable. It means that I will have to do what I came to do originally, at least until we can establish an alibi for you."

"Alibi? Why would I need an alibi. What did you come here to do?"

"Mr. Elliott, I have come here to arrest you for murder. You have the right to remain silent......"

"Murder? You have got to be kidding me! Who am I supposed to have murdered?"

"Why, your fiancée, Shannon O'Loughlin, Mr. Elliott. Your wallet was found right under her strangled body this morning."

Chapter 1

Three months earlier.

"Well, look here. This is interesting." Shannon waved the letter she had just opened in Jack's direction. Shannon and Jack were sitting at the navigation table in the pilothouse of 'Final Option' with their breakfast coffee and muffins in front of them. She had just gotten around to opening yesterday's mail.

"What do you have there?" Jack's face was buried in a travel guide to the British Virgin Islands, making plans for their upcoming cruise to the Caribbean.

"It's an invitation to Sean and Katie's Christmas Eve party. Do you want to go?" Shannon was nodding her head as she spoke, indicating that she definitely wanted to go.

Finally distracted, he looked up from his book. "Of course we'll go. Why would I not want to go to my best friend's party? Besides that, you know Sean's parties are all out, and he'll probably take over his whole club for us."

"Well, that's the interesting thing. It stipulates that the party is black tie, and it will be held at your parents' house." She raised her eyebrows in confusion.

"That *is* interesting. I don't think that has ever happened before." His brow furrowed and he appeared deep in thought. "I wonder what it could mean."

"We are still going to the party, right? I mean, I haven't even met your father yet, and we've been together for ten months now. You aren't ashamed of him, are you?"

"No, of course not. I just haven't yet found the right reason to go over to their house. You know that whatever time we choose to go over, the chances are that Rain and her sleazy ambulance-chasing, attorney boyfriend would be there. Maybe this is the perfect excuse, since other people are going to be there, to take you over to meet him."

"So, do you want me to RSVP to Sean and let him know that we are coming? We do owe your parents a dinner, you know. We never did go over there before our little adventure in the Bahamas. And we did promise your mother that we would come."

"You're right. Seems to me to be perhaps the best way to kill two birds with one stone."

The previous summer, Shannon, who was five and a half feet tall, with straight, auburn brunette hair normally worn in a ponytail that reached down to her lower back, her slim figure augmented by adequate, but not excessive, curves in all the right places, and Jack, her boyfriend and owner of the yacht upon which they lived together, along with many of their friends, had succeeded in locating a sunken Nazi submarine carrying $220 million in gold. Their subsequent retrieval of the gold had earned them a fifteen percent finder's fee from the government; money the whole group could live on, in moderation, for the rest of their lives without having to earn a living. They finished their breakfast and retired to the main salon, which was now much more comfortable and livable since their redesign of the interior of the boat.

Together they had woven their common sense, Jack's practicality and Shannon's until now unrealized flair for color and comfort into an award-winning living space, which they now enjoyed together. The vessel upon which they lived was a Neptunus 70 foot cruising yacht, which Jack had named 'Final Option' when he had bought her after his divorce. To him, the name was full of meaning and maybe a little prophetic.

Practical to the bone, he thought that she was a thing of bewitching beauty, 70 feet of solid, practically bulletproof fiberglass, with a beam of 21 feet and a semi displacement hull which drew only 5 feet of water, an important requirement for cruising in the shallow waters of the Bahamas.

17

She was definitely not a go-fast boat, as so many South Florida boats are. Her twin Caterpillar C32 - 1450 horsepower engines were capable of pushing her along at a top speed of 33 knots but most of the time she would lope along quite happily at 10-12 knots and at 9 knots her 1850 gallons of diesel fuel, supplemented by the new 500 gallon tank, gave her a range of well over 2200 nautical miles, which was sufficient to cross the Atlantic, when it eventually became necessary.

The subsequent reconstruction of the boat by Bradford's Shipyards had been a huge job after the damage caused by the adventure from the past year. Unfortunately it had been a necessary complication to their lives, and had just recently been completed to everyone's satisfaction.

Sitting side by side on the plush sofa, Shannon reached for the remote for the TV, but was stopped in mid-reach by Jack, who looked into her eyes and asked rather shyly, "Would you want to marry me, Shannon?"

Obviously startled, a sly grin formed on her face. Squinting at him and twisting her mouth sideways, she said, "Would I marry you? Now that's an interesting question. All right, let's see how this stacks up. Would I, a beautiful, ultra sexy, 29 year old woman, want to utterly destroy my chances to meet a handsome movie star, or super sexy athlete, or maybe even an old Palm Beach multi-millionaire with one foot in the grave and the other firmly planted on a banana peel? Would I want to give up all those possibilities for a middle aged man with a multitude of faults, who, while admittedly good looking and somewhat desirable, doesn't even know how to ask the right question?"

She raised her eyebrows while looking directly into Jack's eyes, who sat there looking perplexed. He thought for a few seconds until the light bulb finally switched on in his mind, and it showed visibly on his face.

"OK. Will you marry me, Shannon?"

"Yes." Not a trace of hesitation or concern showed in her answer.

Moving closer to her, he pulled a small black velvet box out of his pocket and with obvious relief, he said, "Excellent. Now I won't have to return this to the jewelers."

He opened the box and presented Shannon with a 4 karat, perfectly cut, blue-white diamond, set in an exquisite platinum and gold ring of his own design. He watched her already beautiful face light up with love and affection. With gentle care, he took it from the box, reached for her hand, which was willingly extended, and slipped it on her ring finger. It fit perfectly, as he knew it would, since he had taken one of the few rings she owned to the jewelers with him in order to get the right size.

"Thank you, Jack. The ring is gorgeous; I will be proud to be your wife, and I promise, I will do everything in my power to keep us together for the rest of our lives."

"Damn, here I was, hoping for a few good years and then on to a newer model." It was a good thing he was smiling when he said it; otherwise Shannon would have been a widow before becoming a wife, if that was even possible. She just grabbed the front of his shirt, pulled him down on top of her and started kissing him as if there were no tomorrow.

Naturally, after a while, Jack rose and locked the door to the main salon. He then offered his hand to his new fiancée and they retired to their main cabin, not to be seen again until the next morning.

Dawn arrived at about the correct time for that time of the year. Since daylight savings time had ended some months ago, it was still dark when they got up every day and nightfall arrived far too soon. For die-hard South Floridians, all would have agreed that there was also a decided chill which could be detected in the air; but naturally, the snowbirds from up north would have laughed at that notion.

Against all the odds of it happening, it was Jack who was up first and well into his winter-modified routine of stretching and exercise by the time Shannon rolled out of bed. Normally, it was she, being a morning person, who would have risen first, but as usual, her first stop was the coffee pot where she fixed herself a huge ceramic mug of the eye opener. She then wandered slowly into the main salon, turned on the TV, and sat down to watch the weather report for the upcoming week.

The news was decidedly not good, in fact, it was downright horrible. Another intense cold front was due to hit in a few hours time bringing with it buckets of rain and cold temperatures, into the thirties in some inland sections, and strong, gusty winds. Small craft warnings were out up and down the coast from Jacksonville all the way to Key West. Twenty-to-twenty five foot waves were forecast for the Gulf Stream, and ten-to-fifteen feet near the coast. Unless you owned a cruise ship or an aircraft carrier, the advice was to stay home, which was exactly what Jack and Shannon had planned to do. For the more land-oriented population of South Florida, there were multiple warnings about the risk of flooding in low lying areas, which naturally most of Florida was, the highest point in the state being Britton Hill which was only 312 feet above sea level and was all the way up in the Florida Panhandle. Drivers of high sided vehicles were warned about the risk of torrential rain and abnormally high winds especially on bridges, causeways, and other exposed stretches of open road. Their prospects of spending an enjoyable week doing the things they loved to do outdoors looked dismal, at best.

Jack came into the salon from the aft deck, having completed his much abbreviated morning run. He was dressed from hoodie to toe in the thickest fleece he could find and was still shivering uncontrollably. He had even donned a pair of thinsulate ski gloves from one of the infrequent ski trips to Colorado and Utah that he used to take with his wife before their divorce.

His face lit up like a beacon when he saw Shannon sitting there in her thickest robe, with that huge mug, which could almost be described as a bucket, of steaming hot coffee.

"I sure hope you left some for me, love," He pulled the hoodie down and headed for the galley. "I bet I need that coffee more than you do. It's damn well freezing out there." Jack managed to get out between his chattering teeth.

"I don't understand why you continue to torture yourself trying to stick to your routine when it's this cold. You are going to kill yourself or at least, lose some fingers or toes to frostbite." Shannon, warm in her robe inside the heated boat, smirked as she gently ribbed him for his obsessive behavior.

"Just because you have a metabolism that is always going a thousand miles a minute, don't assume everyone else does. I would hate for you to end up with a fat husband. Besides, if something were to happen to me you would be able to visit the best looking corpse in the mortuary." Jack had always envied Shannon's ability to eat copious amounts of food without gaining an ounce, and all without having to perform any unnecessary exercise. Between dancing, swimming and scuba diving, and just living on a boat with its constant motion, seemed to be enough exercise to keep her figure trim, just the way Jack liked it.

He came back to her with his own mug of coffee, sat down beside her and leaned over to give her a big, loving kiss and a hug, although it was more for his benefit than hers. "So, what are our plans for the week, other than being snowed in, I mean?" he asked.

"Don't really know. You could call Sean and Katie; see if they want to go play some pool, if they are as bored as we are. That would take care of today, at least." Shannon was not quite as good as either Jack or Sean at pool, and only a little better than Katie, but she won her fair share of matches, especially those where she didn't get frustrated. She was at her best when they played couples with Sean and Katie.

"That's a great idea. We do need to get out and socialize. Don't know about you, but I got ten text messages from various friends wanting to know where we were yesterday. I didn't know what to tell them, so I just said we were busy, because I didn't want to give the game away."

"What game?" Shannon seemed a little puzzled.

"Well, our engagement, of course. I suspect you will want to let everyone know in your own time."

"You are right. Thanks for that." One of the things Shannon appreciate the most about Jack was his obsessive passion of always making sure that she was given the choice in everything they did together, and as many options as possible in all of the courses of action they were contemplating. It was called consideration for others and these days it seemed to be lacking in many people.

Jack picked up his cell phone and hit Sean's picture in the list of contacts. It was answered by Sean on the first ring. "I don't know how you knew I was about to call you, but I guess great minds think alike."

"And small minds seldom differ. How are you doing?"

"Bored, and trying to think of something to do."

Sean sounded as frustrated as Jack felt. "We were thinking of coming over and playing pool at your club. We haven't been around there for quite a while and I'm feeling a mite rusty. Besides that, you sound as bored as I feel, and it would be good to see you guys again. What do you think?"

"Sounds like a plan to me. Around noontime then, I'll bring Katie, too. Maybe we could play couples."

"I should certainly hope so."

"See you then."

Jack put down the phone and picked up the TV remote, selected recorded programs and found a Rick Steves' travelogue on the Amalfi Coast in Italy, then leaned back into the comfortable sofa. Shannon crept closer and put her head on his shoulder and snuggled in tight. They actually managed to watch a few minutes of the program before Jack's wandering hand found itself between Shannon's robe and her bare body. Travelling upward, the hand discovered that she had not yet had the time, nor the inclination, to put on a bra, which was just fine with him.

"Is there time?" she wanted to know.

"Of course there is. Noontime normally falls anywhere between 11 a.m. and 1 p.m., and it is not even nine yet." He assured her. "Besides, you know Sean and Katie will wait for us if we're late."

"You are being Mister Macho again, huh. I guarantee you it won't take that long if I have anything to say about it."

"And you always do, don't you?"

Laughing, he went and checked that the door was locked, came back and lifted her up into his arms and carried her to the stairs leading downward into the lower deck. There he put her down gently onto her feet and followed her closely down the stairs to their stateroom. Once there, she untied the belt on her robe, shrugged it off her shoulders and let it drop to the floor. Jack had more than a little trouble shedding all of the fleece that he was wearing, but, as usual, she turned out to be a very willing helper to a very willing subject. As soon as they were both naked, the two of them slipped into bed and pulled the sheets up over their heads in hurried anticipation.

"Where's your ring?" inquired Jack when they were finally leaving for their date, a few hours later.

"I left it in the safe. You know I very rarely wear any jewelry, except on special occasions, and that ring, while it is absolutely stunning and I love it, is not for everyday wear. Besides, it would give the game away before I'm ready to make the announcement. I'll wear it to the Christmas party, though, since I believe that would be the best place to let everyone know what is happening to us, don't you think?"

"Sounds like a perfect plan to me. Apparently, all our friends are going to be there and my parents, if they knew, would absolutely love it. Now, let's get going if we're going, or they will send out a search party for us."

As it turned out, they were only barely fifteen minutes late, well within the bounds of respectability, and managed to make it under the cover of the marquee of the club before the deluge started. They were greeted just inside the door of the Four Leaf Clover by an old friend, Kevin, who was the club's bouncer.

"Good afternoon, Mr. Elliott, Ms. O'Loughlin. Sean and Katie are in the pool room at the back and asked me to tell you to go straight through."

"Hi, Kevin. I thought I had made it perfectly clear to you that I wanted you to address me as Jack, not Mr. Elliott, who as you well know, is my father." Jack admonished him, jokingly.

"Yes, sir, you did, but I have a difficult time with that, sir. It doesn't really matter how long you have been coming here, you are still a customer and I wish to treat you with respect." Kevin replied, a little contrite.

"I appreciate that, but I still want you to call me Jack. Otherwise, I'll have to take you out back and whip your ass. OK?" Jack was being his usual smart-ass self.

Shannon chimed in, laughing, "Now, *that* is something I would like to see." She looked at the 6 foot 6, 300 pound frame of muscle and sinew that was the ex-Marine everyone knew as Kevin, and who was also smiling broadly at that thought.

Mistakenly thinking that everyone was on the same page, Jack took a pretend swing at Kevin's face, only to find his fist enveloped and stopped in mid air by Kevin's ham hock of a hand, which had moved with startling speed. "OK, Jack. You've made your point." he said.

Jack winced a little at the sudden stop his hand had come to in midair. "You know, it's times like these that I'm glad you are on my side. You *are* on my side, aren't you, Kevin?"

"Of course, *Jack*." Kevin was still smiling as he released his grip, leaving Jack rubbing the slight pain out of what he imagined to be his semi-crushed hand.

As Kevin stepped aside, the front door greetings obviously finished, Jack and Shannon made their way slowly through the main dining room and bar, waving at friends along the way, including members of the boat club who had helped recover the gold in the Bahamas and who had also decided to skip boating because of this horrible day. As they entered the pool room, Katie was just sinking the 8 ball in spectacular fashion, leaving two of Sean's balls on the table.

"Looks as if you're as rusty as I am," Jack said, simply as an observation. Sean scowled at him but started to rack the balls in preparation for their first game in quite some time. Katie put down her cue and came sidling over to Jack and snuck in a quick kiss as her welcome. Shannon got one, too. Pool table set up and ready, Sean gave Jack a bear hug and Shannon a kiss.

"Good to see you both. Want to break, or practice first?"

Jack frowned, for Sean was usually much more gregarious than that. Perhaps it was just the weather getting him down.

"I'd just as soon break and start playing, if that is good by you." Jack decided not to make a big deal out of his friend's recalcitrant attitude, at least for now.

"Sure, go ahead."

The first game, surprisingly, was played in almost absolute silence, and ended up with Jack taking a win when Sean missed an easy final shot on the 8 ball that both of them had made a million times. Sean reached for the rack, but Jack stopped him.

"Not meaning to be a father confessor, but what's wrong? You're moping around like a lion with a thorn in its foot."

"Just a problem back in Ireland that I can't get a handle on. Nothing for you to worry about. Anyway, we have some good news for you," he said, obviously trying to cheer himself up and lighten the mood. "Katie and I have set our wedding date."

"Oh, that's great. When is it?"

"January the tenth, and you had better be there with bells on." Sean wagged a lone finger in Jack's face to show that he meant business.

"Why?"

"Because you are my best man, of course."

"Really? Would have been nice if you had told me."

"Well, I'm telling you now."

Jack had been expecting to be asked, but with only a couple of weeks left before the chosen date, he knew he would have to hustle to get all the necessary arrangements taken care of, especially with so many things going on over the holidays. "Well, then, I accept."

Katie, who had been listening, took Shannon's hands in hers, and asked, "Would you be my maid of honor, Shannon?"

"Of course I will, it would be my honor." The two girls hugged, and immediately started making plans.

"By the way, is a verbal RSVP to the Christmas party OK?" was Shannon's first question.

"Yes, of course. You're coming then?"

"You better believe it."

After an inquiring glance, pointing to the table, and receiving a nod from Jack, Sean started racking the balls again. He took the heavy breaking stick, lined up his shot and let fly.

"Nice shot," said Jack, noting that 2 of the solid balls had fallen on the initial stroke.

The game continued, back and forth, both of them making some brilliant shots and some flubs, but Jack was only paying half a mind to the game. Jack repeatedly glanced over at the girls, Katie in particular, and soon she noticed his perusal.

"What?" she said, noting with alacrity the grin that had formed on his face.

"Oh, nothing of any consequence. Just thinking back to the good time we had on the flybridge of the boat on our way to Holiday Isle last year, and you......."

"Really?" With great clarity, she recalled the exhibition she had put on, all on the spur of the moment.

Still smiling broadly, Jack said, "Remember, it was you who said that I had been ignoring you."

"Listen, buster. You have a snowball's chance in hell of ever seeing me topless again." She appeared indignant, but really wasn't since it had been at her instigation.

"Oh, yes, undoubtedly you are right. But you can never take that memory away from me, and I have a *very* vivid imagination." Jack's grin broadened to a full leer.

Sean and Shannon looked at one another, rolled their eyes and shook their heads. Shannon had had enough. "Jack, you really are an ass, you know that?"

"Yes, I know, sweetheart, that's why you love me." He, of course, had a smile on his face when he made that comment.

"Anyway, if you can tear your tiny, depraved mind away from my fiancée's boobs, it's your shot," said Sean, "and just remember, you have the striped balls."

As Jack Walked to the table, Shannon joined in the action when she commented with a giggle, "I beg to differ, Sean, for his balls are definitely solid." Katie and Sean looked at her with utter incredulity, and she simply shrugged and said, "I know from personal experience and extensive research."

After a micro-second, they all broke into uproarious laughter. It was quite a while before Jack was composed enough to take his next shot, which he flubbed badly with a miscue.

"Could you come up with a Dark and Stormy, if I asked nicely, love? I think I could probably play better if I had a little alcohol in my system." He had directed his request to Shannon, but since Sean was nodding his head quite vigorously, Katie took the hint and both women left to get the drinks order.

After his next shot, which he sank, Sean looked around and motioned Jack over to the corner and whispered conspiratorially, "Look, Jack, I'm sorry I'm such rotten company today, but I got some bad news this morning after your call. My brother over in Ireland has been arrested for murder, and I don't know what to do about it. I don't want Katie to know about it because I don't want to spoil our wedding plans."

"I didn't even know you had a brother in Ireland," said Jack, perplexed.

"It's something I don't want to get around. He's not, how should I put this, the most honest of men, just like the rest of my family. He's always been a scallywag and a hell raiser, but I never thought he would sink so low as to resort to murder."

"You know, you've never talked about your family before, and if you don't want to now, I'll understand. But if you need my help with anything, anything, you know I'll always be there for you. You know that." Jack was caught off guard by the information that Sean was giving up freely.

"Yeah, I know. It has always been difficult to talk to anyone about my past. Because of my success here in America, I didn't want people to get the wrong idea about where my money was coming from, so I just didn't say anything about it."

"So are you saying that the money came from your brother's less than honest business?"

"Oh, hell no! He doesn't have two pennies to rub together. The money came from my father, who is ... was quite wealthy. Trouble is, his businesses were not quite legal, either."

"So where is the problem? I mean, if you've been doing all right all these many years, why should it change now?"

"Because our father is the one my brother is charged with murdering. And now, there will be all kinds of investigations, police, lawyers, accountants, you name it. I'm sure to get swept up in it, even though I had nothing to do with it."

Just then, Katie and Shannon appeared around the far corner of the room, bearing trays filled with drinks and finger food for the weary competitors.

"We'll talk about it later. Just don't let Katie know."

Jack caught him by the shoulder as he turned away, toward the girls, and forced Sean to face him. "I don't believe that's the right way to go about it. If it affects you, it affects her, too. You don't want to keep secrets from your future wife, or she *will* find out and wonder about that and everything else throughout the whole of your married life." Jack was deadly serious, and the look he gave Sean showed it.

As the women approached they could sense the tension in the air, and, after setting down the trays, immediately went to their respective fiancés. Shannon spoke up, "OK. What's the problem?"

Jack's answer was a simple nod of the head towards Sean, who sat on the edge of the felt covered table with downcast eyes, their pool game totally forgotten.

"Let's grab that table over there, and I'll explain everything." Sean led the way to the empty table and when everyone was seated took Katie's hands in his own.

"I have some bad news. You remember that phone call I took this morning after Jack called?" Katie nodded. "I was informed that my father over in Ireland had been murdered, and that my brother is in jail charged with his murder." Sean felt Katie's fingers tighten on his, and an extremely shocked expression formed on her face.

"What!!" she cried, "Oh, Sean, I am so, so sorry to hear that. What are we going to do to help?" This was not the kind of reception Sean had been expecting since Katie did not know about his family, either.

"Well, obviously, I have to go back to Ireland, and I want you to come with me. I need to get to the bottom of this situation. My sister only gave me the bare facts without any details, so I don't even know what really happened."

Katie was supportive, even if she was slightly perplexed. "Of course I will go with you, but a brother *and* a sister. You've never mentioned that you had anybody back in Ireland."

Sean hung his head, knowing that he should have filled her in on his family even before their engagement. "Yeah, I know. Until now, it just didn't seem important, since I haven't seen or spoken to them for at least ten years. I actually have two sisters, a brother and a half brother. My mother and my step-mother, and now my father are all dead, but I can't bring myself to believe that

Dylan, my brother, had anything to do with it. However, I guess the police must have some evidence if they've gone and arrested him, and I need to find out what it is and if it's true."

"So when do you want to go?" Katie was already on board.

"The Christmas party is this Saturday, and Christmas Day is Sunday. So we could fly out of here on Monday. How does that sound to you? That way we will be back long before January tenth for our wedding."

Placing her head on his shoulder and wrapping both arms around his body, Katie agreed. "That sounds good to me."

Despite it being the week before Christmas, Jack and Shannon decided to follow the routine that they had held for the past year. Thursday nights, with only a few exceptions, they went to Laser Wolf, a local watering hole with a large selection of craft beers and, as the sign said, No Jerks. Situated in a 1920's white, two story L-shaped building with a walled courtyard, the staff of the establishment, Jacques, Ollie, and Jerrod catered to all the customers who weren't jerks with a carefully cultivated wry sense of humor. Jordan, one of the owners of the Wolf, as it was known to its clientele, worked across the railway tracks at the brewery of his second place, which was called Invasive Species. Jack and Shannon, along with whichever friends happened to be there that night, usually paid a visit to both places, since it was only an easy five minute walk between them.

In a fruitless attempt to try and match Sean's expertise at pool, they usually spent Friday afternoons playing pool against each other at Kim's Alley Bar, where Margie, the magical pourer of alcoholic spirits, was always happy to see them. The willowy brunette was quite often joined by Joyce, the owner of the bar, both of whom verbally offered encouragement to Shannon over Jack, who naturally understood the preference that they showed. Everybody understood that the ribbing was all in good fun. Some of the customers who came on Fridays were friends who also joined in the ribbing.

That Saturday night, being Christmas Eve, saw everyone gathering at Jack's parents' house on a canal in the Victoria Park section of Ft. Lauderdale. Shannon and Jack arrived only a few minutes late in her shiny white Corvette to find a lot of cars there, most of which they recognized. Prominent among them were Sean's Hemi 'Cuda, their friend Janine's fire engine red Porsche 911 and a certain Ferrari, which Shannon didn't recognize, but Jack most certainly did, having last seen it parked in his own driveway at his house in Coral Springs.

"Oh, damn. Sean should have warned me. That Ferrari belongs to that personal injury, slime-bag lawyer Stephan, Rain's boyfriend." Jack was suddenly very anxious to get away since he didn't want Shannon exposed to the scandals of his past life. He took her hands in his and asked. "Do you think we should just leave now and phone in our apologies in a little while?"

Shannon shook her head emphatically. "Let's not leave on my account. I can handle myself, and you've already taken care of him a few times, from what I hear. I don't want to miss out on a party with our friends simply because of his presence."

Jack looked her in the eyes. "OK, but don't say I didn't warn you. This could get quite ugly, especially with what we have to announce tonight."

Shannon smiled, "I can take care of myself; you know you don't have to worry about me."

Jack found a space and parked. Together they walked to the front door of his parents' house, Jack admiring Shannon's long, slim body clad in a clinging ruby red cocktail dress that looked painted on instead of being worn. He, of course, felt like a penguin in his black tuxedo and bow tie, but he had promised Shannon that he would wear it, so there was no way out.

Their ringing of the front door bell was answered by Sean, who, as host of the party, looked quizzically at Jack, not understanding why Jack had not simply walked into his parents' house.

"Merry Christmas and all that, old man." Sean's handshake turned to a bear hug until he saw Shannon. Jack was summarily eased aside as Sean enveloped her in his arms and kissed her gently. A loudly exaggerated cough from behind him brought him abruptly back to earth, and he turned, smiling, to find Katie glaring daggers at him. "Just greeting the guests, my dear."

"Yes, I can see that. How are you two doing?" She walked seductively over to Jack and repeated the greeting Sean had put on Shannon, to everyone's amusement. "Come on in, I think everybody is finally here, now."

As they entered the living room, they were greeted by a multitude of old friends who came over to hug and kiss them. They quickly found drinks being pushed into their hands and the conversations drew them into the tight little circles discussing past events. Some of the people present were a small but pleasant surprise. Members of the Boat Club, who had helped with the recovery of the gold from the sub last summer, were there, along with Charlie Palmer, who was the current U.S. Secretary of the Treasury. Jack glanced around and moaned softly as he spotted Rain, short for Lorraine, who was his ex-wife, and Stephan, her lover, heading their way. They rudely pushed their way into the group of friends who were surrounding Jack and Shannon, and it was obvious that Rain was angling for a kiss from Jack, when he deftly turned to Shannon, and said, "Let me introduce you. This is my ex-wife Rain and her boyfriend, Stephan Goldman. This is Shannon."

Shannon looked at her with amusement, "Hello again, Rain." She only got an abbreviated nod in return.

Stephan, his eyes greedily consuming Shannon's exquisite shape in her clinging dress, stepped forward and thrust out a hand, "I am very pleased to meet you, Shannon."

Shannon's look of amusement turned to one of mild disgust, and she kept both hands at her side.

"I would tell you that I was pleased to meet you, Stephan, but I do really hate to lie." she said quite loudly. "And I have to apologize, but I'm afraid I can't shake your hand since I don't like to touch slimy things. Just one of my childhood phobias, you understand, don't you? Sorry."

His smile slipped quite dramatically, and his hand was lowered slowly as he looked around. All conversation had, of course, ceased abruptly and everyone was staring at him, waiting for his reaction. He nodded slowly at Shannon, pursed his lips and narrowed his eyes, then turned, pushed his way through the circle of gathered friends and walked to the bar where he took a bottle of Dewar's and a rocks glass, filled it with ice and headed out the patio doors into the backyard. He sat down on one of the chairs which had been positioned overlooking the canal behind the home and proceeded to fill the glass to the rim. He finished the first glass in three long swallows and was refilling the glass when he was joined by Rain, who had brought her own glass. She mirrored his actions as she sat down beside him.

Inside the house, the interrupted conversations were slowly starting up again when a voice behind Jack caught him by surprise. He knew immediately who it was.

34

A quiet chuckle preceded the voice, "My wife told me that I would find this young woman feisty and high-spirited, and, as always, she was totally correct."

Jack turned and saw that he had been correct. "Hi, Dad." he acknowledged. "Shannon, I want you to meet my father, Jackson Elliott, Senior. Dad, this is Shannon O'Loughlin."

"I am very pleased to finally meet you, sir." Shannon held out her hand, and was pleased when Jack's father took it in both of his, and smiled glowingly at her.

"And I am so happy to finally meet you, Shannon. You are even more beautiful than my wife was able to convey even in her wildest exaggerations. My wayward son Jack, here is a very lucky man."

"Why, thank you, kind sir. May I impose upon you and call you Senior? I don't think I could get used to calling Jack Junior."

"Hmmm. We are going to have to have a conversation about that, but for the moment, why don't you call me Jackson for now, since I am more used to that name than Jack is."

Anne, Jack's mother, who knew Shannon from their Pier 66 encounter, joined them from upstairs where she had been dressing. As usual, she looked stunning, because one thing she knew about from many years of practice was how to take advantage of her best features while downplaying her few flaws. She positively beamed when she saw Shannon all dressed to the nines. As she approached, she caught her husband's eye, remarking; "Now you see what I was talking about, right?"

"Yes, dear," he confirmed, putting his arm around her shoulder and hugging her close.

Jack smiled at this show of affection from his parents, just as it had always been. He decided it was time, and led Shannon to a raised part of the living room by the fireplace. She knew what was about to happen and surreptitiously slipped her engagement ring onto her finger.

"Could I have everyone's attention, please?" Jack didn't quite shout, but had to raise his voice a notch or two to get past the general hubbub of conversation. He repeated himself a couple of times until the room went quiet, and he noted with satisfaction, that even Rain and Stephan out in the backyard were paying attention.

"I know we are here today to celebrate Christmas, and I cannot think of a better reason for the gathering of old friends and new. Shannon and I just want to take this opportunity, since all our friends are present, to announce to the world that from this day forward, we are officially engaged to be married."

The roar that went up was heard a block away, and everyone rushed over to them with congratulations and well wishes. Champagne corks went flying through the air and soon glasses of bubbly cheer were overflowing. Shannon, who had chosen to wear her ring because of the announcement, was holding court in the middle of the room with many admirers around her. Between toasts, Jack snuck a peek into the backyard and saw Rain sobbing in Stephan's arms. He felt sorry for her, especially that she had made such poor choices, but could not think of a way of helping her out of this particular dilemma. He was distracted by Sean and Katie, who simply could not believe that the secret had been kept from them so effectively. It was only for a couple of minutes that his attention wandered but when he looked back to where they had been seated, Rain and Stephan were both gone from their seats in the backyard. He wondered if he should go and look for them but was faced with a small dilemma of his own making. Somehow, he had forgotten to bring the five bottles of Dom Perignon champagne with them from the boat, and informed Shannon that he was going back to get it. He had almost made the front door when he heard Stephan's Ferrari with its distinctive roar start up and leave and was therefore forced to assume that they had both left. He noted the Ferrari's absence as he drove away toward his boat knowing that he would only be gone for about fifteen minutes or so.

The tall, shadowy figure on the stand up paddleboard made his way down the canal in total silence. He stayed close to the shore on which the Elliott residence was located. At the house next door to his chosen target, he closed on the shore and climbed the seawall with ease. He was just tying his board to a fencepost when an obviously drunk, female voice asked him. "What do you think you are doing? This is private property, you know, and you were not invited."

He stood quickly and faced her, but said nothing, closing the distance to her in three mighty strides. Startled, she turned to run but was stopped immediately when her spike heel dug deeply into the ground.

He was on top of her in a flash, one hand over her mouth and the other dragging her futilely resisting body toward the canal. With as much strength as he could manage, he picked her up and threw her toward the water, but did not quite make it. Her head struck the top of the seawall and her hands were trying to stop herself from falling but as she could not stop her momentum, she fell into the water with only a small splash. He moved quickly to the water's edge and peered over, but could see nothing in the dark. He stayed that way for a few minutes, seeing and hearing nothing until the sound of a returning car made him think that someone must have called the police. Since the last thing he wanted was to be questioned by the police, he made his way back to his paddleboard and silently left.

Jack had finally returned with the bottles of champagne just as the caterers arrived with the food that had been prepared at Charlie's house next door and Jackson announced that dinner was served. When all the guests were seated, it became quite obvious that they were two short, Rain and Stephan.

"Now where could they have gone," Jackson muttered as he rose to go and find them.

"I heard the Ferrari leave about fifteen minutes ago," offered Jack.

After a cursory scan of the house and garden, without any sign of them, it was generally agreed that they had left because of Jack and Shannon's announcement. Their place settings were removed and everyone settled into their respective places and, with much gusto, dug into the food. As usual, the exquisite Italian restaurant over on Federal Highway, which had handled the catering for the party and where everyone, at one time or another, went for happy hour and dinner, had once again outdone itself because the food was hot, delicious and plentiful. Everyone, but Jack in particular, stuffed themselves, figuring that they could always take it off tomorrow.

Dinner, dessert, coffee, brandy, drinks, music, dancing, and a quiet walk in the moonlight down by the canal with Shannon; the night never seemed to end. But end it had to and as their friends drifted off toward their cars, saying their goodbyes along the way, Jack and Shannon said their farewells to his parents.

"Welcome to the family, Shannon, from both of us." Jackson once again took her hand in both of his while Anne put her arm around Shannon's shoulders. Reluctantly they released her and Jack and Shannon were finally able to get into the Corvette and drive back to the 'Final Option'.

Jack and Shannon were rudely awakened the next morning by the ringing of the boat's satellite phone, which was kept intentionally loud to compensate for the noise of the boat's passage through the water, and the sounds of the machinery when running at a reasonable speed.

Jack rolled over and grabbed the handset off the side table, automatically noting the time of 9:05 a.m. on the digital clock beside the phone. *'What the bloody hell now,'* he thought irritably as he brought the phone to his ear.

"Jack, turn on the TV. Rain is dead!" his mother practically screamed in his ear.

"What!!" was all he could manage as he fumbled for the remote, and turned the flatscreen in their master stateroom on and tuned to the local news station.

The news anchor, someone Jack had watched for years, spoke beside an image of the canal behind his parents' house, although at the other end, showing paramedics pulling someone from the water.

"As we reported earlier, this was the scene just after dawn this morning as the lifeless body of a young woman was pulled from the water of a canal in Victoria Park. The body was discovered in the shallows at the end of the canal by early morning joggers who immediately notified police by calling 911. Paramedics who arrived first at the scene were unable to restore life to the woman who appeared to have been dead for several hours. Identification of the woman has been withheld pending notification of next of kin. Police have asked that anyone with any information about this incident to please contact them at the number now showing on your screen. We will bring you more information on this tragedy as it becomes available."

"Jack, the police are here at the house and want to interview you and Shannon." His mother sounded desperate, for this was not something she was used to dealing with.

"OK, Mother. You tell them that we're on our way over right now." He rolled over to wake Shannon only to find her staring intently at the TV. There was a look of sadness on her face that Jack had never seen before, and she started to shake, so he took her in his arms and held her tight until the shuddering stopped.

"Rain?"

"Yes. We need to go to the house; the police are there."

They hurriedly got out of bed and dressed simply in jeans and T-shirts, each taking a windbreaker with them. Jack locked the boat up, and they jumped into the Corvette and drove down Broward Blvd. to his parents' house. The police were waiting for them, two patrol units and an unmarked car parked in the places where all their friends' cars had been parked the night before. A uniformed officer stopped them at the door and escorted them inside once he had checked their identification. He led them over to a detective in a suit and tie, who asked Jack to sit on the sofa while another detective took Shannon into the den at the front of the house, in order for them to be questioned separately.

"Your name?"

"Jack Elliott, Junior."

"Your father owns this house?"

"Yes, for many years."

"Do you know the deceased, Lorraine Jensen?"

"Yes, she was my ex-wife."

"And when was the last time you saw your ex-wife?"

"Last night, just before dinner, right here."

"Describe to me the circumstances."

"She was here for dinner with her boyfriend, Stephan Goldman, and spent a while outside in the garden with him. She was upset because Shannon and I had just announced our engagement. She was crying in Stephan's arms the last time I saw her. Shortly thereafter, they both left."

"Did you see them leave together?"

"No, I didn't see them leave. I had to return to my boat to get some bottles of champagne and just before I got to the door, I heard Stephan's Ferrari start up and drive off. It has a very distinctive sound. When I returned, we looked for them, but since we could not find either of them, I just assumed that they had left together."

"Did you ever see any signs that she may have been suicidal?"

"No, never. Not even during the divorce."

"Tell me about Stephan Goldman."

"I am not the person you should ask if you want an unbiased opinion. He is the one who caused my divorce. Therefore, my opinion of him is very slanted in the bad direction."

"Do you think he is capable of murder?"

"I honestly don't know. I don't know him that well, nor do I care to."

"OK. Is there anything else you can think of that might help us in our investigation?"

"Not at this moment. Are you treating this as a murder?"

"Right now, it's just a fact gathering investigation. We'll have to wait and see what the coroner has to say about how she died. Thank you for your time, Mr. Elliott."

Shannon was just coming out of the den while Jack was rising from the sofa, and they both saw Sean and Katie being escorted in by the uniformed officer and turned over to the detectives. They went out the patio doors to join Jack's parents in the garden.

Jack went over and put his arm around his mother's shoulders. She had obviously been crying, but for now at least, she just looked immensely sad. "How are you doing, Mom? Are you all right?" She looked up and nodded her head, but she just couldn't manage to put on a smile.

Jackson came back from the edge of the canal, where he had been studying something on the ground intently. "Come with me, Junior," he said, leading Jack down to the canal. When they got to the spot which he had been examining, he pointed to a dark stain on the edge of the seawall facing the canal. "Is that what I think it is? It looks like blood to me."

"I think you're right. I'm going to get a policeman." Jack was up and gone before Jackson could restrain him; he hoped that this was not going to affect their lives adversely.

Jack walked back up to the house and entered the living room through the patio doors just as the detective and Sean were standing up and shaking hands. "Thank you for your time, Mr. Brady."

Jack interrupted and addressed both of them, "Please come with me, there is something down here I think you need to see." He turned and led them down to the canal where his father waited for them.

Pointing, Jack said, "I'm no expert, but that looks like blood to me."

"And those torn up patches of grass look like skid marks. None of that was here yesterday before the party, or I would have noticed." Jackson was fastidious in maintaining his property, and knew every inch. The detective called one of the uniforms over and placed him on guard duty while he called for a forensics team. He then asked Jack to come back into the house with him.

"I have called and asked Stephan Goldman to come by ASAP to give his statement, and I would like you to sit in on the interview. I know it's unorthodox but I think he would be much more inclined to stick to the truth with you present. I've had dealings with him in the past and he's the kind of person who would lie, even if it was unnecessary, don't you think? Would you mind staying?"

"No, of course not. Anything to help get to the bottom of this. And I agree with you, he is definitely not the most trustworthy individual in the world, I have personal experience with that." Jack could already feel his hackles rising, and hoped he had the opportunity to catch the man in an outright lie.

They were interrupted by the throaty roar of the Ferrari pulling into the driveway, and moments later Stephan rushed into the room.

"Where is she? What have you done with her, Jack? I told her not to stay here." Jack was taken aback. Either Stephan didn't know about Rain's death or he was an Oscar winning actor.

The detective stepped between them, "Please sit down, Mr. Goldman. I have a few questions for you, and then we will tell you everything. OK?"

After Stephan sat down, the detective's first question was, "When was the last time you saw Lorraine Jensen?"

"Last night, here at the party."

"Tell me all about it."

"Everything was fine until Jack announced his engagement to Shannon and then she went to pieces. We had both had too much to drink and I was trying to console her by once again asking her to marry me, and I guess it was the wrong thing to say at that time. She told me she had never wanted to marry me, and that she had only kept me around as an escort until Jack changed his mind and took her back. I was very upset about that and I told her that I didn't appreciate being used and that it was over for us. Then I left." Stephan looked extremely worried, almost as if he suspected that something very unpleasant was coming down the line.

The detective then shocked Jack with his next question. "Mr. Goldman, I am going to ask you the same question that I asked Mr. Elliott. Do you think that Jack is capable of murder?"

You could almost see the wheels turning over in Stephan's mind, but he finally said. "No, I don't think so. If he was, I think I would have been dead when he caught us in his bedroom."

The detective nodded at this statement agreeing to the logic of it. He then broke the bad news. "I'm sorry to be the one to tell you this, but Lorraine's body was found at the end of this canal earlier this morning." The detective must have been a veteran, because he was watching Stephan's face the whole time he was talking. Even he, as well as Jack, was surprised by the reaction. Stephan took one huge breath, and burst into tears, bending over at the waist and sobbing into his hands.

It took a full ten minutes for Stephan to compose himself, and he finally muttered, more to himself than to try to explain his reaction, "I guess I really loved that little girl."

Jack asked, "Where was she when you left?"

"Down by the dock. She was crying again and she kept looking back toward the house. She was walking around in small circles and kicking at the ground, hugging herself, and muttering curses." Stephan shook his head, and wiped his eyes on his sleeve. "I wish now I had stayed with her."

"Did she seem suicidal to you?" The detective asked.

"I'm not an expert, but, no, she just seemed angry. Pissed off, if you know what I mean. She had just lost two men who cared for her, at different times, in one night. Who knows what her thoughts were?"

Just then, the forensics team arrived and the detective took them down to the seawall, and after about ten minutes, returned carrying something in an evidence bag.

"Either of you recognize this?" holding up the bag.

Stephan spoke up, "Yes, that's the heel off one of the spike heeled shoes Rain was wearing last night."

"We found it immediately when we got down to examine closely the skid marks in the lawn. It had been driven straight down into the lawn and had snapped off at the base of the shoe."

"So what does that mean? What are you thinking?" Stephan seemed still to be a little dazed and emotional, for his questioning of a police detective seemed a little out of line. The detective, however, was magnanimous and answered Stephan's questions.

"What I think happened here; it was just a stupid accident. I believe Lorraine was walking back and forth on the lawn in a foul mood when the heel of her shoe went deep into the grass and stuck there. She tried to wrench it out and when the heel broke, she lost her balance, striking the back of her head on the seawall on her way into the water. She was knocked unconscious and drowned before she could regain her senses. It seems, to me, an unfortunate accident, such a tragedy."

"So we are free to go?" Stephan asked.

"Yes, and as far as I'm concerned, unless the coroner comes up with something to dispute my theory about what happened, I don't think I need detain any of you any longer." The detective seemed satisfied that there would be no extraordinary circumstances to worry about. "Just don't leave town until I have his report."

Sean jumped in immediately, "My fiancée and I have tickets to fly to Ireland on an urgent family matter tomorrow morning. I can't see how our remaining here could possibly affect the coroner's ruling, and we will be back in a week. We still have our wedding to plan for on January tenth."

The detective hesitated, looked around at the people in the room, and said, "Since, according to witnesses, you and your fiancé never left the room, I don't see any reason for you to postpone your trip, but please get in touch with me when you return, if only to get the final outcome on this case."

"Yes, sir, we will certainly do that." Sean's voice revealed his relief at not being restricted in his travels.

The detective turned and followed the forensic team, who had finished their collection of evidence, out the door, collecting the uniforms along the way. They were followed closely by Stephan who, having said hello, expressed his condolences to Mr. and Mrs. Elliott, also left without bothering with goodbye.

Sean, Katie, Shannon and Jack ended up staying for lunch, even though nobody felt like eating, and then they, too, left the Elliott family home in Victoria Park, which now did not seem like such a welcoming place.

For all concerned, Christmas Day was a day of mourning.

Chapter 2

The next morning, Sean and Katie left for Ireland, with Shannon and Jack there to see them off. Jack made a point of taking Sean aside and telling him, "You keep me informed about what is going on. You know I'm always there for you, right?"

Sean was somewhat taken aback, but remembered the adventures that they had been through together the summer before. "Don't worry about me; I can take care of myself. And Katie, too."

"I know that; all I'm saying is that if you need me for anything, I'm there for you. O.K.?"

Grasping Jack by the back of the neck, Sean brought him closer and almost whispered, "I know and I appreciate it. You are the best. Man, that is. You had better be ready. I'll be back soon and I expect everything set up for my wedding, you know what I mean?"

"Yeah, yeah. You're always expecting others to do the dirty work for you. Just be careful over there, you never know what's going to happen. Don't get yourself tangled up in anything you can't get out of, you know?"

"I hear you, brother, I'll keep it clean."

Two hours before flight time, after hugs and kisses, Sean and Katie gathered their carry-ons and wound their way through the designated pathways leading to the TSA inspection stations, passing through without a problem. They waved a final farewell and then they were gone, swallowed up by that bureaucratic maze colloquially called an airport, where bags check in and are never heard from again.

As they were leaving the airport, headed for their car, Jack remarked, "I sure hope he finds what he is looking for. I don't like him this way."

Having indulged in some duty free shopping and indulged in a long, drawn out breakfast, Sean and Katie arrived at their gate just as the first boarding call was made, and were quickly seated in their first class seats at the front of the Boeing 747, spending a few moments getting comfortable.

"You know, you didn't have to spring for first class seats on my account; I'd have been just as comfortable in business class or even coach." Katie remarked.

"What's the use of having money if you don't use it to make yourself and other people happy?"

"Seriously?" Katie was having a little trouble following Sean's logic.

"Sure, by buying these seats up front, we freed up two cheaper seats for some folk who needed to get to Ireland for New Year, didn't we?" Sean beamed a wide smile at his reasoning.

"I guess."

It was a 12 hour journey from Ft. Lauderdale to Dublin Airport in Ireland, with a layover at New York's JFK Airport. Counting the lost time flying against the earth's rotation, their arrival was late in the evening and after going through customs, they finally walked into the concourse around midnight local time.

Sean was not surprised to find his sisters and his half brother waiting for them at the baggage carousels for he had texted them that he was coming. For Katie, though, it was a surprise since Sean had had no contact with his family for at least 10 years.

Kathleen, Sean's older sister, immediately stepped forward and hugged and kissed Sean, saying, "Welcome home, brother, I've missed you."

Sean's younger sister, Erin, joined in the group hug while his half brother, Brendan, stood where he had risen from his chair. His face, Katie saw, revealed nothing; not joy, anger, compassion or disgust, only resignation. He walked slowly forward, but made no move to join in with the hugging trio. He looked at Sean, glanced at Katie, shrugged his shoulders, turned and walked out of the building toward the car park.

Kathleen untangled herself and announced, "We'll carry this on at home. C'mon, I've a motor waiting." She turned and strode off, confidently knowing that everyone would follow her.

"Motor?" Katie was confused.

Sean smiled, "She means a car. Things are called by different names here than in the States."

It was but a short hour's drive through the winding roads and lanes to reach the Brady family home nestled in the low, rolling hills of the countryside north of the Irish capital city.

"Never thought I'd see this place again," muttered Sean, as they rounded the last bend and caught their first glimpse of the structure, illuminated by the car's high beam headlights.

It was not, by any stretch of the imagination, an imposing or impressive house; it was just big and blended gracefully into the rocky landscape. Two stories in height, half timbered in weathered wood and stone with a dark gray slate roof, it looked as if it had stood on that spot for a thousand years and been neglected for all of that time. A sense of foreboding hung over the place like a suffocating blanket.

Katie leaned forward between the front seats from the rear bench where she had been sitting between Sean and Erin ever since they had left the airport. Kathleen drove and Brendan occupied the other front seat. From the silence in the car during the trip, it was obvious to her that she had landed in the middle of a strained relationship between Sean and his siblings. Still a little uncomfortable at being the only stranger in the group, Katie withheld any comment on the state of the building, preferring to keep silent rather than taking the chance of being misunderstood, for she had still not been properly introduced to the rest of the family.

Kathleen braked to a halt in the circular driveway directly in front of a large, unpolished wooden door that was obviously the main entrance of the house. A single, quite dim light bulb in a weatherproof housing provided the only illumination after the headlights had been extinguished. It was barely adequate to see by to unload the trunk of the car, or rather the boot, as she was told later. They collected their luggage and followed Kathleen into the house. As soon as Kathleen hit the interior light switch, Katie stopped dead in her tracks and dropped her suitcase out of sheer surprise. She felt as though she had stepped through a time warp, or maybe fallen down a rabbit hole. The living room which lay before her was as ultra modern as any she had seen before in her life. The white leather couches and armchairs contrasted sharply with the smoked glass and polished chrome and sandal wood coffee tables, end tables and bookcases, which were filled to overflowing with beautifully bound volumes. The flat screen TV must have been 80 inches at the minimum and was enhanced with the most expansive surround sound system she had ever laid eyes on. She had no doubt it sounded as good as it looked. The polished light wood floors also contrasted with the smooth off-white walls which were literally covered with exquisite paintings which, to her eye, looked extremely expensive. The area was illuminated with a series of hi-hat recessed lights and position-able spotlights aimed at the appropriate artwork, and muted, concealed strip lights. Several modern art table lamps stood on the end tables near the couches. She was blinking for perhaps the twentieth time, when Sean moved up behind her.

"My father had somewhat eclectic tendencies when it came to home furnishings," he whispered to her.

"It's just such a total contrast to what is outside, to the whole building and even the countryside." She turned to him and smiled. "I really like the effect; it's almost like having your cake and eating it, too."

He turned and faced the group assembled in the living room, looked directly at Brendan, and said, "Now that we're all together, I think it's time for introductions. This is my fiancée, Katie. Katie, this is my older sister, Kathleen; my younger sister, Erin; and my half-brother, Brendan."

Kathleen and Erin both came over and gave Katie a hug, but Brendan just nodded.

"So you're his fiancée, hey?" Kathleen asked, which brought a nod and a big smile from Katie. "So might I venture a wild guess and assume that you won't mind when I tell you that we only have one guest bedroom vacant upstairs, and you two will have to share?"

The smile broadened into a huge grin, and Katie replied, "I guess we can work out something; maybe a board or something between us."

Kathleen grinned, too, and said, "Somewhere up in the attic, I'm sure we could find one of those old fashioned iron chastity belts, if you'd like?"

Now it was Sean's turn to grin, "Too late! We're going to bed to sleep because we have to be up early to go see Dylan. Anyway, I am too jet-lagged for anything else."

"They won't let you see him before 11 am, so sleep in if you can. I've made up the east bedroom for you." Kathleen called after them as they wearily made their way up the stairs. When they reached the bedroom, there was no question of unpacking. Throwing their suitcases in one corner, they stripped off all their travel clothes and tossed them on the two chairs in the room. Climbing into the Danish Modern design sleigh bed, and after a quick kiss, they laid their heads on the pillows and were instantly asleep. An hour before dawn, something caused Sean to come half-awake, but finding Katie's naked body next to him, he rolled over into a spooned position with her and fell back to sleep.

Sean was awakened by a loud knocking on the door to their bedroom and Erin's voice announcing, "Breakfast in ten minutes, don't be late!"

"All right. All right! I'm up already." He threw off the light sheet which had covered their bodies during the night, thanking his dead father for putting in central air and heating into the old building. He sat up, but that was as far as he got because of the sight of Katie right beside him. She was still asleep, but, of course, she was naked and once more that wonderful sight took his breath away. He reached over and gently shook her shoulder, marveling at her beauty as she rolled over onto her back, slowly coming awake. She opened her eyes to find him staring at her, and then grinned, raising her arms above her head in a long, drawn out stretch before grabbing the hair on the back of his head and pulling him down on top of her. He put up a feeble attempt to escape, but soon played his only card. "Breakfast in five minutes," he managed to gasp as he came up for air.

He saw the confusion register in her eyes as she glanced to both sides, then relief when she realized where she was. "Gotta go," she said and jumped out of bed and headed for the bathroom, aware that Sean, as always, was watching her every move. She gave her ass a cute little wiggle as she closed the door on him, and, groaning, he fell back onto the bed.

Eventually, they both got dressed and headed downstairs to breakfast. "What time is it, anyway?"

"Don't know. My watch is still set on Eastern Standard Time, but it says 6 o'clock. That would make it, let's see, 11 am local time."

"Isn't that the time the jail is open for visitors?"

"Yeah, but I imagine it is open for a long time after that."

They were greeted cordially and shown their places at the table. Katie, seeing the amount of food on the table, innocently remarked, "What time does the army get here?" The question was answered with blank stares, until Sean explained the difference between an American breakfast of cereal and coffee, and an Irish breakfast of bacon rashers, pork sausage, fried eggs, white pudding, black pudding, toast, fried tomatoes, fried mushrooms, baked beans, hash browns, liver and brown soda bread.

Looking at Sean, Kathleen smirked, "You know, Katie, if you are going to marry Sean, you are going to have to learn to cook all of this and a lot more besides. Don't forget, this is only for breakfast; you wait until you see lunch, high tea and dinner, not to mention special holidays. You've a steep learning curve ahead of you, girl. Fortunately, you have me here to teach you. What are you doing for the next month or two?"

"Really?"

"Yes, and we can start today, while Sean meets with his brother in the jailhouse. I don't imagine you would want to intrude on the meeting of two brothers after ten years, especially under these circumstances, would you?"

"No, I guess not, unless you need me there, Sean."

"Much as I want you to meet Dylan, I think it would be better if I went alone this first time. Maybe later, if we can get him out on bail, you can meet him here at the house, okay?"

"Sure, just be careful, please."

"Of course I will. In the meantime, what Kathleen said makes a lot of sense. I'd love to have a breakfast like this at home in America," he said as he wolfed down the last of the enormous plate that had been placed before him. Katie had tried everything, but in determined moderation since a girl still had to mind her figure.

"Erin will drive you to the jail," Kathleen said.

"She drives now?"

"Of course I do," Erin cried, "You've been gone ten years, Sean, and I grew up while you were away. I am 22 now and I can do a lot of things I couldn't when you left." She turned away, ashamed at her outburst. Sean, realizing that he had upset her, stood and took his little sister into his arms. "I keep forgetting how long it's been. Forgive me, Poppet, I didn't mean to hurt you."

At the sound of his childhood name for her, Erin's eyes misted over and she grabbed him in a fierce bear hug, and cried softly. "I never understood why you had to go away; I thought you hated me and couldn't wait to get away from me. You never called to see if we were OK, you never came for a visit; it was as if you were ashamed of us, as if we were the worst people in the world and you never cared for me. It was as if you were dead. Where were you all the time I was growing up and missing you so much? Where?"

Sean was stunned, gob smacked as they say in England, never realizing that his decision to leave for America had had such an effect on his little sister. Now that it was out in the open, it was obvious, of course, but at the time it seemed to be the easiest and most sensible way to go. Putting his arm around his little sister's shoulder, he led her out of the kitchen into the living room and sat her gently down on one of the white leather couches. Sitting down next to her, he took her hands into his. He looked into her tear-streaked blue eyes and almost wept himself.

"Poppet, I'm not going to make any excuses for myself. I didn't realize how badly this would affect you, or I would have found another way. Our Pa and I agreed that this was the best way. The others were told what happened, but I guess that Pa thought that you were too young to understand and that you would not get so emotional if you saw that the others were in agreement with his decision. I can see now that he was wrong and I was wrong, too, for not contacting you for all these years and allowing you to feel sad and bitter because I was not there for you. Nothing can make up for all those years but from now on, I promise that I will be here for you if and when you need me. Now that the statute of limitations has run out, I can come and visit you as often as you want, or you can come to the States to visit me. What do you say to that?"

Having listened to this speech, Erin had only one question, "What statute of limitations?"

Sean hesitated, for this was not something he wanted brought up again. "Just a figure of speech, Poppet. I didn't mean it literally. It's just a legal problem that kept me from coming home for too many years."

Erin stopped and thought for a moment. Showing just how grown up she had become during the intervening years, she leaned back into the couch and suggested, "If we are going to help Dylan, perhaps we had better get going now. But just so you know, this conversation is far from over. There are things you are hiding from me, and I will find them out, sooner or later."

"We will talk tonight, Poppet. But you're correct; we have to help Dylan right now. Let's go."

They got up together from the couch, said goodbye to those in the kitchen and left the house headed for the car. She never looked at him on the way out, but as she slipped her hand into his, she murmured, "I do love you, Sean, and I'm so glad you're home." That short statement brought tears to his eyes, tears he had suppressed for ten years.

It was a scant twenty minute drive from the house to the jail, but the way Erin drove, they arrived there in twelve. Sean made an offhand remark about her trying out for Formula One racing, and she beamed a huge smile his way and informed him that she had already won the Formula Two title two years running, and was the test driver for the Midlands Formula One racing team. The surprise on his face must have been evident, because for the final few minutes of the ride, she was spouting facts and figures of racing at him as fast as she was driving. When she finally screeched to a stop outside the jail's gates, she wound down and drove demurely into the parking area. "I'm staying here, I'll see Dylan when he is able to come home." she announced.

Sean exited the vehicle and walked to the main entrance where he went through the necessary procedures to protect the inmates, the visitors, and the guards from each other. He finally wound up in a windowless room with two doors, one on each end, a table, and two chairs facing the opposite doors.

He was sitting in the chair facing the prisoner's door when they brought his brother in. The look of astonishment on his brother's face told Sean that nobody had bothered to inform Dylan that Sean had come home from America. The scar across the front of his face only an inch above his eyebrows showed Sean how close he had come to losing his brother as well as his father.

"So, the prodigal son returns. Bearing gifts, I hope. Like a 'get-out-of-jail-free card, maybe?" Dylan hadn't changed over the intervening years; he was still the smart-ass, wise cracking jackass he had been when Sean had left ten years ago.

"Maybe a get-out-of-jail-on-bail card is the best you can hope for." Sean stood and embraced his brother, because, even after ten years apart, they still felt the need for physical contact to assure that each was there for the other. "Sit down and tell me what happened."

They sat. "I've been assured that there are no listening devices in here, this room being usually reserved for the lawyer-client confidential consultations, so you can talk to me freely."

No hesitation. "It was the Corcoran brothers, Timmy and James. They ambushed us, me and Pa. Shot him dead and tried to kill me, too. He was able to get off one shot, and the police are saying that was the shot that grazed me across my forehead and knocked me out, and the crummy .38 they found in my hand was the one that fired the bullet that killed Pa. You know, even after ten years, that my gun has always been a Glock; hell, even the police know it's a Glock, since it is registered and I have a carry permit. They even did a gunshot residue test on me that came up negative, but they are not willing to give up on their pet theory. One of the Corcoran brothers must have taken the Glock and pressed that .38 into my hand while I was out. Sean, you have got to get me out of here, my life has already been threatened and the only way to stop from being dead was to get myself into solitary confinement."

"OK, OK! Details, anything I can use to get you out on bail."

"Ha! The way they have me wrapped up on this, it'll take a shit-load of money to get me out on bail."

"Dylan, I'm your American brother. I *have* a shit-load of money, and access to more, if necessary."

That shut him up, if only for a second. "This is all bullshit, anyway, there's no way that they can prove I shot Pa. It wasn't even my gun, dammit. And they haven't a clue about any motive."

"OK, I'm convinced. I'll get you out of here tomorrow; just hang in for one more night, all right?"

"Hell, it's not like I have any choice in the matter. If they don't get me tonight, I'll be here tomorrow."

57

They finished their conversation and a few minutes later, the guard arrived to take Dylan back to his cell. After Dylan's door was locked, Sean's door was opened from the outside, and he was ushered out to face all the other visitors on their way to see their own detainees when a man approached him. His attire screamed lawyer, and, sure enough, the man turned out to be Dylan's attorney.

"Mr. Sean Brady?"

"Correct." Sean answered.

"I am Rory Carmichael, Dylan's attorney, and incidentally your father's too. Dylan's bail hearing is scheduled for 10 a.m. tomorrow morning, right here. Do you think you will be able to attend and is there any way you can you help us with the bail?"

"Yes, I will be here, and I do have some resources, but as to if I can help, that depends entirely on the judge, don't you think?"

"I know the judge we have been assigned and he is a fair man. If we can convince him that Dylan is not a flight risk, he will in all probability set bail but it will be astronomically high, seeing this is a murder case."

"Then we will see you in court tomorrow, and I will bring all the character witnesses I can round up to testify on his behalf, if necessary."

The next morning, just after ten, they were all gathered in the courtroom for Dylan's bail hearing. The prosecutor, a small, fat man, laid out a good argument for keeping the prisoner confined until his trial, but Rory had a few choice comments of his own. The judge listened attentively to both sides of the argument, then, without comment, set the bail at two million Euros, cash or bond. Dylan's face fell as he heard the amount, convinced he was going back to jail, but Rory stood up and announced that Sean was able to come up with the full amount.

It took a couple of hours, but Dylan was finally reunited with his family that same day. As they walked out of the courthouse, Sean took Dylan by the arm and led him aside. "Now, I want you to stay out of trouble, stay away from the Corcorans, and stay at home, away from the 'businesses'. Understand me?"

"Yes, little brother, I understand you completely. I'll make sure that you get your money back."

"Good, now get in the motor and go home with Kathleen. I have a few things to take care of; then I'll see you there." Sean turned and walked toward Rory Carmichael as the rest of the clan piled into two cars and left for home, leaving the last car for him.

"Might I have a word with you, Mr. Carmichael?"

"Of course, Mr. Brady. But please call me Rory."

"All right, Rory, and I'm Sean. I'm a little lost here in Ireland; I've been in America too long. You don't happen to know a good private investigator, do you?"

"Only the best. Shall I set up an appointment for you?"

"That would be a splendid idea. As soon as possible, if you would."

Rory immediately excused himself, walked away a few paces, and started dialing on his cell phone. After only a few verbal exchanges, he walked back. "She will see you in twenty minutes, and her office is just around the corner. I'll walk you there."

"She?"

"Yes, Sean, she. Her name is Samantha Beckett, but don't call her Sam. Her friends call her Maddy, but only if she asks them to. She is the absolute best in the PI business, but she will only take a case if she wants to and if she thinks she can help her client, who, in this case, is you."

They walked for all of two minutes, around the corner from the courthouse, and found, in an older building which had been restored to its former glory, the office they were seeking as indicated by the polished brass plaque on the front door. Sean took particular note of the exact wording. 'Samantha Beckett, Esq. Private Investigations.' it read.

They loitered around outside for a few minutes, until it was time for the appointment, then opened the door and entered the office. Sean was pleasantly surprised. The small outer waiting room looked a lot like the ones he had seen for years in movies depicting private eyes from the forties and fifties, with wooden floors, wainscoting on the walls with chair rails and heavy overstuffed furniture upholstered in plaids and tartans. There was even a coat rack with an honest to goodness Burberry trench coat hanging on it. The only lighting, apart from the rippled glass windows, came from a small but elaborate chandelier in the center of the small space. The only incongruous note was the open door leading into the inner office, which had a sleek, ultra modern look to it. Dominating the room, however, was the woman behind the desk who was now rising to greet them. She was at least six feet tall, slim and attractive, her long blonde hair flowing down her back as she made her way over to Rory, and gave him a kiss which was much more than mere hello.

"Hi, Maddy, I've brought you a new client."

"So I see. I'm Samantha Beckett, Mr. Brady. I'm pleased to meet you." She held out her hand, which Sean promptly took in both of his and they formally shook hands, with Sean holding on for just a smidgeon too long.

"I am very pleased to meet you, Ms. Beckett. But how is it you know my name?"

"Well, I *am* a private investigator, and….. Rory told me on the phone. You can call me Maddy if I can call you Sean, but don't you dare call me Sam."

Rory was standing there, shaking his head, "Wow, it took me three months to get to call her Maddy, and you do it in thirty seconds. Unbelievable."

Maddy smiled seductively, "Yeah, but you are not cute, like he is."

"Well, at least I got a kiss. Anyway, I've got business to attend to, so I'll leave you two to hatch whatever plans you have in mind. Sean, call me if you have any questions, anytime." With those closing remarks, he turned and walked out the door.

Maddy showed Sean to the chair before the desk and walked to her chair behind it and sat down.

"Now that all the pleasantries are out of the way, how can I help you, Sean?"

Sean gave her the Cliff Notes version of Dylan's predicament, all the way up to the bail hearing that morning and ended by saying, "much as I would like to stay and investigate this myself, I have business back in the States. I can only stay a few more days, and I'd like to spend them with my family, for obvious reasons. So I'll leave the investigation to the professionals."

"Wow, do you mean to tell me that you paid two million Euros, cash, to bail Dylan out of jail?"

"Yes, of course, he *is* my brother."

"Remind me later to pad my bill a little. You certainly seem like you can afford it." She was, of course, smiling sarcastically when she said it.

"I don't mind paying top money for results. I just hope you can find something that will keep him out of jail and put the Corcoran brothers behind those bars."

"I certainly will try to do my best, and I already have several ideas."

He stood up, gave her a twenty five thousand Euro retainer along with all his contact information, and she escorted him to the front door where they once again formally shook hands.

Sean walked the two minutes around the corner to where he had left his car parked, programming Maddy's information into his cell phone as he went. But as he approached the car, he saw someone waiting for him, leaning on it. He hesitated slightly, slowing his walk as he recognized the man as being the last person he wanted to encounter. He felt a hand from behind push him forward and a rough voice declare, "C'mon now, Sean, yer old friend, James, wants to see yer again."

He turned his head and looked straight into the forehead of Timmy Corcoran, who was at least six inches shorter that he was. He adjusted his view downward, "I'd forgotten what a short little bugger you are; you know it *has* been a while." That earned him a scowl and another shove in the back.

He shrugged his shoulders and walked straight up to James Corcoran, declaring, "You better call off your pipsqueak, before I ram his hand so far up his ass, he'll be able to chew his fingernails, from the inside!"

James made a dismissive gesture with one hand, and Timmy backed away a short distance; he then looked Sean square in the eye, "Seems we have a problem here, Sean. One you have just made worse. Hiring that female investigator was not the smartest move you've ever made. I can see you coming all the way home to bail out your brother, but hiring someone to pry into our business; that just isn't done. It'd be better if you call her from America and fire her before she gets messed up."

"Thank you for your unsolicited advice. You'll forgive me if I ignore it. Now, get out of my way."

Sean pushed James away from the car, unlocked it and climbed in. He started the engine and put it into Drive. As he was about to pull away, Timmy stepped in front of the car, pulled aside his jacket and revealed the Glock, Dylan's Glock, in his belt holster. He eased off the brake pedal and as the car crept forward, Timmy took a couple of involuntary steps backward and then spun out of the way, laying a boot into the door of the car as it passed. Sean, being unarmed, kept going, accelerated and was soon far enough away to resume normal breathing again.

As he drove, he speed dialed Maddy and warned her about the threat James had made. She told him not to worry, that threats were something she encountered every day. Apparently, she could take care of herself.

The two Corcoran brothers watched him until he disappeared from sight, and then Timmy turned to James, "So, what do you think? Is he going to be any trouble?"

"No, I doubt it. That bitch he hired won't find anything 'cause there's no physical evidence left to find, and neither of us is going to say anything, right? So he'll hang around for a few days with his family, and then he'll tuck his tail between his legs and run back to America, just like he did the first time. Our little Sean just doesn't have the balls for this business. C'mon, let's hit the pub for a pint, and then head home."

Sean was still a little shaken by the time he arrived back at the house, and Katie noticed immediately. After a downplayed account of what had happened, she held him tight and whispered soothing words to him, as a mother would to her upset child. He didn't really need the words, but he appreciated the cuddling and let her continue.

"Sean, you just wait until you see what I have planned for us tomorrow." Erin shouted, running up to him as soon as she spotted him coming into the living room.

"Tell me, Poppet."

She grabbed his hand and dragged him down onto the couch with her and started laying out all the plans she had put together while waiting for him to return. "First we're going to do the culture thing by visiting the quadrangle of Government Buildings in Dublin City, University Church, which sits alongside St. Stephen's Green, the Sean Walsh Memorial Park in Tallaght, the Irish Museum of Modern Art, and the National Library of Ireland. Then we're going to do some interesting things at Balbriggan Beach, visit the Lambert Puppet Theater and Museum; then go to Phoenix Park, which is the largest enclosed city park in Europe. Its area is 1,752 acres and is home to the official residence of the President of Ireland, called Áras an Uachtaráin, and also the Dublin Zoo. Then, finally, we get to do the fun things by going to the Dawson Lounge, which is Dublin's Smallest Pub, for a pint. We'll have dinner at Bewley's Grafton Street Café and Restaurant. It's Ireland's longest established and largest café and serves excellent food. After dinner, we'll grab some cocktails and the view at the Marker Hotel, which has a panoramic rooftop lounge where you can see all of Dublin Bay. Then we'll come home and decide what to do the next day."

"Wow, do you think we can do all that in one day?" Sean was already feeling tired, and was thinking of going to bed early, to catch up on his sleep.

"We can if you're not too old to keep up with me!" she challenged him with a smile and a fun poke in his ribs. He grabbed her shoulders and they started fun wrestling on the couch. Suddenly remembering that she was ticklish, he reached out for her waist just as she turned and he ended up grabbing one of her breasts instead. He recoiled instantly, throwing both his hands into the air and shifting backwards as far as he could. "I'm sorry, I didn't mean to......"

She gave him the oddest look at his words and reaction, and then started laughing uproariously. "Oh, come on, Sean. It's me, your little sister. Yes, I'm all grown up now, and I have boobs now; so what? I was only twelve when you left and it *has* been ten years, remember? And besides, you've seen me naked before, so what's the big problem?"

Katie, who was sitting in a chair across the coffee table from them, smiled and silently laughed at Sean's embarrassment, for his little sister had taken exactly the right attitude to diffuse a potentially awkward situation.

"Yeah, but not lately," Sean said, feeling somewhat relieved. He did note, subconsciously, that his little sister had grown into a tall, slim, beautiful woman from the slightly chubby adolescent she had been when he had made his forced trip to America. What he couldn't understand was why she chose to hide the fact by wearing baggy oversized clothing that did nothing to enhance her appeal. "Perhaps, I should stop calling you Poppet then, since you've obviously outgrown your childhood name."

"If you do, I'll never speak to you again. I love your nickname for me and you are the only one who uses it and it makes me feel special." With that, she leaned over, took his face in both her hands and planted a hugely exaggerated kiss on his forehead, while simultaneously pulling him toward her. "Give me a hug, big brother, and make me feel safe again, like you used to do. I missed you so much, and now Pa is gone and I miss him, too."

Sean, without a word, folded her into his arms and gave her a tight, drawn out hug while feeling a mist coming to his eyes. He could feel her against him, sobbing quietly and finally letting her emotions take over. Katie, watching them, realized once again why she loved this man so much. They sat like that for quite some time, locked together in their emotions, until Kathleen came out of the kitchen and announced that dinner was ready.

After dinner, over brandy and cigars, Sean and Dylan compared notes about what had happened over the past ten years. Dylan was very impressed how well Sean had set himself up in America, and when the tale of the gold laden Nazi submarine came up, he suddenly went very quiet. "You were never privy to the story, because you were too young at the time, but our father told me a story of how, when he was nineteen or so, he helped to load wooden boxes onto a Nazi sub on the Dingle Peninsula." Dylan was shaking his head.

"You don't suppose…?"

"It would only make sense; after all, he spent the rest of his life running guns for the IRA."

"Wow, unbelievable." Sean's head was reeling with the possibilities, but could think of no way to check the veracity of the story; at least not at this time.

The next morning, before they left for their day's adventures, Sean placed a call to Dylan's attorney. "Rory, is there any chance that Dylan could come to my wedding in Florida on the tenth of January?"

"I sincerely doubt it, his bail agreement specifically states that he stay in Ireland. But I'll talk to the judge; he's an old friend of mine, and I'll try to get a dispensation. I'll call you back when I have an answer."

"Good enough. I'll talk to you later."

As Sean, Katie and Erin piled into the car, Dylan and Kathleen having decided to remain at home, Brendan approached the car. "I am going to stay home, too" he said. "If you are going to be drinking, I would only be a hindrance to you. Besides, I've been to all those places." Before anyone could speak, he turned and stalked off back into the house, hands in his pockets and his eyes downcast. Katie was shocked; for those were the first words that the nineteen year old teenager had spoken in her presence.

Sean was astonished, "What was that all about?"

"Unfortunately, being the youngest, and only a half-brother, he feels quite frequently left out of everything. He usually overcompensates. I used to feel that way sometimes, too, but I learned the hard way that it doesn't make much of a difference to anyone except for yourself." Erin glanced with sorrow toward the door that Brendan had gone through, "I only hope he figures out things the way I did, before he alienates everyone."

There was a small, dark cloud over their heads when they finally set out, but it soon dissipated in the excitement of new discoveries, and they found, due mainly to the compact nature of the Irish capital, and the M1 Motorway, that Erin's plan of sightseeing was actually quite feasible. They marveled at the history of Ireland, seen through exhibits and displays specifically designed to present the important highlights in the most favorable light. They were wandering through the Dublin Zoo when Sean's cell phone went off, and they quickly found a park bench upon which to perch.

"Sean Brady," he answered.

"Sean, this is Rory. I have you on speaker phone with Judge Hamilton. He has some questions for you. Is now a good time?"

"Yes, it's not a problem. We're at the Dublin Zoo, but we are seated away from other people. How can I be of service?"

"Mr. Brady, Rory tells me that you are to be married on the tenth of January in America, and that you have asked that your brother be allowed to attend. Is that correct?"

"Yes, my lord. My request is of a personal nature, and is not intended to take away from the court's authority. We have been apart for ten long years and it would mean a great deal to me to have him present at my wedding. I would, of course, assume all responsibility for his appearing before the court at the appropriate time. Since I put up the two million Euros bail, it would be in my own interest, too."

"I do understand, Mr. Brady. Rory has explained the circumstances to me. In the spirit of the season, I am inclined to grant permission to your brother on a couple of conditions. If I allow him to travel overseas, he is to be remanded into your custody, and you will be responsible for having him appear before me in my chambers on the sixteenth of January. Otherwise, I will issue an arrest warrant not only for him, but for you, too. Do I make myself crystal clear?"

"Yes, you do, my lord. I *will* have him here before you on the sixteenth."

"Very well. I will give the necessary papers to Rory, and Dylan will be free to attend your wedding. And may I say, congratulations to you and your bride, I hope you both have a long and happy life together."

"Thank you, my lord, for both of the wishes you have granted me today. I hope the same for you."

Sean sat in stunned silence for a moment, and then considered the ramifications. He could only hope that this would work out for the best and not the worst. He decided to keep the news to himself until all the family members were gathered at the house, but he did go ahead and make the necessary reservations.

They finished Erin's plan for the day, and they were all well fed and watered by the time they arrived back at the house. Immediately upon entering, Dylan handed Sean a sealed envelope, with a questioning look on his face and raised eyebrows. "Rory delivered this for you this afternoon. Does it concern me?"

"Yes, it does. In fact, it concerns all of us, so I want us all in the living room so I can explain."

Sean went to the fridge and grabbed a bottle of champagne and six glasses, brought them to the living room and instructed

Kathleen to pour six equal measures. She was taken aback, but complied. When all, including Brendan, had full glasses in their hands, Sean explained. "You are all aware that Katie and I are getting married on the tenth of January. I am now telling you that, if you wish to come, you are all invited."

Dylan immediately said, "I know everyone else has their passports, we need them to go as far as England, but I can't leave the country. You know that, Sean, it's in the bail agreement."

"And in this envelope we have your passport, and a dispensation letter from the judge allowing you to fly to America to attend my wedding, as long as I have you back here on the sixteenth."

"It's a miracle, a Christmas miracle." Dylan was overcome, and Sean was shocked to see tears appear in his eyes. He had never seen his older brother cry before.

"Our flight is at noon tomorrow, so if you need to notify your bosses about your trip to America, you better do it now. Here's to the Brady clan, finally all together again. Slainte!"

They all toasted, even Brendan took a sip, but made a face and gave it to Erin. "This stuff is horrible, I'm never going to end up a drunk, I can tell you that." he said.

Everyone laughed, and Brendan finally grinned, feeling that even he now belonged. Of course, once he got started, you couldn't shut him up.

Shortly after noon the following day, the entire Brady clan, and Katie, the 'to be Brady' hanger on, were comfortably seated in the first class section of a British Airways 777 headed for New York, with connections to Ft. Lauderdale, Florida. In fact, they pretty much took over the forward part of first class, since it being between Christmas and New Year, their section was sparsely populated, and the few people in first class soon joined in the fun that the rollicking Irish people were having. Everyone got off the plane in New York, a little wiser, a little drunker and a lot happier. The later flight to Ft. Lauderdale was a great deal more subdued, with several of them falling asleep before the flight had even left the ground.

Chapter 3

'Final Option' glided silently toward its assigned mooring. Despite the fact that both engines were running, the modifications that had been made during the refurbishing of the yacht following the Bahamas incident made the vessel almost a stealth ship at idle speed. On the flybridge, Jack maneuvered the 70 foot vessel between several smaller boats already tied to the small, round, white floats that formed the mooring field just a short distance from the marina at Dinner Key in Miami.

Since the current on this particular day was stronger than the wind, he slowly approached the floating line attached to the buoy from down current, engaging and disengaging the clutches on his engines in order to keep the boat moving at a snail's pace.

Perched on the bow of the boat, Shannon had a long boathook in her hand, and had placed the head of it only inches above the surface of the water, in order to catch the loop of the mooring line when the boat finally nudged its way up to within grabbing distance. The boat's mooring line, which would be tied to the buoy's mooring line, had been run through the fairlead and secured, the free end only inches away from where she stood by the boat's bowrail.

As the boat's forward momentum finally allowed her to reach the line, she expertly snatched it from the water and secured the vessel to the mooring buoy. Jack shifted the throttles into neutral and allowed the current to drift the vessel away from the buoy until it reached the length of the combined mooring lines. Shannon walked back to the aft deck, replaced the boathook into its holders and climbed the aft stairs up to the flybridge. Having double checked the security of the mooring, Jack was in the process of shutting down the engines and instrumentation when she arrived, grabbing him around the waist from behind and planting a kiss on the back of his neck.

Without turning, he said, "Well done, love, we'll make a sailor out of you yet."

Her only reply was a "Hah!" and a playful punch to his shoulder, as she released him and sat down in one of the three Stidd helm chairs positioned in a line on the forward part of the flybridge. This arrangement allowed the helmsman, or woman as the case may have been, to converse freely with two others without having to turn around. Jack finished securing the boat and then sat down beside her in the center Stidd chair.

"You should have let me go and catch that mooring line, Jack," said Sean, who was seated at the table with the rest of his family. "I feel useless just sitting here."

Turning around toward the table, Jack said playfully to everyone's amusement, "You *are* useless, Sean, but Shannon needs as much practice as she can get. Don't forget, it'll only be the two of us when we go to the Caribbean in a couple of weeks. That's the reason why I let her drive the boat on the way down, too."

Sean's family, Dylan, Kathleen, Erin and Brendan, slathered in SPF40 sunscreen to protect their decidedly white, delicate Irish skin were all grinning from ear to ear, and it wasn't all from Jack's joke, but mainly from the experience of going to dinner by 70 foot motor yacht. Sean's intended, Katie, was also laughing but in a subdued kind of way. With only 10 days to go before their wedding, she was not about to do anything to spoil it. After the proper introductions at their arrival in Ft. Lauderdale, Sean's Irish relatives had been absolutely overjoyed at Jack's suggestion of a short Florida Key's trip in his boat, and this first stop on New Year's Day at Dinner Key was already filling them with excitement. After sampling the shopping at CocoWalk, they had planned a dinner at Monty's Stone Crab and Seafood before returning to the boat for the night, so they might continue their journey in the morning refreshed and ready for more adventures. New Year's Day at Monty's was a tradition for Jack and Sean, back in the days when Jack came with his now deceased ex-wife and Sean came with whoever he was seeing at the time. It was the same deal as the annual Columbus Day Regattas they used to attend.

It took two trips to get everyone ashore because the 15 foot Novurania RIB that was 'Final Option's tender was not big enough to take them all at once. Jack ferried Sean and Katie along with Erin and Brendan ashore on the first trip, then came back for Dylan, Kathleen and Shannon. After locking up the boat and setting the alarm, they all reunited by the dockmaster's office, with whom they left the tender and walked the short distance to CocoWalk. While the intention was to do a little shopping at a unique shopping complex which the visitors simply did not have in Ireland, very little shopping was actually done. Swimsuits, cover-ups and a few small souvenirs were the main things, although Erin seemed to take an inordinately long time for her selection of a bikini she would probably never wear back home. Mostly they just wandered around, marveling at the unusual, for them, selection of objects for sale, window shopping and people watching.

Jack found himself walking between Shannon and Erin, and asked Erin, "So do you have any plans for your future? Have you decided what you want to do with your life?"

Erin seemed a little surprised by his question, but answered, "No, nothing definitive yet. I don't know if Sean told you, but I am a test driver for the Midland F1 team, at least for this year. After that, we'll see. I honestly don't know if they will ever let a woman be a Formula One driver, but I intend to find out."

73

Jack was impressed, "Well, I am a huge F1 fan, so I'll be watching for you."

She laughed, "Well, at least that's the plan for now. I especially like the travel because, even though the people are different, they are still the same, although some of them do speak weird, if you know what I mean."

"Yes, I know. Sometimes for the better, but not always. I remember the same feelings when I first went to Europe, how things were different, but still the same." Jack gave an involuntary shudder, remembering a long-ago trip to Europe with his ex-wife, who was so recently deceased.

With the morning having been spent cruising slowly down to Miami, and the afternoon crawling along to its inevitable conclusion, it was decided that an early dinner was called for. They walked slowly through the park along the shoreline until they got to Monty's. By invoking executive privilege, Sean, as another bar and restaurant owner, was able to get them a table for eight outside on the deck overlooking the marina, the expanse of Biscayne Bay, and in the distance, 'Final Option' resting serenely at her mooring.

Not long after ordering cocktails for everyone and a soft drink for Brendan, who looked 21 but was still underage, the delectable crustaceans for which the restaurant had been named were brought out and greedily consumed. It was expensive but worth every penny.

Completely sated, they made their way back to the tender and after the necessary two trips, gathered together on the flybridge in the evening glow provided by the full moon. Cocktails, and at Dylan's insistence, a Lite beer for Brendan, lubricated the conversation.

Dylan spoke up, "So, Jack. How much has Sean told you about what is going on?"

74

"Not much. Hell, until a couple of weeks ago, I didn't even know any of you existed."

"That much I expected; he has always been very close-mouthed. Anyway, you should know just who you have aboard, in case you want to change your mind. I was arrested for murdering my father, but I swear to you that I didn't do it. I know exactly who did it because they tried to murder me, too, but they missed. They probably figured that the next best thing to do was to try to frame me for the murder."

"That much I have heard about. If Sean and your other siblings are willing to accept your word for your innocence, I don't see why I should doubt it. Here in America, you are innocent until proven guilty in a court of law. Although some people *have* been considered guilty by the media; despite never having been charged with anything. But having spent a little time with your family, I don't have any fears for our safety as far as you are concerned. I have known Sean for a long time and if he trusts you, to be honest, so will I."

"And so will I." Shannon spoke up. "Nobody has ever said what happened to your father's body, after he was murdered."

"The police released his body to us and we buried him before Sean was informed about his brother's arrest for the murder. I never expected Sean to come over to Ireland, so we didn't delay the funeral. I found his phone number in Pa's ledgers, but I was just contacting him to inform him of our father's death. Now, of course, I'm extremely glad I took the chance and rang him, seeing the way things have worked out." Kathleen appeared to be the spokeswoman for the group, since even Dylan had fallen silent when she had started speaking.

"What's going to happen to us now?" Brendan asked, surprising everyone, since he had been silent for most of the day, only exchanging pleasantries when absolutely necessary. The beer must have loosened his tongue. Or maybe, for the first time, he felt he was being included in serious conversation.

Sean said, "Well, we are going to enjoy ourselves on this mini-vacation and then we are going to have our fabulous wedding on the tenth. Then we are going back to Dublin, so Dylan can report back to the judge on the sixteenth. After that, Katie and I are going on our honeymoon in Europe, and when we come back, I am going to try to get all of you into America, if that's what you want."

"And if we just want to stay where we are and carry on?" Kathleen asked.

"Then that is what you must do. I'm just offering you the option." Sean grinned, looking at Jack. "The final option."

"Seriously?" Jack shook his head, "If that's the best you can do, there's no hope for you."

"Hey, lighten up; I learned that from a master. You!!"

"No, really," Jack retorted sarcastically.

"Anyway, all I'm saying is that you have plenty of choices and you don't have to be in a hurry picking one. Now that we're together again, we'll work things out, one way or the other, and that's the way I want it to stay. We will deal with the hurdles as we come to them, okay?"

Jack shifted uncomfortably, "By the way, while you were gone, we had Rain's funeral. Her parents insisted and I didn't want to call and upset you, since you were all tied up in Ireland. The coroner ruled that it was an accidental drowning. They found particles of concrete dust in the gash in her head and scrapes on one hand. It was her blood on the seawall and there was brackish water in her lungs. Her blood/alcohol level was over twice the legal limit and the supposition is that she caught her heel in the grass, twisted and broke it off, lost her balance, and fell into the canal. It appears she tried to save herself by reaching out with one hand as she fell, but she struck her head on the seawall, knocking herself unconscious. She apparently drowned before she could regain consciousness. Without any evidence pointing to anything but an accidental death, the detective who called with the information told me that we were all free to travel and the case was officially closed."

"Well, that's one dilemma out of the way. Poor Rain, she was so sweet, but she just kept making the wrong decisions all the time. Now what we have to deal with is Dylan's problem." Sean was getting morose, and that was never a good thing.

"With all due respect; that's a problem that we are not going to solve tonight, so I suggest that we finish up our drinks and head for bed. Everyone agree?" And everyone did.

The sleeping arrangements for this cruise were quite simple. The main stateroom was Jack's and Shannon's, the forward one being occupied by Sean and Katie. The guest stateroom was claimed by Kathleen and Erin, while the two settees in the main salon, having been converted to hide-a-beds, were where Dylan and Brendan would be hanging out. The arrangements suited everybody.

Standing alone on the flybridge of the yacht, wrapped in a thick white terry cloth robe which was firmly sashed at the waist, Shannon watched the brilliant red fireball rise out of the ocean as it heralded yet another beautiful, cloudless day. She loved these mornings, especially the quiet ones that she could share with Jack. He, normally, would be there with her, but for some reason, this morning she just couldn't get him motivated enough to join her. Hopefully, this morning was simply an aberration and he would not forego their special time together on any kind of regular basis.

"Top of the morning to you, lassie," a voice behind her announced softly.

Startled, she turned and saw Dylan at the top of the aft stairs, standing and looking at her and not the sunrise. "Oh, you scared me for a second. Good morning to you, too."

He simply nodded and moved to the rail, glancing at the rapidly rising sun clawing its way into the sky to begin its daily journey. She suddenly felt slightly apprehensive, knowing that beneath her robe she was wearing nothing at all, and it must have showed on her face, for Dylan noticed it immediately as he turned back to face her.

"Don't you worry, Shannon, you have nothing to fear from me. I am not that kind of man, lusting after what clearly belongs to someone else. Besides, I have enough trouble of my own without adding Sean's and your Jack's wrath to it. I would rather stand beside both of them than against them."

Shannon breathed a small sigh of relief, and smiled at him. "Do you love mornings, too?"

He chuckled at the thought, "Not really. While I appreciate mornings, to me it really only means that I have made it through another dark night somewhat intact. I usually like to sleep in late, but that was something that couldn't happen this morning, since I was so rudely awakened by a large herd of draught horses galloping on my ceiling at an ungodly hour."

"Sorry," she said. She had tried to be especially quiet that morning, slipping out of the pilothouse door and walking down the side deck to the aft stairway, rather than crossing the main salon as she normally would have done had Dylan and Brendan not been sleeping in there. Then, realizing that he was pulling her leg, she said, "Besides, it's time for everyone to be getting up if we are to start our adventure today. We still need to get breakfast before we leave."

"I'll see you in a while, then." He said as he preceded her down the aft stairs. "I'll get Brendan up and clean up the salon."

She slipped back in through the pilothouse door and started to descend the stairs to their cabin, when she met a freshly showered Jack coming up. Seeing what little she was wearing, he normally would have ravished her right there on the stairs, but being acutely aware of the number of guests they had on board, settled for a quick peck on her lips. "Good morning, sunshine, I'll get breakfast going."

She rolled her eyes at him, knowing that his idea of 'getting breakfast' meant pouring himself a mug of coffee from the automatic coffee maker and carrying it to the flybridge, "Really?" He just shrugged his shoulders and carried on up the stairs into the galley; doing exactly the very things she had expected him to do.

As he sat on the flybridge, coffee in hand, he mentally planned out the day they were about to enjoy. One by one, all the others appeared with their own coffee or tea and settled in spots of their own choosing as the day rapidly warmed up from its nippy start. It was, after all, January in Florida and one had to expect lower temperatures. Why, sometimes during a hard winter, it actually got into the fifties, almost unbearable for true thin-blooded Floridians. If you got cold sitting and watching the snow report from up north on TV, you were accepted as a true Floridian.

Kathleen and Shannon got busy with cooking breakfast, with Katie and Erin subbing as servers. Soon the delectable smells of the Irish breakfast Kathleen was preparing permeated the boat and the delicious tastes generously filled the stomachs of the diners. Finally, nobody could eat another bite of the abundant fare, and all vowed to skip lunch. The dishes were loaded into the dishwasher and they prepared to get under way.

Sean and Jack, being Floridians, had dressed sensibly in shorts and T-shirts but Dylan and Brendan had chosen to wear jeans, something they were soon changing out of since the day's heat was increasing rapidly. The girls all disappeared below decks to change into their travelling clothes.

Jack went to the flybridge and started the engines and electronics. Once the engines were warm and the electronics had cycled through their respective start-up programs, he nudged the boat forward until Sean was able to reach the mooring connection which had held them fast all night. Once free of the mooring buoy, he reversed out into the channel and set a course for the Featherbed Banks where the Columbus Day Regatta was held every year. Sean finished tidying up the foredeck and joined the others by the helm on the flybridge.

The girls finally made an appearance, one by one as if by design, each one expecting an evaluation of the outfit they had chosen to wear. Kathleen went first, dressed in a very conservative one piece swimsuit. She exuded a quiet confidence in her manner, despite the fact that this was the first swimsuit she had ever worn.

Shannon came up the stairs next in her radically cut, black racing one piece. She was sexy as all get out, she knew it, and it showed. Sean and Jack had seen this one before, but Dylan and especially Brendan, looked floored, wide-eyed and chins drooping. Their hearts had slowed only a little before Katie came bouncing, and I mean bouncing, up the stairs. She was wearing the tiny, dusky rose bikini that Jack remembered from their first trip to the Keys, and a wide, leering grin formed on his face. She caught his expression and walked straight over to him, and grabbing her top between her breasts, announced, "Wipe that stupid grin off your face, Mister, this top stays on this time," emphasizing her words by pulling on the top to illustrate that it was firmly attached.

"Yes, I can see that, but I still have my memories." Jack tried unsuccessfully to quit grinning but his next smart-ass comment was cut short by the loudest wolf whistle he had ever heard Sean produce. He turned to find out the reason for the interruption. Erin, forgotten in the commotion of Katie's pronouncement, had snuck onto the flybridge without anyone noticing and was standing shyly at the back of the group. Hidden beneath the baggy pants and loose fitting sweaters she constantly wore, there was a slim, sexy, 22-year-old siren who more than adequately filled out the small, bright red bikini she had chosen to buy the day before.

"Whooee, Poppet, you *are* all grown up, girl. Who would have thought that my little sister could look this good?" Sean was digging himself deeper and deeper into the hole he had created for himself, but he was partially rescued by Brendan, who only uttered one word, "WOW!!!!"

Jack had a questioning look on his face, "Poppet?"

Erin turned to face Jack, "That's Sean's childhood name for me, and it's his alone. Only he is allowed to call me Poppet and I love him for it, even if he chooses to use it in a condescending way."

"Oh, come on. Ten years ago, you were ripe with puppy fat, and were not very proud of yourself. Now you hide yourself in baggy pants and sweaters, when there is a model class woman waiting to take the world by storm. Who would have thought that such beauty lay behind such plain wrapping? Not I. That is all I meant to say." Sean was trying desperately to worm his way out of his faux pas, but was not succeeding until Brendan, acting in a way that was totally out of character for him, suddenly reached out for Erin's waist and started to tickle her.

She let out a squeal, and turned on him, "You cut that out! I've already been groped by one member of this family, and once was enough!" Even as she said it, she turned to face Sean, only to find him with his face lowered into his hands and thoroughly ashamed of himself. Her mood swung instantly from one of annoyance to one of consternation, and she rushed over to him, took his head in her hands and buried his face between her breasts, crying, "Oh, I'm so, so sorry, Sean. I know it was an accident and you didn't mean it, and I know you still feel guilty about it, but I want you to stop it, OK?" She lifted his head, "OK?" And all he could do was nod his head weakly, and keep from grinning. She saw his thinly disguised attempt to hide it, looked puzzled for a split second, looked down at her own breasts and then realized what she had done, and started laughing uproariously.

All tension immediately disappeared from the entire group. In the middle of the commotion, Brendan stood up and cleared his throat quite loudly. When he had all of their attention, he announced, "Well, if she can stand up for herself, so can I. I don't want to be a half-brother any more; I want to be a fully fledged brother in this family. Now that Pa is gone, I think I deserve that much."

Shock and perhaps a little guilt followed the pronouncement, but Erin was the first to recover. "Welcome to the family, brother," she said, smiling and gave him a huge kiss and a bear hug.

"Thank you, sister, and I just want to say, Sean is right. You really are beautiful, and not only physically. You are overall, a beautiful person. If you weren't my sister, I could really go for you." Brendan was looking a little ashamed about his sudden emotional outburst, but Erin took his hands and said, "Why, thank you, little brother. I believe that's the nicest thing you have ever said to me."

As the eldest, Dylan and Kathleen were sitting at the table looking rather perplexed. Dylan stood up, "We will now vote. All who want Brendan to be a full brother say 'aye'."

A heartfelt shouted chorus of ayes rang out across the water.

Jack and Shannon, of course, remained silent, until Dylan swung on them, "And what say you two?"

Jack said, "We are not members of the family."

"You are now, whether you like it or not. Now, what say you?"

Jack looked Shannon in the eyes and together they said, "Aye!"

Kathleen jumped up immediately and said, "I think we ought to celebrate. I know it is still morning, but this is an exceptional day. Eight Mimosas coming right up."

"Make that seven," Jack said.

"It's his day; Brendan can have one, too."

"I meant me."

"One is not going to kill you, mister-stickler-for-the-rules. From the stories Sean has been telling me, the whole bottle of champagne would not affect either one of you."

"Telling tales out of school again, Sean?"

"Had to build up your reputation somehow, you sure as hell weren't going to do it on your good looks."

Everyone paired off again, and Kathleen went below to mix the drinks. Jack scanned the area, but being a weekday morning, there were few recreational boats on the water and none were near them. Shannon had sat down in the Stidd chair next to him and was holding his hand; Sean and Katie were in the process of removing the cover from the notorious Jacuzzi, which had been the scene of much hilarity and a little debauchery during the last Keys cruise. Jack doubted it would happen again, but as they slipped into the water, Jack heard Katie giggle.

During the rebuild of the boat, Jack had designed and had Bradford's build a champagne flute carrier for the dumb waiter from the galley to the flybridge, and it arrived now bearing the promised libations. After Kathleen distributed the drinks, she joined Dylan at the dining table.

Brendan sat down next to Erin, and slipped his arm around her waist. She flinched, but when it became apparent that he wasn't going to tickle her again, she relaxed. Jack heard him saying softly, "that was the best tickle ever. You see what we have now; a complete family."

Jack turned, and said sarcastically, "Yeah, the Brady Bunch."

Sean and Katie both laughed, while the rest looked at Jack uncomprehendingly.

"Sorry, it was the title of an old American sitcom from way back when, about a family with a bunch of kids. As I recall there were three brothers and three sisters in that one, too."

"But we only have two sisters."

"In nine days time, you will have another sister, because Katie will be one, too."

Jack raised his glass high, "A toast. To the Brady Bunch!"

"The Brady Bunch. And their friends." They all drank. Even Jack.

All day long they followed the Intracoastal Waterway south and west until around five in the afternoon when they anchored in ten feet of water only a half mile from the Lorelei Restaurant in Islamorada. They tendered ashore to the restaurant's dock, two trips again, and had a 'comfort food' dinner and some drinks while listening to music performed by a local Keys group, who by any standards weren't half bad.

After a pleasant evening, they tendered back out to the yacht and gathered together on the flybridge for a nightcap, sitting around discussing, in great earnest, Keys and South Florida fashions. Dylan had found Jack's stash of genuine Hawaiian shirts, made in Hawaii, not in Indonesia like Tommy Bahama shirts, and sold by a small beachfront store in Lauderdale-by-the-Sea.

Dylan had thus acquired himself a whole new wardrobe, courtesy of Jack, for it was indeed Jack's wardrobe, and was determined to wear them all before he went back to Ireland. After he showed up wearing the first one, Erin and Brendan joined in the sacking of Jack's and even Shannon's wardrobes. Brendan's fit was comparable to Jack's but Erin was still a little small for Shannon's shirts, except for the bosom part, where she left Shannon somewhat wanting. No one minded the extra volume, though, since Hawaiian shirts are meant to be loose and worn out. It did make for a colorful collection of Irish men and women whenever they went out.

After what everyone agreed was the appropriate amount of camaraderie, they all partnered up and retired to their assigned staterooms. Jack and Shannon both agreed that it was amazing what a difference one day on a boat could make to certain situations and relationships, and they both hoped for that kind of result in Dylan's case back in Ireland. It was certain that the Brady Bunch was going to be a much more close knit family from this day forward.

Chapter 4

Knowing that they only had a manageable distance to travel until they reached Key West, everyone slept in late the next morning. Indeed, it was Brendan who woke first, and throwing on a pair of shorts, he went for a walk around the decks of the boat. Seeing nothing unusual or alarming, he brewed himself a cup of tea, ascended the stairs to the flybridge, and seated himself on the helm seat, watching the world start up around him. He marveled at how different the islands here were from the ones back in Ireland, their low lying, mangrove covered, flat landscape contrasting sharply with the storm-eroded, grass covered, rocky tall spires of the islands off the coast of his home, that he had grown so used to seeing.

Although most of the islands he had seen here were populated, there still seemed to be an abundance of vegetation which, while not tall, seemed lush and all-encompassing. It seemed that the plants made up for their lack of height by their sheer impenetrability. He could not imagine having been an explorer trying to make a passage through that seemingly solid wall of extravagant growth.

It took the better part of an hour before the rest of the company decided that it was time to finally get up and join in the celebration of a warm winter's day. When they all were settled with their coffee, tea, bagels and other light breakfasts, Sean went forward and raised the anchor and they were off. The boat followed the sinuous path of the Intracoastal Waterway southwestward to the south of the bulk of Florida Bay, but north of the island chain itself until they passed under the Seven Mile Bridge and exited into the Hawk Channel, which would take them all the way to Key West. All were dressed in typical boating attire -

shorts, T-shirts, swimsuits and bikinis - and were prepared to spend a relaxing day just cruising along working on their suntans.

Books, paper or Kindle, sprouted like weeds in an untended garden, and soon all were absorbed in their own little fantasy worlds. Brendan and Erin were on the sunpad forward of the pilothouse, Sean and Katie occupied the dining table on the aft deck, and Dylan and Kathleen were hanging out on the flybridge with Jack and Shannon.

"You know, I've never thought about living on a boat like you do. I was brought up believing that boats were for fishing and other work, except for the cruise ships where you took your holidays, if you could afford it." Dylan observed. "It seems to be a very comfortable way of life, even if it is expensive."

"It is a great way to live, and it is actually less expensive than it seems." Jack pointed out. "Once over the initial costs, it can be quite economical."

"How so?"

"Well, this boat initially cost four million dollars when new; I put down a million, and got a loan from the bank for the rest. I sold my home in Coral Springs for half a million, so I only had to raid my savings for the other half. Due to a stroke of good fortune, the bank was recently paid off in full, so now Shannon and I own it free and clear." Jack could see that Dylan's brain was working overtime, and he waited patiently for the next inevitable questions to come, and they did.

"But the dockage, insurance and fuel to run this boat must be exorbitant. How can you justify spending that much extra just to live on the water." Dylan hadn't had time to think it through, so Jack explained.

"Actually it costs the same or less to live on a boat. With a house, you have taxes, insurance, utilities, maintenance, grounds up-keeping fees, transportation, etc., etc., ad infinitum. On a boat, you have dockage fees, which are usually a whole lot less than the taxes you would have to pay on a four million dollar house; fuel for the engines and the generators, usually a lot less than your typical electricity bill; insurance, which surprisingly enough, is less than on a house of the same value; maintenance tends to be a little higher on a boat, but that is offset by the fact that we make our own electricity with the generators, and our own water with a reverse osmosis water maker. We have no grounds to keep up, and our transportation is the boat itself, the fifteen foot Novurania tender, a three-person Yahama jet ski, two Vespa scooters we keep on board, our two Segways, two bicycles and our two Hydrospeeders. When we need a car or truck, we simply rent one for the day." Jack took a deep breath, for he was not used to stringing so many words together in a single speech.

"O.K. I'm with you so far. But does it have any advantages?"

"Of course it does. You can go anywhere in the world that you want, at least where there's water deep enough to float your boat, and take your home with you. A great advantage if you happen to live next to a lousy neighbor, who throws wild parties, won't invite you and won't shut up, no matter how many times you call the police. On a boat, if the guy next to you is incompatible to you, you simply raise the anchor and move somewhere else. Try doing that with a house. Also, if you want to save on costs, you simply find a nice anchorage somewhere, like where we were last night, which cost us nothing, and stay there until you run out of fuel or food, whichever comes first. Then you spend one day at a marina, refuel, and spend the day restocking your food supply, and you are good to go for another month or longer. And even anchored out, you still have the tender to take you ashore for shopping, a restaurant meal, entertainment, or the hospital in case of emergency." Once again Jack paused for a breath.

Dylan was left processing all the information he had just received, and looking mighty thoughtful doing it. Kathleen was also looking thoughtful, though a little worried.

"And you could go anywhere you wanted in this boat?"

"Sure. After Sean and Katie's wedding, Shannon and I are taking this boat to Tortola, in the British Virgin Islands, then when we come back, we'll go up to New England and maybe the Great Lakes, and next year, we are planning a trip to the Mediterranean. During the refit the boat went through not so long ago, I took the opportunity to modify it a little. I fitted a new 500 gallon long range fuel tank in addition to the standard 1850 gallons; I put in a wireless remote control system allowing me to control the engines and bow and stern thrusters, and the anchor from up to a hundred yards away; and I fitted a satellite radio in the pilothouse so I could talk to people even from the middle of the Atlantic. The boat is now set up to travel anywhere in the world."

Conversation lapsed and then, shortly after lunch, Key West appeared on the horizon and everyone disappeared below decks to freshen up and change clothes. On their way into the port, they had to dodge past a just-docking cruise ship and Jack wondered idly how many of the ship's passengers they would see in town, and how many of them would be fleeced by the time they left for their next port of call.

Jack had phoned ahead to secure their slip at the A&B Marina, and soon they were backing into their assigned spot. Jack was showing Dylan how simple it was to operate the remote control while Sean handled the stern line and Shannon was on the bow line. The two spring lines would be added once the yacht was positioned correctly to take advantage of the folding boarding steps they carried with them. Once everything was in place, Jack shut down the engines and instruments, and after connecting the shorepower cables, he also shut down the generator. He had earlier turned off the watermaker when the gauges showed the water tanks to be full, so they didn't need to connect to shore water supply. As always, Jack securely locked up the boat and set the alarm system before they began their explorations.

The quirky, eclectic nature of Key West came as quite a culture shock for the Irish men and women, even as it felt so welcoming and wonderful to the Americans, who had been there before. The obligatory first stop for Jack was, of course, the Schooner Wharf Bar, where for years, his Cuban friend Hector had been cutting and rolling by hand Jack's favorite rum flavored cigars in his little stand inside the bar, and the others just followed along. Every other month, Jack received in the mail twenty five of the cigars and promptly sent two hundred dollars to Hector. But this afternoon, Jack was disappointed to see that his friend was not there, his place having been taken by the man's daughter, Consuela.

"Hi, Consuela, where is Hector? He's not sick, is he?"

Startled, she turned to Jack, "Oh, Señor Jack, I'm so sorry. Hector died a couple of months ago, and I took over the business. Are my cigars not good for you?"

Jack was shocked, for he had not noticed any difference in the cigars he was receiving now as compared to all the ones he had received in the past. He leaned over and kissed her cheek, "I am shocked and so sorry to hear about Hector. He was a good man; he raised you right and taught you well. Your cigars are just as good as his were and you can keep sending me my order, but from now on, you send them to my friend, Sean, instead of to me, because we are going to be cruising in our boat down in the Caribbean for a while and Sean will know where I am. Is that OK with you?"

"Sure, Señor Jack, you give me the address, I send them to Sean."

Sean, who had been standing right behind Jack during the exchange, handed Consuela one of his business cards. "You send them here, and I'll send you the money and I'll make sure Jack gets them."

"OK, Señor Sean. You buy some, too?"

"Sure, you send me twenty five every other month, too." Sean knew of Jack's weakness for the cigars, and quite often pilfered one of the supply Jack kept on the boat.

All of them trooped into the bar and found a table upstairs amongst the treetops and all the kitty cats that populated Key West, almost to overflowing. Many were of the six-toed variety, descendants of Ernest Hemmingway's six toed cats who still hung out at his home, now a museum to his work and life, but some were clearly imposters and hanger-ons, there only for the food they could beg off the unsuspecting tourists. In this regard, the begging from unsuspecting tourists, the cats weren't the only perpetrators, as a fair portion of Key West's human inhabitants seem to be in the same line of business.

A little finger food and a beer later, they were on their way again, and after a quick stop at not only Sloppy Joe's but at Captain Tony's, both of which claimed to be the oldest and the original, Jack led them to The Porch, his favorite since he was an aficionado of craft beer, and this place had them all, and great atmosphere to boot.

They spent a respectable hour at The Porch, consuming a couple of Belgian Triples, and then Jack led them a long way off the beaten path to the Green Parrot Lounge. There were not many tourists, out there on the outskirts of the downtown area, but there were quite a few locals hanging out. There was a band practicing for that night's performance, but unfortunately it was not the blues band Jack was hoping to see. A quick drink and then a long walk down Whitehead Street brought them to Mallory Square on the waterfront, just in time for the daily Sunset Celebrations. Clowns and unicyclists competed for space and attention with trained cat antics, escape artists and chainsaw jugglers in a strange spectacle of haphazard vocations designed to separate dazzled tourists from their hard-earned money. And, for the most part, they seemed to be succeeding.

As it does every day, the sun finally set on the quirky comedic chaos of Mallory Square and as the tourists, as well as the artists, if one's imagination could stretch that far, began slowly to dissipate, Jack led them back toward A&B Marina and the upscale Commodore Restaurant. Given that the service was prompt, the food was decidedly superb, and the atmosphere was very relaxed, the time spent was well worth it. The meal was easily the most expensive of the trip, but justifiably so because of the quality.

At the bottom of the stairs, a slight quandary occurred. Brendan voiced a desire to return to the boat for some much needed sleep since he had been the one who was up first that morning and he didn't need any more to drink. The boy had been matching everyone drink for drink all day, and Jack secretly suspected that this was not his first escape into the world of alcohol, despite his being underage.

With the boat's key in hand, and the clicker programmed with the alarm code locked into its electronic brain, Brendan walked slowly down the dock, while the others retreated toward an old cigar and rum store Jack remembered well from previous trips to this Sin City of the South. On the bar's second floor rooftop, they imbibed in highly illegal, for the moment, but highly desirable Cuban cigars, and a variety of classic Caribbean Island rums. It was well after midnight when they finally stumbled back to the boat, to sleep, perchance to dream and to survive the hangover which was sure to follow such a marathon day. Jack would later recall this night as the one that caused his eventual downfall.

They spent the next two days exploring Key West and its immediate surroundings. They had time to visit Fort Zachery Taylor, the Martello Towers, with even a trip on the high speed ferry out to Fort Jefferson for lots of snorkeling and scuba diving. There was even time to do some shopping and Erin picked up another bikini, this one a deep cobalt blue with bright white accents, and it was even skimpier than her red one.

They left Key West bright and early Friday morning for the high speed run down the Hawk Channel to Ft. Lauderdale, because, as Jack explained with Sean nodding agreement behind him, you didn't want to be in Key West for the weekend because of the chaos that inevitably erupts between the locals and the visitors. The 'Final Option' cleared out of Key West harbor just before seven, hung a left at the outer marker buoy, and accelerated to thirty three knots. Jack was well aware of the prodigious amount of fuel that the engines were consuming, but he was unconcerned because, for some unfathomable reason, he was anxious to get back to the place he called home.

It was just before noon, as they were passing South Beach in Miami, that Erin asked Jack if there was anywhere they could stop and go swimming at the beach.

"Sure, we could go in through Haulover Inlet; there's a marina there we could tie up at and then go to Haulover Beach, the southern part is OK." Jack said.

"Sounds great, I want to get my new bikini wet. What's wrong with the northern part?"

"Oh, nothing is wrong with it, it's just, well, it's a nude beach. You know, clothing optional."

"Seriously, in America? I didn't think that was even possible." Erin looked incredulously at Jack, as if she had just discovered the meaning of life, and didn't believe it.

"Hey, c'mon. We have a lot of nude beaches in America. There was one in Key West we could have gone to, but I didn't think that was what you wanted to do." Jack was furiously trying to think of a way of discouraging her, but for the life of him, he couldn't come up with one sound reason.

"So let's go, Mister, or is your puritanical attitude going to hold you back forever?"

"That sounds a lot like a challenge, young lady."

"Take it however you like; I want to go swimming at the nude beach. You can stay on the namby-pamby southern part if you want to, but I want to go swimming."

"OK. If that's what you want, that's what you'll get." He adjusted the course of the boat fifteen degrees to port and shortly they were lined up with the entrance of Haulover Inlet.

As they were closing in rapidly with the shore, everyone noticed and came rushing to the flybridge expecting the worst. When they saw Jack standing at the helm and still fully in control of the boat, they relaxed but remained somewhat perplexed.

Sean walked over to Jack, "What's going on? Do we have some kind of a problem?"

"You tell me. Your little sister wants to go swimming and get her new swimsuit wet at Haulover Beach."

Sean suddenly looked anxious, "North or south?"

"North."

"And you told her about it?"

"Yes, but apparently, that's why she wants to go."

"And you're going to do it?"

"Anything for my guests." Jack gave Sean an appropriate shrug of the shoulders.

Erin stepped between them, "You two stop talking about me as if I am not here. I want to go. Nobody else has to come. If your prudish American sensibilities won't let you get out and enjoy

94

yourselves, that's your problem. I'm European, where the attitude on nudity and sex is much more relaxed and accepted. More of a 'ho hum' than an 'oh, boy'. If you know what I mean."

Dylan spoke up for the first time in this discussion, "Just what is the problem with this beach, anyway?"

Sean and Jack spoke in unison, almost in harmony. "It's a nude beach."

Dylan's brow knitted and his eyes narrowed and for the first time since Jack had met him, he sensed the power and anger in the man. "Erin, I don't want you to go to this place; I don't feel you would be safe."

"Thank you for your concern, brother; I do appreciate your feelings. But I'm a grown woman now and I have to make decisions for myself. This probably is no big deal to you, and it really is *no big deal*, but it's something that I've decided that I want to do, and you have no say in the matter. I will do as I want and *nobody* can say that I can't."

Dylan acquiesced, "I can't stop you, but I won't go with you. You're on your own."

"Me, neither." said Kathleen, looking pointedly at Sean.

Sean said, "I'll go with you, Poppet."

Katie said, "And I'll go with my man."

Sean looked over at Jack, who shrugged and said, "What the hell. It might be interesting."

Shannon said, with a huge grin "And I'll go with my man, if only to keep him out of trouble."

Everyone suddenly looked over at Brendan, who was standing to one side with a big grin on his face, and he said in typical teenage fashion, "Oh, hell, yes. I'll go. I wouldn't miss this for the world."

During this discussion, Jack had been guiding the boat toward the marina, and he grabbed the wireless remote for the boat and proceeded down the aft stairs to the deck. He quickly and deftly guided the boat into an empty slip and stepped onto the dock to tie up the lines as Sean threw them to him. When all was secured, he told all the participants on this adventure to gather only a minimum of things for it was a long hike across what was a sizeable parking lot, which seemed surprisingly empty, and across Highway A1A, until he realized that it was still Friday.

Donning their swimsuits and cover-ups, and carrying their towels in beach bags, they set out across the asphalt towards the beach. Despite Jack's warning, it wasn't that much of a hike; he had just exaggerated it to try to change Erin's mind. But they could see it hadn't worked. Where they emerged was still on the southern part of the beach. A little way to the north they could see the fence across the beach designating the clothing optional part of the white sand. Erin, a grin on her face, turned directly north and started marching.

"This looks nice, don't you think?" Sean called to her receding back.

"I think this looks better up here." she called back.

Shrugging his shoulders and out of options, Sean follow her along the sand, finally resigned to his fate. The others followed along, only a few paces behind.

Erin reached the fence with its stern warning that they were entering a clothing optional area and that those who were easily offended should turn around and go back. She turned to make sure that the others were following her and then crossed the threshold. It didn't feel any different there on the other side of the fence, but she felt she had made a commitment. She had taken a stand, stood up to the other's objections, and felt that she had to, for better or worse, trust her own judgment and carry on regardless. She turned again to be sure that the others had made that same commitment and was relieved to see that they had, for they were only a few paces behind her on her side of the fence.

She continued on, scanning the horizon, noting the lack of crowds with a sense of relief. She kept walking 'til she was what she judged to be halfway between the lifeguard towers and somewhat away from other people. She laid her towel on the sand, unfolding and straightening it at a precise ninety degree angle to the shoreline. Brendan, coming up behind her, laid his down next to hers exactly six inches away, so as not to crowd her. Sean and Katie lay their towels parallel to the shore, with the corners touching, and Jack and Shannon put their towels on the sand parallel to the shore on the opposite side to Sean and Katie's. Then they all stood on the end of their towels, looking at each other with uncertainty.

Sean was the first to break the silence, "So, whose idea was this?"

Erin, suddenly very unsure of herself, nevertheless summoned up the courage to answer, "I believe the original idea was mine."

"Then, little sister, might I suggest, that you go first?"

Now, of course, it was crunch time. She had always felt very unsure of her attractiveness to men; that was the reason she always wore the baggiest clothes she could find. But the comments that Sean had made when he had first seen her in a bikini, combined with the consternation she had seen on his face when he had accidentally grabbed her breast, made her feel a little more confident in her mind.

"If you insist," she said as she slowly reached behind her back, unfastened the clasp on her bikini top and gently pulled it over her head and dropped it on her towel. She then hooked both thumbs into the sides of her bikini bottom and slowly slid the small triangle of cloth down to her ankles, where she gracefully stepped out of it and kicked it backward to join her top. She was naked but somehow she didn't feel ashamed, not even nervous, which was surprising to her since there were, if not strangers, at least acquaintances, looking at her naked body and assessing her attributes, but she didn't care. She then placed both hands on her hips and, facing them, asked, "Well?" looking straight at Sean. He, naturally, was standing there open-mouthed because he truly believed that she wouldn't have had the nerve to actually go through with it, and now that she had, he was at a loss about what to do. His salvation came in the form of Brendan, who shouted, "Hell, yeah. You really are a big sister," as he pulled his boardshorts down to his ankles and stepped out of them. He was clearly looking at her breasts, which were impressive, to say the least.

They all turned to look at him, a well proportioned young man who was also very well endowed.

"Just so you remember; I'm your sister. Don't get any funny ideas." Erin said, but she couldn't keep her sense of loss out of her voice.

Katie, in her usual role of the instigator, didn't even comment or hesitate. She just untied the top of her string bikini, threw it on her towel and pulled her bikini bottom down to her ankles and stepped away, placing one fingertip on top of her head and performing a graceful pirouette, completely naked.

Jack, being the smart ass he was, commented, "Katie, you realize you just lost the bet, right?"

"What bet," she said, perplexed.

"The bet we made at the pool table, when you said that I'd never see you topless again. Somehow, I think this more than qualifies, don't you?"

She hesitated only slightly, "I guess. What exactly was the bet we made?"

"I don't remember, but I'll think of something."

"Yeah, I'll bet you will."

"There you go; betting again."

Sean, in the meantime, having removed the Speedos he inevitably wore and thrown them on top of Katie's bikini, stood and listened to this verbal exchange while pointedly looking at Shannon, who was still wearing her black lycra one piece racing suit, which most of the time looked painted on instead of worn especially when it was wet.

She reached behind her neck and unfastened the clasp, bent over at the waist, bringing the suit down to her ankles as she went. She took one step backward, leaving the rumpled garment on the ground, intertwined her fingers and slowly straightening her willowy body to its full height, and while bringing her arms above her head and standing on tip toe, turned a full 360 degree circle. Even Jack was impressed at her poise.

Jack heard a sharp and prolonged intake of breath from Sean at the sight of a naked Shannon before them, and turned toward his friend with an 'Oh, really!' look on his face.

"Hey, don't look at me that way. This is the first time I've seen Shannon naked. She is one of the few women in my life who I never got to sleep with." Sean was trying desperately to explain his reaction, and digging another deep hole for himself.

Katie punched him on the shoulder, "And what am I, just another one of your conquests?"

"No, you are the only one I have ever wanted to marry." he said glibly.

"Oh, you sly fox. You always have the right answer right on the tip of your tongue, don't you?"

"Well, I *am* Irish, and I *do* have the gift of the gab." He laughed and pulled her naked body to him and gave her a long, drawn out kiss while holding her tight in his arms. She resisted at first but soon relaxed and enjoyed his embrace.

All eyes shifted to Jack, who simply shrugged his shoulders and dropped his boardshorts on top of Shannon's black swimsuit. Jack had never thought of himself as God's gift to women, but he did notice that Katie was peering over Sean's shoulder and her eyes widened momentarily, then cut quickly to Shannon, who stood with a Mona Lisa smile on her lips indicating she understood how Katie was feeling. His attention, however, was drawn to Erin, who had pursed her lips and inclined her head ever so slightly and was giving Jack much more than just a passing glance. Jack, of course, was also enjoying his view.

Erin suddenly yelled, "Let's go swimming. Race you!" Immediately, the three girls jumped up and raced for the water, boobs bouncing in the breeze. The guys were slower off the mark, but had almost caught them before they reached the waterline. They all hit the water almost simultaneously, dove under and came up laughing and splashing. Jack found Shannon a few feet away and swam to her, while Sean and Katie came up side by side, taking hold of each other and squeezing tight. Erin surfaced and found Brendan standing close by, but a respectful distance away. She gazed into his eyes, perplexed by his sudden shyness, then slowly walked over to him, and kissed him lightly on the mouth. "I love you, little brother," she said, noticing with a certain alacrity that her nipples were hardening and standing at attention. '*It is probably the coldness of the water,*' she thought to herself, but said, "I am still your sister; so don't you be getting any ideas."

He grinned, "I love you, too, Erin. Don't worry, nothing will happen. But you can't stop me from being a man, though." With that she laughed at him, splashed water in his face, then turned and dove into the water, swimming away from him as fast as she could. When she started feeling a bit breathless from the exertion, she rolled onto her back, allowing her legs to slowly sink below her body, and looked for Brendan, certain he was following. She was astounded when she found his face only two feet from hers, and he suddenly lunged and kissed her, then placed his hands on her shoulders and pushed her below the surface. She only had time for a quick breath, but it was enough. He released her immediately and she surfaced laughing and giggling. Together they swam side by side back to the group, and any tension that there had been before was totally dissipated by the time they returned.

The two engaged couples still clung to their respective partners, whispering sweet nothings into each other's ears. It wasn't long before they all started heading for the beach since the January water was quite cold, at least by South Florida standards. They walked back to their towels hand in hand, even Erin and Brendan, who had established an unspoken agreement between themselves as to how close was proper.

They lay sunning themselves for over an hour, laughing, talking and smearing each other with SPF40, since the sun's rays were very strong. Jack finally spoke up, "I hate to be the one who ends this adventure, but we have to get the boat back to Ft. Lauderdale today." Everyone agreed that it was time to leave and started donning their swimsuits and cover-ups. Towels were shaken out and disappeared into the girls' voluminous beach bags. They then proceeded, couple by couple, to walk back toward the fence. Brendan stopped at the fence and said, "Wait, I want a photo of this occasion." He walked up the fence line toward the lone figure lying face down on her towel, and asked, "Excuse me, do you think you could take a photo or two of my friends and I?"

She rolled onto her side, scrutinized him for half a second, and with a bright smile on her face, said, "Sure, it would be a pleasure." She stood, completely naked, walked over and took his cell phone from him and followed him down to the lifeguard tower where the others waited. Brendan was amazed at his luck, for the petite, slim blonde that followed him was absolutely gorgeous, seemingly uninhibited, and filled out in all the right places. All he had wanted before was a photo to remember this day, but no longer. His mind was already racing, conjuring up and discarding varied scenarios to prolong this chance meeting.

They arrived at the tower and she took a dozen or so shots of the group posing, laughing together and hamming it up before holding the phone toward Brendan, who reluctantly took it from her.

"Can't I convince you to stay for a while longer?" she said, tilting her head to one side, causing her long, blond hair to cascade across one shoulder, "You know, it's kind of lonely here with no one to talk to."

He nearly fell when his knees went rubbery, but he said with much regret in his voice, "I wish I could, believe me, I really wish I could, but Captain Ahab over there insists we get the boat back to Lauderdale tonight; and I am but a lowly passenger."

"Lauderdale? I don't suppose you could give me a lift back, could you?"

Brendan couldn't believe his luck, "Let's see."

He walked straight up to Jack, and with his best pleading face firmly in place, asked, "Could we please give her a lift back to Lauderdale?" Jack had already noticed, with not a small amount of amusement, the desire in the boy's body, and was not about to ruin his chances.

"Sure, I don't see why not; we have plenty of room."

The smile on Brendan's face threatened to outshine the sun as he turned around toward the blonde, who was already walking back to the group. Brendan was nodding his head, as she reached him, and she said, "I guess we had better be introduced if I'm coming with you. I'm Kelly Jorgensen."

He shook her hand, "Hi, I'm Brendan Brady. Let me introduce you to this terrible crew. This is our captain and the boat's owner, Jack Elliott, and his fiancée, Shannon. My brother, Sean and his fiancée, Katie, and my sister, Erin."

"Your sister?"

"Yes, she's my big sister. She's all of 22 and I'm 19."

"I'm sorry, and I don't mean to pry. But I saw you two out there in the water and it didn't look like brother and sister to me."

"Well, I understand what you mean. But since it was our first time at a nude beach, we were unsure of how to act. I'm not ashamed to say that I was shy and embarrassed at first, but we worked it out, as you can see. But tell me, weren't you hesitant your first time?"

"Oh, yes. It took me ages sitting on the other side of that fence, gathering up the courage to cross the line; but once I did, I got over the jitters quickly and from then on I enjoyed myself. Of course, I didn't have your support system of brothers, sisters, and friends, since I was all by myself."

Jack interrupted the discussion, "Well, we have to get going; if you're coming with us, you have 5 minutes before we shove off."

"Aye, aye, Captain," she saluted and took off at a run back to her possessions, got dressed in her bikini and cover-up and shook out her towel, folded it into her beach bag and was back in under two minutes.

They wandered back to the boat across the parking lot, talking amongst themselves. Brendan kept close to Kelly, peppering her with questions, until Erin started to feel a little miffed and left out. With startling insight, she suddenly realized that this was the way Brendan must have felt all those years when he had been excluded from sharing fully in their family gatherings. For no apparent reason, she felt guilty, but promised herself that she would make it up to him somehow.

They were approaching the marina when Kelly suddenly let out a gasp, pointing to the boat. "Is that huge yacht yours?"

With an unaccustomed sense of pride, Jack replied, "Yes, or should I say, ours. Mine and Shannon's."

"She is beautiful. WOW." Kelly was awestruck and it showed on her face. She grabbed Brendan's arm for support and pulled him close. "I am so glad you stopped to talk to me."

He looked her directly in her eyes and murmured, "Believe me, so am I."

They boarded the boat, introduced Kelly to Dylan and Kathleen, and prepared to get underway. The engines and electronics were fired up and soon all was ready to go. Jack stepped to the helm on the flybridge, only to be hip blocked out of the way by Shannon, who took the controls and dared, with slitted eyes, for Jack to object. Discretion being the better part of valor, he made no comment as she neatly exited the slip, powered into the Intracoastal Waterway, which she followed under the Haulover Inlet bridge and into the open ocean, increasing the revs on the engines until they were doing 30 knots and headed for Port Everglades. Brendan and Kelly, lost in their own little world in the corner of the dining table on the flybridge, talked animatedly of their past lives and were hardly aware of the comings and goings of the other people on the boat.

Dylan and Kathleen, standing on the other side of the flybridge, were acutely aware of the changed dynamic of the whole group. Everyone seemed more friendly, loose, cooperative and appreciative of one another, and secretly, they both wished that they, too, had joined in with Erin's impulsive move to take a trip to a nude beach. They watched as their little brother, seemingly without being aware of it, charmed Kelly to the point where she was hanging on his every word. This young man, who for years had railed against their every attempt to find him a girlfriend, now appeared to be most comfortably assured in the company of a member of the opposite sex and loving every minute of it. Of course, they were not privy to the circumstances of the meeting which taken place on the beach, so their confusion was understandable.

Dylan was not too sure that the young girl Brendan had chosen to befriend was necessarily the right girl for his younger brother, but he intended to find out. Despite Kathleen's attempt to stop him, he walked over to the table and seated himself right next to Kelly, as close as convention would allow.

"So, Kelly, tell me all about yourself." he said, deftly ducking the daggers Brendan was throwing his way with his angry eyes.

"What do you want to know?"

"Your life story, if you have the time. If you want to be a part of this family group, we have to know more about your history; don't you think that's fair?"

She hesitated, looked at Brendan with pleading eyes, and said, "Sure, if that's what you want. It's a pretty simple story, actually. I was born twenty years and three days ago in Madison, Wisconsin to Danish immigrant parents, who doted on me. They gave me everything I ever needed, a loving home, a balanced upbringing, and the best education they could afford. They encouraged me at all times to do the best I could at whatever I chose to do. Everything I am, I owe to them. I moved here to South Florida two years ago, and am currently working full time as a paralegal for a law firm in Plantation."

"It's Friday, why aren't you working?"

"I took a week off to celebrate New Year's and my birthday, January 4th, but I have to go back to work on Monday, come hell or high water."

"You *do* realize that Brendan is only 19, don't you?"

She stood up suddenly to her full height of five foot six, and looking down at him because he was still sitting, said in her most pleasant and calm voice, "And that makes him less than a year younger than me. Not an insurmountable difference, wouldn't you agree?"

Brendan was shocked to say the least, for he had never before seen Dylan at a loss for words, obviously deeply embarrassed, and groping for the words that didn't seem to come.

Dylan stood, his six foot five frame towering over the blonde woman in front of him, who continued to challenge him with her eyes even though she now had to look up. She saw his haunted eyes flicker hesitantly, scan momentarily across her scantily clad body, and then, like a deflating balloon, he seemed to sag visibly.

"Welcome to the group," he said gruffly as he retreated toward Kathleen, "I'll reserve judgment about the family part until we know more about you."

As he walked away, she collapsed into Brendan's arms, "He's scary," she said.

"Don't worry about Dylan. He's going through a rough period right now. In fact, we all are. You see, our father was murdered a few weeks ago, and we're trying to make the best we can of the situation."

"Oh, Brendan, I'm so sorry. I hope I haven't contributed to your pain."

"No, exactly the reverse. You've given me something to hope for again." With that, he folded her into his embrace and held her tight, wondering what was to become of this prickly, but delightful situation.

All too soon, Shannon was making the sweeping left turn into the entrance to Port Everglades. She headed north on the Intracoastal, at idle speed, into the New River, and then west up the river to their berth in the heart of Ft. Lauderdale. They would be docked right by the Downtowner, which was their favorite watering hole and hangout of their many friends, who would undoubtedly be most happy to see them again.

As soon as the boat was secured, locked up and alarmed, the whole company marched over to the Downtowner, and proceeded to overwhelm the bar and the kitchen with their orders. To everyone's delight, the blues band Jack had been hoping to see at the Green Parrot in Key West, the ACB, was just taking the stage to provide the evening's entertainment. To all, the evening as well as the week, was now complete.

Chapter 5

January the tenth arrived with a roar and snuck up on everyone, just like a tornado in a Kansas wheat field. They were all expecting it and had planned for it, but it still took them by surprise. After the trip to the Keys, everyone, seemingly with a new bond between them, pitched in with the last minute details concerning Sean's and Katie's wedding and it appeared that all of the bases had been covered but, as always, there were a few of those little glitches that the gremlins created which nobody was expecting.

The bachelor party, organized by Jack and held at Sean's Four Leaf Clover bar was a resounding success, with literally hundreds of people spilling out of the bar itself into the parking lot, and, in a few cases, onto the street. This was not a good thing since it was a busy thoroughfare, and there were some near misses, but eventually the bouncers managed to keep everyone in check within the property boundaries. It was lucky that Jack had planned it a few days before the actual wedding day because there was a large percentage of the population that was severely hung over and headachy for those next few days; it almost seemed that an epidemic had descended over the town. Even Sean, the hard drinking Irishman, seemed adversely affected, for he was incommunicado for the next few days. This was unusual, given the fact that he had been a bar owner for over ten years, and was used to wild and rowdy parties. Of course, this *was* the first time that he was going to be married, so maybe he was just drowning his sorrows.

Katie's bachelorette party, arranged by Shannon to be held in the Maxwell Room at the Downtowner Saloon, was similarly successful. The number of secretaries, barmaids, and assistants to the presidents of various companies around town who had called in sick the following day had been astounding, and afterward it was only with extreme difficulty that anything got done in the days following that party. Not to say that everyone was falling down drunk; let's just say that everyone had a truly memorable time.

But the best news actually came as an interruption to the wedding rehearsal. Sean, having forgotten to put his cell phone on mute, received a call which, as soon as he saw the caller ID, he said he had to take. He walked away, out of earshot, and everyone was shocked, for Sean was not known for his phone etiquette. Everyone helped themselves to another drink, and stood around talking until he returned.

The smile on his face was overwhelming, like that brilliant ray of sunshine that finally breaks through the black threatening storm clouds at the end of the tumult and sends a silver shaft of hope for a better tomorrow onto the land. "Gather around, one and all, for I have glad tidings to tell you."

Jack smiled, for he knew that Sean was one of those people who secretly believed that they had lived before in another life, and his was the renaissance period. Thus it was his propensity to speak in Olde English when the occasion warranted it.

"Dylan, my brother, you are now, even in the eyes of the law, an innocent man."

If someone had dropped a bomb in the middle of the group, nobody would have noticed. They all stood perfectly still, frozen in the position that they were in and looked at Sean, open mouthed, waiting for the other shoe to drop. He seemed oblivious to the confusion he had caused, walking up to and slapping Dylan on the shoulder, followed by a bear hug, which effectively broke the hypnotic state everyone was in.

Sean, holding Dylan by his shoulders, explained his bombshell news to everyone present, "That phone call I just took was from Maddy, the P.I. I hired in Ireland. Using the information she got from Dylan's lawyer, Rory, who had been able to find out everything that the police knew, she utilized her own underground network of informants to verify the information I was able to share with her about the Corcoran brothers, both of whom we already suspected. She was able to disprove the alibi Timmy Corcoran had given the police by interviewing his so-called friends, who wanted nothing more than to see him locked away. She turned all her evidence over to the police who raided his house and arrested him. After a thorough search of his home, they were even able to find the clothes he had worn that night, which hadn't yet been washed, with gunshot residue still on them, *and* they also recovered your registered Glock in his possession. After his arrest, he also implicated his brother, so both of the Corcorans are cooling their heels in the slammer. The Judge still wants to see you on the sixteenth, but he says that all charges against you have been dropped."

"That is the best news you could have given me," said Dylan, who felt as if a great weight had suddenly been lifted from his shoulders. His whole family was dancing around him, hugging and kissing him with relief and joy. Sean noted with pride that this was only the second time he had seen his big brother cry, this time with relief, and he felt proud that he had a small hand in the outcome. Dylan staggered over to a table and sat down, and asked someone to bring him a Jameson's. Not a glass, but the whole damn bottle. Wedding rehearsal forgotten, he was determined to drink someone under the table, and from the looks of it, he had plenty of takers.

The next day, the wedding went off without a hitch. The weather cooperated, with only a slight breeze, a temperature in the low seventies, and no precipitation. The area outside the Downtowner was cleared of tables, and a temporary if smallish chapel was set up and cordoned off so only the invited could enter. The many folding chairs had been set up in rows from the landing stage of the dock all the way to the bridge at Third Avenue. The Maxwell Room had once again been chosen as the venue for the reception.

The guests started arriving around one for the three o'clock wedding and just hung around talking and joking amongst themselves. Jack was pleased to see that Brendan had invited Kelly to attend the wedding with him, for he found that he had taken a liking to the happy and intelligent young lady Brendan had found for himself. He noticed that Dylan and Kathleen were done up in their Sunday best and talking to all the other guests in animated tones, and seemingly enjoying the company of the people with such different lifestyles from their own. The only jarring note he found was Erin, who stood alone at the river's edge looking wistfully at the passing boats. She was all dressed up and looked beautiful, but a sad smile on her face told of her apparent loneliness for she seemed to be the only unaccompanied woman there. Jack, being chivalrous, walked over and put an arm around her shoulders, which seemed to lift her spirits, at least for the moment. She smiled at him and said, "Almost time to gain a new sister, isn't it?"

The organist arrived at two and set up her equipment and speakers, and the minister arrived at two thirty and immediately started setting up the small lectern which would serve as the altar. By three, the only ones missing were the bride and groom.

"If those two have run off and eloped, I'm going to shoot both of them," grumbled Jack. But he need not have worried, for at that moment, Sean appeared at the gate to the courtyard beside the restaurant and signaled him over. Jack hurried over, secretly admiring Sean, who looked like a model out of GQ and was probably the most dressed up Jack had ever seen him. Shannon followed Jack, knowing that Katie would not be far behind Sean. And she was right.

The organist started playing and Sean and Jack walked that long road down the aisle between their guests until they stood facing the minister, both looking extremely nervous.

Jack leaned over to Sean, and whispered, "Cell phone?" which caused both of them to jam their hands into their pockets and put them on mute.

'Here comes the bride' started and all heads turned in the direction of the gate through which Sean and Jack had exited. The vision in white that greeted their eyes was truly amazing, for none had seen Katie looking so beautiful and radiant, and yet so calm, happy and self-assured. She even outshone Shannon, following a few paces behind her. As she proceeded down the aisle regally, like a princess meeting her prince, her sheer enjoyment of the moment showed in the smiles she had for everyone, but her eyes were firmly fixed on her prize waiting before the minister, shuffling nervously from foot to foot.

Just as a great ocean liner must eventually make landfall, her deliberately measured progress finally ended with her standing beside Sean, and the ceremony began with the usual, 'Dearly beloved...', and ended with the usual, 'You may now kiss your bride.'

As the ceremony ended with a long and passionate kiss, all hell broke loose, and the cheering was uproarious, for there were many in their crowd of friends who sincerely believed that this event would never happen. Not that any of them would have wished less than total happiness for Sean and Katie, but until now, the chances of Sean getting married had been estimated to be at about the same as winning the Power Ball lottery.

Somehow, while working for Sean at his club, Katie had worked her elfin magic and Sean had fallen, hard, for her feminine wiles.

A shower of rice, which the pigeons would enjoy later, engulfed the happy couple as they walked hand in hand down the aisle toward the 'Final Option', where they would change into more appropriate attire before joining the others for the reception in the Maxwell Room. Jack and Shannon accompanied them onto the boat and extracted from Sean a solemn promise to lock and alarm the boat before leaving, and then they joined the crowd thronging toward the awaiting food and drink.

For Sean and Katie, the dinner, drinking and dancing, as well as the roasts and toasts, lasted until ten pm, when they drove slowly out of the Downtowner's parking lot in Sean's Hemi 'Cuda bound for Sean's house, while for the others, the party would last 'til midnight.

Jack and Shannon staggered back to their boat well after that, having stayed to help with the cleanup, a fact much appreciated by the staff of the restaurant. The only jarring note of the evening was when Jack turned his cell phone back on and noticed the number of missed calls and text messages he had waiting for him. As he scrolled down the list, dismissing some outright as unimportant, and making a mental note to call others back in the morning, he noticed an unusual text message that had come in at 3:12 p.m., during the ceremony. Shannon was sitting beside him on the lounge in the main salon when she saw him go deathly pale and still. "Jack, what's wrong? Are you OK?"

"No, I'm not." he replied, turning the phone toward her.

She couldn't believe what she was reading, 'I hear the weather in Tortola is nice. Horst'. She went as pale as Jack, but managed to blurt out, "So, that crazy son-of-a-bitch managed to escape after all."

"So it would appear, unless someone is playing a very stupid joke on us."

"We'll have to cancel our trip to the islands, then?"

"NO! No way am I going to let that jackass run our lives for us. I'll call Charlie Palmer in the morning and he can get the CIA and the FBI onto this guy, but we are still going to go on our cruise. Just don't tell Sean and Katie, I don't want to spoil their honeymoon in Europe. OK?"

"OK, I guess. But let's stay away from Tortola until they catch him. There are plenty of other islands to explore."

The next morning, Sean and Katie, along with the rest of the Brady Bunch, having been sent off by Jack and Shannon, virtually took over the first class section of a plane bound for New York, and eventually Dublin, Ireland. To say that the group was ecstatic would be an understatement for they were all excited to be headed home, especially with Dylan's newfound status of free man.

Coming in through the main entrance channel two days later, 'Final Option' and its crew cruised slowly and serenely into Nassau Harbour. The day before, they had returned to the cave on Eleuthera where they had found the sunken submarine the year before. The purpose of their dive through the tunnel was to retrieve the five bars of Nazi gold they had left behind when they had returned the 297 bars of U.S. gold to the government. Jack made a phone call to the Atlantis Marina announcing their imminent arrival, and before they had even got to the high twin bridges leading to Paradise Island, Jack had started his right turn into the short canal that led to the marina. When the marina came into sight, Jack's face broke into a huge smile at the sight of his reserved slip with Capt'n Pete's 165 foot Feadship 'Triumph' in the next slip beside him. This was the former 'Shillelagh', belonging to Senator O'Malley, and bought by Capt'n Pete off the estate after the demise of the Senator. Shannon was also smiling at the prospect of seeing the old man again, along with their other friends.

Maneuvering and docking was quickly accomplished, and once secure, Jack and Shannon made their way onto 'Triumph' and were enthusiastically greeted by Capt'n Pete, who introduced them to all the members of his new crew. It turned out that there were even a couple of members of the crew that Jack knew from his years of boating in South Florida, and one that he definitely counted as a friend and who was serving as the first mate, a position formerly held by Horst Keller under Capt'n Pete.

After checking in with the harbor master at the resort, Jack, Shannon and Capt'n Pete relaxed with snacks and drinks on board the 'Triumph' while awaiting the arrival of Birdman, Moses, Janine and Courtland, all members of the crew who had found the sub and the galleon the previous summer, and who were scheduled to arrive in Nassau on commercial flights throughout the afternoon. Jack had spoken to Sean and Katie before their flight to Ireland about his plan to reveal the galleon to the officials of the Bahamian government, and had gotten their approval before making a call to Government House, requesting and confirming an appointment with the Bahamian Minister of State for Culture for ten a.m. the next morning. He had also dropped some pretty blatant hints to the astute Appointments Secretary that what would be discussed might be of special interest to the Prime Minister and perhaps even the Governor General.

Over the course of the afternoon, all the others arrived, two by two, except for Charlie Palmer, who arrived with an escort of two secret service agents. After checking into their respective rooms, they all dumped their luggage there and gathered together in the skylounge on 'Triumph'.

The vote was unanimous: dinner was first, and then on to business. The former was accomplished at one of the many fine restaurants at the Atlantis resort, and the latter back in the skylounge on the big Feadship. Later that evening, over cocktails, Jack laid out his plans for the following day, including contingencies just in case the Prime Minister and/or the Governor General actually did show up. After listening to Jack's proposals for an hour, and bringing up many points for discussion, the vote to adopt Jack's plan was again unanimous. They all retired that night excited by the prospects that the next day's meeting might bring. Jack's only disappointment was that Sean and Katie could not be there, but naturally the honeymoon came first for them. They had been told of Jack's plan and had agreed wholeheartedly that this was not something which needed to be put off any longer.

They were actually early for their appointment the next morning, and were asked to wait in the outer office. At precisely ten a.m., they were ushered into the inner office where the Minister awaited their arrival. He stood up, his hand extended as he walked out from behind his desk as they entered, surprise spreading across his face as they all filed into the room. When the door finally closed behind the last of them, he smiled and welcomed them.

"My name is Randolph Buckley. How may I be of service, Mr. Elliott?"

"I believe it is entirely the other way around, Mr. Buckley. I believe we can be of service to you, if you have the time to listen to our story."

"You have me intrigued, Mr. Elliott. Please sit down and continue, and if I may, I'd like to record this conversation." He retreated back behind his desk, producing and switching on a small voice recorder.

When everyone had found a seat or a place to perch, Jack started his agreed upon tale. "Last summer, the people you see here today, and two others who could not be here today, came to the Bahamas on my yacht, 'Final Option', in search of a German submarine, commanded by the father of this man, Capt'n Pete Olsen-Smith. The German Captain had been shipwrecked here in the Bahamas, and the sub had been sunk."

Jack was interrupted by the Minister, "Yes, we are quite aware of your trip to the Bahamas last summer, as we are of your leaving the Islands without clearing customs. This is a *very* serious offense, one which could result in confiscation of your boat, which you have so conveniently brought back to us. There will be two policemen waiting to talk to you at the conclusion of this meeting. Please go on."

Jack let out the breath he had been holding in a huge sigh. "Well, yes, we do realize that we committed an infraction of the rules with our hurried departure; however, you might want to change your position on that after you have heard the rest of the story. Needless to say, we did indeed succeed in finding the submarine, but to our immense surprise, we also found in the same location in Bahamian waters, a sixteenth century Spanish galleon," he paused for effect, and looked the Minister directly in the eyes as he said, "loaded with treasure!"

The Minister sat bolt upright in his chair, his eyes had gone wide and he was unable to utter a word.

Jack smiled, "Now might be a good time to bring in the Prime Minister or the Governor General if you think they might wish to hear the story first hand. I can wait."

The Minister reached over and mashed down an intercom button. "Please call and ask Orville and Michael to join us at their earliest convenience. Stress urgency." He released the button and sat back, coldly regarding Jack and his friends. As the seconds stretched to minutes, he found himself unable to control his impatience and began to fidget with various objects on his desk. Jack regarded him with amusement, knowing he had one Minister under his thumb, and allowed himself a small smile of encouragement.

Ten minutes later, the door was thrust open violently, and two important looking men entered. They went straight to the desk and buttonholed the Culture Minister. "Randolph, why did you call us out of our meetings, and who are these people?"

He just stood there looking sheepish, and then shook his head, and pointed at Jack. They both turned to Jack, questioning looks in their eyes and consternation on their faces.

"Hello, I'm Jack Elliott, and I have a story for you that I am certain you *will* want to hear."

Jack quickly explained the revelations up to that point, including the threat to his freedom and that of his boat, and by the time he had finished, both men were sitting down, enthralled. As a finishing touch, Jack took his time opening the manila envelope he had brought with him from the boat. He extracted the contents from the envelope, six photographs that he had printed from the boat's computer showing various carefully selected views of the submarine, the galleon and the golden throne downloaded from the underwater digital camera he had carried with him during the retrieval of the sub's gold. None of these carefully edited photos showed the gold which had, of course, disappeared. He handed over the prints to the two men who couldn't believe their eyes, judging from the expression on their faces.

"So you see that our bending of the rules about clearing customs last summer was not an attempt to deprive the Bahamas of the treasure we had found, but to allow us time to assess the situation before we decided what the best way was to handle it. If we were simply thieves, we would have dismantled that golden throne and disappeared, and you would be none the wiser. It is still in the same position where we found it. Instead, we have voluntarily presented ourselves and our evidence to you so you can decide what to do with it." Jack could see that the two men were relaxing and already making plans for the treasure.

"Jack, I'm Orville, and I'm the Prime Minister. He's the Governor General and his name is Michael. You have already met Randolph. In private, we are always on a first name basis, because we feel it helps to maintain a more cooperative atmosphere. We would like to keep this discussion friendly because I think that you all deserve our thanks for bringing this discovery to our attention."

Jack interrupted him, "We, however, were not the first to find this galleon. It was discovered, 40 years before the submarine came along, by your own ex-Governor General, John Jefferson Beaumont and his adjutant, Stanley Gresham, in 1904. Unfortunately, both men lost their lives in the attempt to bring their discovery to the world. The Governor, who is the skeleton seated on the golden throne, is represented here today by his grandson, Mr. Moses Beaumont, and his great-grand daughter, Miss Janine Beaumont, and their attorney, Courtland Williams."

Both men rose and shook hands all around, uttering words of condolences.

"Now let's get down to business. I'm sure you want something for your trouble." Orville said, clearly taking charge of the situation, and overshadowing both Michael and Randolph.

Again, Jack spoke for the entire group, "You are right, but you will be surprised by what we want. On the off chance that you would be accommodating, we all discussed this very thing last night. First, naturally, we want to be fairly compensated for our discovery of this historic and valuable find, and my negotiator for that discussion is my friend, C. Bryant Palmer, the U.S. Secretary of the Treasury."

All three men looked startled as Charlie stood up and smiled at them.

"Mr. Secretary, I had no idea you were even in the country. Welcome." Orville stammered.

"I'm afraid that it was Jack's idea, incognito, you know. It is his version of a security backup." Charlie's smile was a little askance.

Jack took over again, "Secondly, we naturally want to clear Governor Beaumont's good name and set the historical record straight. I understand there was a question regarding some shortfall in the treasury around the time of his disappearance, and he was blamed for it, throwing a shadow over the whole Beaumont family's good name. That accusation has to be written out of the history books, and an account of his expedition as recorded in his journal inserted in its place. That's only fair to the Beaumont family." Jack noticed that all three men were nodding their heads in agreement.

"Thirdly, I would like to see a monument and a museum dedicated to the late Governor be built to house the treasure of the galleon, to be situated where the cave is located and the cave opened up as a tourist destination, providing much needed jobs in the area. Both the ship and the sub should be left in situ and a pedestrian walkway built which would allow the public to view them inside the cave, which is a wonder in itself since it has cathedral-like qualities. I would further ask that Moses and Janine Beaumont, and Mr. Williams be retained as consultants on the building of the museum to their exacting standards."

His presentation finished, Jack sat back in his chair, smiled and folded his arms across his chest.

"I personally cannot see any difficulty with complying with any of those conditions, but naturally it will have to be brought up in committee and discussed before a commitment is reached."

Orville glanced at his two colleagues, and got no objections from either. "You do realize, I'm sure, that you haven't given us the location of the cave."

"Once an agreement is drawn up, agreed upon and signed by all concerned, you will get the location of the cave. Rest assured though, it is in an already popular tourist area, so no extra infrastructure will need to be built other than a road to the museum which will sit above the cave."

"This has all been recorded, so I will have the agreement drawn up and try to have it ready by tomorrow, so you can all come back and sign it. You have no idea what a pleasure it has been talking to you." Orville, Michael and Randolph stood up as one and shook hands all around.

"And the two policemen outside?" asked Jack.

"Will not bother you." added Randolph.

They all marched out of the office and back to well-deserved bottles of champagne on the 'Triumph'.

"What now?" Shannon asked, already slightly tipsy from the on-going celebrations on the flybridge.

Jack thought for a few moments, and then said, "Well, after we get everything taken care of tomorrow, there will be no need for us to stick around, so I want to continue on our cruise into the Caribbean, to St. Thomas first and then to Tortola. After the negotiations, Charlie has to go back to Washington, but Moses, Janine and Courtland ought to stay on to oversee the plans and the building of the museum. I am sure they can stay on this boat with Capt'n Pete. What do you think?"

She just smiled brightly, "Sounds like a plan to me."

Chapter 6

Horst Keller sat morosely on his barstool at the Soggy Dollar Bar on the island of Jost Van Dyke in the British Virgin Islands. He was already part way through his third Jameson's on the rocks, without a water back, and it was not even two in the afternoon. His concentration was elsewhere, many miles away, but not a long time ago. In fact, it seemed like only yesterday that his world had come crashing down around his ears, and it was all due to that jackass, Jack Elliott. He felt once again that uncontrollable rage coming over him, as it had many times in the last few months. Ever since his miraculous escape from the Senator's crashing helicopter, which had almost taken his life as well as the Senator's and the pilot of the chopper, he had been determined to live for only one thing. To exact his revenge on the people that had foiled his plan to secure the gold from the sunken WWII Nazi submarine, but especially on Mr. Jack bloody Elliott.

In between his blinding rages, where he was liable to smash anything and anyone in sight, and often did, he had entertained many moments of clear lucid thinking. He had spent many of these moments attempting to come up with a plan to take his revenge on the person he blamed for all his abysmal luck this past year. So far any plan with even a 50/50 chance of success had eluded him and driven him to yet another drink, which was pushing him one more step closer to alcoholism.

Reflecting on the past couple of months, as he often did these days, he once again thanked his good luck at escaping the helicopter crash without any injuries. It was the thing that allowed him, because of his strength and determination, to avoid capture on that fateful afternoon. He had swum to the far side of the crashed helicopter and utilizing the height of the waves at the time, had managed to avoid detection until the Senator's yacht 'Shillelagh' had arrived on the scene. With all the rescue boats in the vicinity of the crash, and with the 'Shillelagh' hove to a little way away, it had only required a small amount of luck to be able to swim to the big boat and sneak aboard unnoticed via the aft swim platform. He had been the captain of the boat, and with his knowledge of the layout of the boat, it was not difficult for him to find a hiding place in the lazarette where no one could find him without a thorough search of the vessel.

Unfortunately, with the Coast Guard cutter on the scene, there had been no way to extricate himself from his self imposed confinement until much later that night. In fact, it was very early the next morning, after the yacht had docked at Pier 66, when he was finally able to retrieve his personal effects from his cabin. He also had the combination to the ship's safe and before leaving he helped himself to the contents of that safe, including the Senator's $200,000 mad money and a Glock 9mm automatic pistol. The one thing he had taken which he valued the most was the Senator's 'little black book', which contained his Swiss and Cayman Islands numbered accounts and passwords that had been set up and funded over the course of many years, and which the Senator would not now be needing.

He was also able to retrieve a complete set of forged papers for his new identity, which he had bought several years ago with a lot of foresight on his part.

He had snuck off the boat as dawn was showing its brilliant face on the eastern horizon, and had walked up 17th Street. Halfway to Federal Highway, he had managed to flag down a taxi, which took him up to Palm Beach. His destination was the home of a foolish acquaintance of his from a few years back, who owned a very fast 38 foot Cigarette Top Gun race boat. Even with the boat valued at over half a million dollars, the man insisted on leaving the boat tied up to the dock behind his house with the keys sitting in the ignition. That man was just asking to have his boat stolen, and Horst was quite willing to oblige him.

Having no trouble at the man's house since nobody was home, Horst, in his newly stolen boat, cleared the Palm Beach inlet just before 11 a.m., and set a course for Bimini, intending to go from there across the flats to Nassau, the capital of the Bahamas. Once there he could catch a commercial flight to anywhere in the Caribbean using his new identity, since he had felt it too risky to use the forged papers in the States. The risk of detection of his forged documents, and the opportunity for bribery were much more favorable for him in the Caribbean. Halfway across the Gulf Stream, he gathered together his U.S. issued passport, driver's license and any other identifying papers, placed them in a zip-lock baggie along with the Glock he had stolen and heaved them all overboard. He breathed a sigh of relief when he saw his former life disappear below the waves. He was glad the gun was gone because he didn't like guns very much, preferring his physical prowess to any threat a gun might make. His enemies tended to agree that, in his case, a gun would be overkill. There would never be a case of armed assault that the authorities could bring against him.

Horst, in his new identity of Anton Kohl, had spent the next two months crisscrossing the Bahamian chain of islands. Taking the mail boat across to the various islands, he had stayed in nondescript, out-of-the-way hotels and boarding houses, eaten simple meals in lower class restaurants, and imbibed his liquor in local bars that the tourists didn't even know existed. After the luxurious lifestyle to which he had become accustomed, it was a minor hardship but one that he accepted and even welcomed, due to his rough and rugged new outlook on life.

It was toward the end of December that Anton (Horst) Kohl decided to move on to new stomping grounds. He had visited most of the inhabited islands in the Bahamas with the exception of Eleuthera, where he felt there was too much of a chance of being recognized and to keep at bay, at least for now, the bad memories of the place. He took the mail boat from Freeport, where he had been staying for the past few days, to Nassau. A slow taxi ride to the international airport, and the purchase of a plane ticket to Ft. Lauderdale convinced him that his documentation was going to stand up to the scrutiny of the officials. His German passport, his German issued international driver's license, his two credit cards, which he had been making small purchases on for the past few years, all issued in the name of Anton Kohl, and the approximately $150,000 in cash left from the Senator's mad money insured that he would at least survive for a while, if not prosper. There would always be time to plunder the Senator's numbered bank accounts later when it became necessary. There remained only one thing to accomplish before disappearing for good. His rage, which had festered over the past few months, demanded that he take his revenge on Jack Elliott and his beautiful girlfriend, the one he had lusted after so many times after seeing her in that tiny bikini on the Senator's yacht. To this end, he was now headed back to Florida over the Christmas holidays.

Since he was not working at anything other than keeping himself from being apprehended, he had had a lot of time to think, an activity that was now accompanied by the consumption of large amounts of alcohol. He had found that, as his thoughts grew even darker, his drinking grew in the same or greater proportions, but he seemed unable to control it.

He had seen, of course, all the newspaper reports of the crash of the Senator's helicopter, and had heard all the radio and television stations, with their whispered innuendo about conspiracy plots, but he had never seen his name mentioned, being just the anonymous captain of the boat along with the unnamed helicopter pilot, who had died in the crash along with the Senator. At first it had bothered him, being considered to be so worthless by the press as to not even rate a name when he'd died in such a spectacular fashion. But soon reality set in and he was grateful that he had not been named since he was trying to keep a low profile, even if it was with a different name.

It was at about this time that his thoughts of rage started to manifest themselves into physical violence. His plane was not due to leave until 6 am the next morning, so instead of hanging around the airport as he should have done, he took a taxi downtown after depositing his bag in an airport locker. With 20/20 hindsight, it turned out to be a very bad move.

He went to one of those restaurants that everyone avoids unless they have no choice; filthy dirty, bad food, bad service but still high priced, designed to lure the sucker tourists in. Naturally, his was the only white face in the whole place, and even the waiter, who was depending on tips to live, casually suggested that the place two doors down might be more to his liking. This was a suggestion which he chose to ignore. Soon, as the food arrived with a more of a thud than a flourish, everyone in the place was aware that this man was not here to eat, but to cause trouble, and the more the better. Consequently, they all left him alone, even when he shouted obscenities at the poor waiter and finally threw the remainder of his food on the floor, breaking the 20-year-old plate in the process. The waiter timidly brought him his bill, and started cleaning up the mess. He paid the twenty five dollar bill, left a one cent tip for the waiter and walked out. All the patrons breathed a huge sigh of relief and went back to their own food.

Anton, for he had started thinking of himself by that name, walked out of the restaurant, more pissed and aggravated than when he went in, and started cursing as he navigated his way back to Main Street. He glared at people headed in the opposite direction to him, and several times he got an angry stare in response, but no one seemed willing to challenge him. He walked the entire length of Main Street, looking for something, or someone, to break but found nothing. It was only after the third pass of the alleys and backstreets that he finally noticed that two teenagers at the middle of a particular street suddenly became alert as he walked toward them. They both stepped out of their doorway as he approached.

"Hey, man. I got what you're looking for, right here." the taller of the two said, indicating the small glassine bags he was holding.

He kept on walking toward them, but he appeared to angle his stride in order to pass them on the street side of the sidewalk. "I don't need any of your fuckin' shit. Go away!" he snarled.

The tall Bahamian smiled, revealing the gold inlays in his teeth, "Well, now, man. I don't think you understand. You can either buy our shit, or you can leave all your money down there on the sidewalk and leave with nothing. It's your choice. Either way, we end up with all your money. Ain't that right, Shrimp?"

Anton stopped, and just looked amused, staring at the two drug dealers like the vermin they were.

Glancing quickly around, he noticed that the odds had suddenly changed dramatically from two to one to six to one, for at each end of the street, two more teenagers had appeared.

"If you think that you and your pipsqueak friends can really take my money, why don't you come over here and try, Little Shrimp and Big Shrimp?" He walked slowly toward them, allowing them to fall back into a defensive position to allow their friends ample time to close the gap between them and the end of the street, where their friends still stood, unsure of what was happening. He suddenly lunged forward, grabbing the bigger man by the throat and slamming his head hard against the brick wall behind him, an action which rendered him immediately unconscious, while simultaneously sweeping a leg out, catching the smaller man at knee level, breaking one knee and toppling the man to the ground. He lay writhing on the ground, screaming in agony while the others closed in from either end of the street.

The four others rushed up the street, two from each side and stopped 20 feet away, all their eyes focused on their fallen comrades. Instead of attempting to effect an escape, as they had expected him to do, Anton stood his ground, and softly murmured, "So who is next to fall?"

They quickly got his drift, and beat a hasty retreat back down the street, leaving their fallen comrades to their fate. He walked over to Small Shrimp, who had stopped screaming because he knew what was coming; or at least, he thought he did. Anton deliberately kicked him in the head, rendering him unconscious like his partner and sparing him the pain to come, at least for the moment. He kicked at the ribs on both sides, cracking several of them, broke the other leg and stomped down hard on both hands, breaking a lot of delicate bones. It would be quite a while before this guy played piano again. He then turned and meted out the same punishment to Big Shrimp, and with his rage finally dissipating, turned and walked down the road toward Main Street. The police, not having any witnesses willing to step forward, would ultimately write this episode off as a gang related beating and close the case. The two men would spend months in the hospital while their bones knitted and, most importantly, neither would ever participate in the drug trade again, one becoming a museum tour guide and the other a taxi driver.

He whistled a happy tune as he rejoined the few people still in the downtown area. He found an open bar, had several drinks and around midnight caught a taxi back to the airport. Since his flight left so early the next morning, he did not bother with a hotel room. He retrieved his bag from the locker, found a quiet corner in the departures lounge and fell asleep, his head resting on his bag. It was not the first time he had spent the night in an airport, nor was it likely to be the last.

A little after six the next morning, he was seated in the last row of economy class of an old, as in had-seen-better-days, Boeing 737 as it lifted off the runway into a clear blue sky above the spectacular sunrise. The plane was only about half full, so he was able to raise the armrests and stretch out across three seats, and grab another hour of sleep before they landed in Ft. Lauderdale. He was careful to follow the old soldier's maxim, 'sleep, eat and have sex whenever you can, because you never know when your next opportunity will come'. He firmly believed in being prepared, which didn't make him a boy scout, but simply smart.

He was actually pleasantly surprised how quickly he cleared customs and immigration, setting aside his fear that his forged documents would not hold up to close scrutiny.

He took a taxi to a tourist hotel on 17th Street, and over an excess of alcoholic beverages, managed to track down Jack's parents' house in Victoria Park. Reasoning, correctly as it turned out, that Jack and Shannon would be at his parents' house on Christmas Eve, Horst made plans for a surprise visit to settle old scores. He bought a stand up paddleboard and spent many hours paddling around the canals in Victoria Park until he knew the layout intimately.

On the designated evening, he quietly paddled his way to the house, only to be startled by the number of people who had gathered there. He almost turned and left, but his rage would not let him. Unfortunately, just as he was tying up, he was confronted by a drunken bitch getting on his case. The rage was in full swing which caused him to quickly lash out. He really didn't mean to kill her, just silence her, but that was just how it worked out.

Seeing what he had done, Horst made immediate plans to get out of town, the rage be damned. Unfortunately, flights were booked solid and it was three days before he could find a flight from Florida to San Juan, Puerto Rico.

When he arrived, a taxi ride down to the old city near the El Morro Fortress, and a short search later, he found a clean but reasonably priced hotel and booked in for three days. He figured that was enough time to plan out his next move.

Never one to sit brooding in his room, the first day's excursion was to the most imposing of San Juan's many attractions, the El Morro Fortress. As he thought about his options for the future, he wandered through and marveled at the huge size of the ancient fortifications. The area of grass in front of the main buildings must have been at least half a mile square and he wondered idly how long it would take to cut it using a push mover. Of course, seeing no wheel marks or any signs of a regular pattern of mowing, he wondered if they had developed a strain of grass which only grew to three inches and stopped. That would certainly put a lot of landscapers out of work, wouldn't it? The only disconcerting note to his exploration of the fortress occurred when he was walking along the top of the wall and almost to the end of the fortress, where one of those one man watch towers anchored a bend in the wall. Apparently someone, presumably a homeless person, had decided that this was an ideal place to take a dump. It was fresh and stank to high heaven; and was off-putting enough that he cut short his explorations and wandered back into the narrow streets of Old San Juan.

Since it was lunch time as indicated by his rumbling stomach, and having skipped breakfast, he found, tucked away in an almost hidden alleyway, a bar/restaurant calling itself the 'American Bar'. He ordered a light lunch and his first Jameson's on the rocks of the day, reflecting on the name. It seemed that every island in the Caribbean, and for that matter, every tourist destination in Europe, had a place called the 'American Bar', to where the American tourists, being the sheep they are, would invariably flock. He shook his head, greatly amused at the thought, until he realized that he was one of the flock; today at least.

During his morning walk he had been thinking of possible destinations to which he could travel with a minimum of fuss, and had tentatively settled on the British Virgin Islands. The U. S. Virgin Islands were close by, but were in a different jurisdiction, and it seemed to him, the BVIs were a more laid back, relaxed and slow-paced place than the USVI's more hectic pace. Through discreet questioning, he found out that a ferry service ran from San Juan to Road Town, on the island of Tortola in the BVIs, and he was determined to take that ferry to what he hoped was his final destination, at least for a while.

With a sudden flash of insight, he realized that it was New Year's Eve, Christmas having occurred during his extracurricular excursion to Ft. Lauderdale, and he could already see the staff of the restaurant preparing to close up early in preparation for their celebrations. He didn't wish to leave a lasting impression as the customer who refused to leave, so he paid his tab and wandered out into the alleyway and sat down on a seat the local council had provided for the use of tourists. All around him, people were bustling about tending to the activities leading up to the parade and fireworks planned for that evening. He decided, instead of heading back to his room, to stay and join in the festivities, maybe even help, if he found someone who needed it. He wandered through the streets of Old San Juan, helping where he could, holding a rope here, erecting a barrier there, helping to manhandle a display onto the face of a building and thoroughly enjoying himself for the first time in a long time. His help was greatly appreciated by the people he helped and they were not hesitant to tell him, asking him back to join them in the celebrations once the parade started. One startlingly beautiful senorita even propositioned him outright, but even after saying to her that he'd be back, he knew he wouldn't. And she probably knew it, too.

Once the parade started, he wandered the streets, never going back to the ones where he had helped, but finding lots of people with the holiday spirit. They had set up booths, stalls and family enclaves along most of those streets, and were dispensing good cheer and spirits to all and sundry, even strangers. He had always been a whisky drinker, but what he was being offered here in the Caribbean was, naturally, rum. After a few polite refusals, he decided to take the plunge, accepting a shot passed to him by an older Hispanic gentleman, who smiled a toothless grin at him, and they saluted each another. Compared to his only foray into the world of rums being an occasional Dark and Stormy, a combination of Gosling's Black Strap Bermuda Rum and Gosling's Ginger Beer, this particular shot was typical, a bland rum from Bacardi, which had a distillery right across the bay from where he stood. However, as the night wore on, some of the rums he tasted were of exceptional quality. He particularly enjoyed the banana vanilla rum distilled by Madouda on the Dutch side of the island of St. Martin.

As the evening wound its way toward midnight, he started working his way back toward the pretty senorita, the one who had been so bold as to suggest a liaison between them even before she knew his name. Maybe it was the rum affecting him, or maybe it had been too long, but he felt an old familiar stirring in his loins that, try as he might, he could not ignore. Much to his surprise, he did actually find the spot of their encounter, only to find the object of his search entwined in another man's arms. She noticed his approach, and with a look of utter regret on her face, shrugged her shoulders and turned away. He didn't for the life of him understand why he felt such a sudden loss of affection since he didn't even know her name, but as he turned away, he heard the crowd counting down. Ten, nine, eight, seven, six, five, four, three, two, one. Happy New Year!!!!

The crowd cheered, the fireworks erupted and everyone started dancing, drinking and grabbing people and kissing complete strangers. Chaos reigncd supreme. He felt himself being pulled and tugged from all sides, being kissed and hugged in the utter confusion that followed. And yet, in all that commotion and confusion, he felt a sense of calm and tranquility that he had not felt for a long, long time, and he hoped that this was indeed, a new beginning that would be better than the last year, which had been a complete disaster. While he regretted the loss of the gold from the submarine, his access to the Senator's numbered bank accounts more than made up for that loss.

It was long time after midnight when he started his lonely journey back to his room, having imbibed a great deal more than he should have. He wasn't actually weaving, but his path did have a slight curve to it, kind of like a long ocean wave with a mile or more between crests. You knew you were going up and down but it was so gentle and took so long, you just seemed to be standing still. He could already see his hotel in front of him, not half a block away, when suddenly he felt something amiss. A hand snaked out of a doorway, grabbed him and slammed him against the wall of the building, turned him around and a fist arrowed its way into his solar plexus, doubling him over, and collapsing him to the sidewalk. Under normal circumstances, he would have bounced right up to face his adversary, but the combination of months of inactivity and an excess of rum in his belly came close to rendering him helpless. He lay there compliantly, gathering his strength and composure, as hands went through his pockets looking for cash or credit cards. He heard the curse of exasperation escape his assailant's lips and the frenzied words spoken in a whisper to him. Even though he didn't speak Spanish, the meaning of those words was abundantly clear. 'Where is your money?'

"Gone, spent. I'm going to my hotel to get more," he cried, trying to sound more desperate than he really was. He had had the wind knocked out of him, and was momentarily disadvantaged, but his assailant had made a fatal error. He had badly underestimated the size, strength and resilience of his target, and he had stopped the attack long before his opponent was down and out. The rage bloomed and Anton was going to make him pay dearly for that flaw in his assailant's thinking.

The young, well built Hispanic considered this statement for a moment, and then leaned down, got in Anton's face and hissed in accented English, "We will go to your room and you will give me all your money, understand? And if you try anything, I'll cut you up bad." He showed Anton the lethal looking switch blade knife he was holding, open and locked, ready for action. Anton nodded vigorously and, indicating his hotel, he replied, "It's just down the block. I'll give you everything, just don't hurt me." He wondered briefly if he was laying it on too thick, but the thug was too preoccupied to notice the admittedly poor performance of his victim, and was glancing around to see if anyone else was aware of what was going on.

By the scruff of the neck, the mugger raised Anton to his feet and started marching him toward the hotel, totally unaware in the subtle change in his victim's demeanor. Anton actually helped, by certain barely noticed body movements, to put himself in an advantageous position as compared to his adversary. He had hardly risen to his full stature when he struck, immobilizing the knife hand, stepping down hard on the mugger's instep and delivering a stiff hand to the throat. The man went down without a sound, his larynx crushed and his ability to speak stopped cold by his inability

134

to breathe. His eyes were wide open when he died, unable to understand what had just happened and why this injustice had happened to him. As Anton turned and walked back to his hotel, his rage subsided, leaving another victim to be found by police in the morning. The still-open switchblade lying by the body would be reason enough to quietly shove this case to the back burner.

Anton stayed another two days at that same hotel, walking during the day to various attractions, and enjoying the vibrant nightlife in the downtown area. His hotel proved to be in an area where a lot was always happening, and he sincerely regretted having to move on. But, bright and early the morning of the third of January, he was standing on the side deck beside the pilothouse of the ferry taking him to Road Town and grinning from ear to ear at the thought of going to sea again. As they cruised out of San Juan harbor, they passed the imposing bulk of the El Morro fortress, and his thoughts turned, once again, to the pretty little senorita from New Year's Eve and his regret at his inability to hook up with her again. But as always, he put his past behind him and he looked forward to an uncertain, to be sure, but hopefully happier, future in the BVIs. The wind in his hair, and the waves causing the boat to seesaw a little brought back to him that here, now, he was in his element.

He cleared customs in Road Town without any problems, and when he discreetly inquired about boats for rent, he was directed to Sunshine Charters. It was a fairly small operation, a varied assortment of only fifteen or so boats, but most of them were high end. He chose a 50-foot Sunseeker flybridge model, which was quite a few years old but had been kept in ship shape condition. He was pleased that he had had the foresight to get a captain's license in the name of Anton Kohl, for it allowed him to skip the introduction to boating classes and the check ride that was mandatory for non-licensed renters. By nightfall, he had moved aboard the boat with the intention of leaving in the morning.

He went for dinner at a local bar/restaurant that was a known hangout for the crews who manned the many private and charter yachts that frequented the area. Road Town was the capital of the BVIs and therefore the natural clearing-in port for foreign flag vessels. He had chosen this bar because he was trying to get up-to-date information from these crew members as to where the good cruising areas were. Naturally he had the nautical charts of the area, both paper and electronic, and had cruised many private yachts in these waters many years before, but there still was no substitute for current knowledge. He finished his bar food dinner, which turned out to be quite good, and he was only on his second Jameson's when he spotted the one person in the bar for whom he had been looking.

Compared to the majority of patrons of the bar, she would have been considered an older lady, being somewhere in her mid thirties, and if she was a stewardess, she was probably at the tail end of her career in yachting. Although quite pretty, she sat alone in one corner of the bar, ignored by the raucous crowd around her. Anton picked up his drink, indicated to the barman that he was joining the lady, and, seemingly casually, strolled toward her. She did not notice his approach until he was quite close, but seemed mildly alarmed when he stopped before her.

"Excuse me, I wonder if you could possibly help me?" he said, putting on his most pleasant face, which he knew from past experience, probably looked as if he had just bitten into a particularly tart lemon.

She hesitated for a split second, and then indicated the seat beside her, saying, "If I can. Mr.?"

"I'm sorry, I am Anton Kohl, and I am very pleased to meet you, Miss?"

"Captain Elaine Banks, at your service."

"Ah, even better. You will forgive me, I hope, but I am afraid I mistook you for a head stew, given the distance the children around here are giving you. I should know, because I am also a yacht captain."

She actually smiled for the first time at this comment on the current population of the bar, and it was actually quite pleasant. "Really?" she said.

"Indeed, USCG Unlimited." He sat down where she had indicated. "But to business, may I refresh your drink before I pick your brain?"

She seemed genuinely amused at his obvious advances, "Sure, why not?"

He signaled the waiter for another round, and then proceeded straight to his enquiries. "I am trying to find out the nicest spots around here to go cruising by myself."

"In what kind of boat?"

"I've chartered a Sunseeker 50 flybridge, and I think I want to stay within the BVIs to save the hassle of customs. I have the rest of January, and I just want to relax and hang out."

"OK. Well, there is the Soggy Dollar Bar, in White Bay, on Jost Van Dyke, that's a great place. Bit more commercial than it used to be, but a great place, nonetheless. Then there's the Baths on Virgin Gorda. The Top of the Baths restaurant is fabulous, and the granite rocks piled on top of each other in such an incongruous way really are a sight to see. Right here on Tortola is Cane Garden Bay, maybe one of the most picturesque spots in the BVIs. If you want to spend a night at a marina, Soper's Hole Marina is one of the best around. Nanny Cay is also great. If you want to stay in a resort, and can afford it, Scrub Island or Peter Island Yacht Club would be the place to go. Salt Island is where the wreck of the 'Rhone' is located if you're into snorkeling or scuba diving, and if you want to spend several days by yourself, but want to have civilization close by, North Sound on Virgin Gorda is where you should head."

While sitting there listening to her dissertation, their drinks had arrived and he handed her the Dark and Stormy she had ordered. His head was fairly swimming, finally remembering all those many different places from years ago. "Well, it sounds like I will have to take another month to see all these places."

"These islands are special; once you see them, you don't want to leave, and if you have to go, you can't wait to get back again." She looked rather wistful as she made this pronouncement, as if she didn't ever want to leave. "So how come you are so foot loose and fancy free at the height of the yachting season?"

"Ah, well you might ask. It would be because of my summary termination from my last place of employment, a situation which I am not prepared to discuss at the moment, if ever. Let me just say this; a great injustice was done and I was left holding the... ah, sticky end of the stick, if you catch my drift."

"But that's terrible. To condemn someone unfairly is inconceivable, but since you still speak of yourself as a captain, can I assume that it didn't affect your license?"

"Yes, thank heavens, my license hasn't a blemish on it; the problem was a strictly non-marine related situation that my owner and I didn't see eye to eye on, and guess who won?"

She looked at him kind of funny, as if making a decision, and said, "I run that 120 foot Westport called 'Island Escape' docked at the end of Pier 1 in the marina; it's a fractional time share yacht run by a company in Ft. Lauderdale, and they are always on the lookout for large tonnage captains with experience since they have several 165 footers being delivered shortly. I'd be more than happy to give you their business card, if you are looking for employment."

"Later," was all he said.

"Now you're assuming that there's going to be a later, aren't you?"

"In that case, give it to me when I'm leaving."

She picked up her drink, which she had only been sipping, and upended it, finishing it in several mighty gulps. Placing the empty glass on the table, and smiling wickedly, she said, "Well, if you're not leaving, I'll have another of those. Please."

He made a circle above the table with his hand, the universal signal to the waiter for another round. He then placed both elbows on the table and his chin on the palms of his hands, fixed her in place with a wry smile that reached his eyes and sent unmistakable signals her way. "So tell me all about yourself."

She flushed slightly at his scrutiny, but took a deep breath and began, "Well, I was born…"

Hours later, sitting side by side instead of across the table, they both realized that the bar noise and the music had gone from chaotic to merely frenzied, and the crowd had gone from 'searching for the one' to 'resigned to going home alone'. She glanced at her watch, and muttered, "Oh, God, I've got to go."

"In that case, my lady, let me escort you home. By a strange coincidence, my boat is on the same Pier 1 as yours. So don't use the 'out of your way' excuse."

"I wouldn't think of it, kind sir, and I accept your invitation."

As they left, Anton caught the waiter's eye and threw a couple of hundred dollar bills on the table, which earned him a huge smile and an exaggerated bow from the waist from the man. It was but a leisurely five minute walk back to the marina from the bar, and as they were walking down the pier, he stopped at his boat, saying, "This is me, how about a nightcap?"

139

"I really shouldn't," she said, but seeing the look of disappointment on his face, added, "but I will"

He led her up the stairs to the aft deck, where they both kicked off their shoes, and then he slipped an arm around her waist and guided her toward the salon doors, which he unlocked and led her inside the darkened salon. Halfway to the galley, she suddenly stopped and turned to face him, still trapped close by his arm around her waist. She put her arms around his neck and impulsively kissed him, hard and longingly, her tongue darting into his mouth and her body pressed up against his, with no air between them. "I have wanted to do that all night long," she said huskily.

"You should have said something, and then we wouldn't have wasted all that time drinking and talking, and really gotten down to business. But you know, you *are* right, sometimes it *is* better to wait. But tonight is not that night."

He held her out from him at arm's length, and looked curiously at the dress she was wearing. He smiled and said, "You know, all night I've been wondering; just how do you get in and out of that dress?"

She grinned at him, knowing his game, and then surprising him by saying, "It's quite simple, really. You reach under your hair, find and undo the clasp, pull down the zipper in back, and shrug your shoulders and it falls right to the ground, like so." She was standing before him in a pair of sheer, almost transparent panties, and nothing else, the nipples on her generous breasts already beginning to harden and not feeling the least bit embarrassed or ashamed about it, but instead feeling good, knowing what was to come.

Chapter 7

Her eyes came slowly open the next morning, and she wondered momentarily where she was, since the daylight streaming into the room revealed unfamiliar surroundings. Turning her head revealed the smiling face of Anton on his pillow next to her, his eyes upon her drinking in her beauty and with a sudden rush, the events of the past night hit her with a pleasant impact that put a smile on her face, too.

"Good morning, sleepy head," he greeted her gently.

Her eyes suddenly went wide, the sunlight making her realize what time it was, and she threw back the covers and jumped out of bed, stark naked, and made a beeline for the head, saying, "Oh God, I've got to go."

His amused comment, "now where have I heard that before?" stopped her in her tracks and she turned around to face him, glared at him for a moment, and stuck out her tongue at him before continuing on her way.

She was only gone for a few minutes, and when she emerged she immediately started dressing. "I have charter guests arriving at 11 a.m., and I've got a boat to get ready for them," she said. She rummaged in her purse for a couple of seconds, came up with two business cards, which she placed on the bedside table, "one card is for the company, the other is my own personal card, in case you want to get together again." She looked at him wistfully for half a minute, then turned and disappeared up the stairway toward the deck. Anton lay there with a self satisfied smile on his face, mentally trying to calculate how long it had been since he had spent such a wonderful night with a beautiful lady, and he failed miserably. He then promptly rolled over and went back to sleep again.

It was well after noontime when he finally threw off the cloak of sleep along with the wadded up sheet that threatened to strangle him. He was sweating profusely, not only from the temperature in the cabin due to the outside door which she had accidentally left open, but from the return of his recurring nightmare. The one in which he was falling out of the helicopter, hitting the water and watching the bubbling fluorescent trails of the razor-sharp compressor blades from the disintegrating jet engines coming directly at him. More by luck than evasion, none had hit him then, and none would hit him in his nightmare, but just the thought of being sliced open by one of those blades made him shiver involuntarily. He found himself surprised to remember that last night, when she lay in his arms; he had slept like a baby and had not had the nightmare. He finally got up, went to the fridge, retrieved a bottle of beer and popped the cap. He consumed half the bottle in several large gulps, noting with a certain amount of regret that the slip where her boat had been last night was now empty. He surprised himself by hoping that everything had gone well and that she had been able to salvage the situation without any trouble.

Breakfast/lunch was another beer, some cheese and crackers, and a slice of dill pickle. His culinary habits had suffered a mighty blow since his involuntary separation from the Senator's service, and he had not yet been able to force himself to stoop so low as to cook for himself when there were others to do it for him. He sat at the dining table with his 'lunch', studying the two business cards she had left. The company on the business card he recognized immediately, Deep South Fractional Yachts, owned by a megalomaniac tyrant who ran his company like a dictatorship, who had little idea of what yachting was all about, but somehow, despite his almost complete lack of business sense, social graces, sound reasoning or financial acumen, had convinced a number of millionaires to invest their hard-earned capital in his fleet. He must be Irish, since he had the gift of the gab, and his glib promises were viewed by the town as the prelude to his demise.

The other card was the one that interested him the most, hers. Under the title, 'Island Escape', and a stylized drawing of a 120 foot Westport yacht, was listed her name and title, her cell and satellite phone numbers, her email, Facebook, Twitter, LinkedIn and Skype addresses. He had no idea if or when she might return here to Road Town, for the conversation had not turned that way, but he knew that he wanted to see her again. As he sat there he pulled out a pen and paper and tried to recall all the places she had talked about at the bar. He found himself intrigued by the possibilities, but one place, for some inexplicable reason, jumped out at him. Soggy Dollar Bar on Jost Van Dyke, so named because the place didn't have a dock, and forced patrons to swim ashore with their dollars in their swim trunks. He remembered it from years ago, and it seemed a perfect place to go, so when his lunch was finished, he started the preparations to move his boat there.

Sitting on his barstool at the Soggy Dollar later that day, something snapped him out of his daydream, and he glanced quickly around to see what it could have been. He saw nothing out of the ordinary, as if the patrons of the bar could, by any stretch of the imagination, be called ordinary. He did notice, along with everyone else, the arrival of a shapely young woman who was just entering the bar from the beach area. He looked, did a double take, then a triple take, shook his head and rubbed his eyes, but the sight was still the same. It was Shannon.

'Oh, god, they have found me already.' he thought.

The majority of the bar under the roof was in deep shadow and she was coming in from the bright sunshine, so he made the reasonable assumption that she had not seen him yet. He was already in a corner, his usual place since he was still very aware that he was a fugitive from the law, but now he tried to crouch down and cover his face. He couldn't bring attention to himself by getting up and walking away, especially since he had an open tab, and the barman was sure to inquire where he was going. It seemed that he was trapped.

She walked into the bar area, blinked a few times trying to get her eyes accustomed to the dimness inside. She hesitated, surveying the bar, and spotted an empty stool two down from Anton, and moved in his direction. She sat down in that stool just as the man between them got up and left. Anton kept his head down, leaning his chin into the palm of his open hand, trying to cover as much of his face as possible. Between his slightly spread fingers, he watched her look at him totally without recognition. *'It is Shannon,'* he thought to himself, but he couldn't understand why she hadn't recognized him. To his surprise, she produced a pack of cigarettes, shook one out and put it in her mouth. She then leaned in his direction and asked, "Excuse me, do you have a light?"

Startled by her question, but being like a boy scout, he produced a lighter and replied, "Of course I do, Shannon. How are you doing today? Are Jack and the boat here, too?"

After her cigarette was aflame, she looked at him as if he had lost his mind. "I'm sorry, but I think you must have me mixed up with someone else. My name is Tamara, my friends call me Tammy. And who is Jack, and what boat?"

The tension totally drained from his body, and he quickly assessed the situation, not believing his luck. "I can't believe how much you resemble my friend Shannon, and Jack is her fiancé and they live on a boat in Ft. Lauderdale. I thought for a moment that they had brought the boat down here for the winter."

She shook her head, "You seriously want me to believe that? I'm sorry, but I've heard better pick-up lines than that."

For some reason, Anton wanted her to stay, since obviously, she was not Shannon. "No, please. It's not a pick-up line. I have a picture of Shannon here on my phone. I even have video. You'll see what I mean; you could be her twin sister." Even as he was blundering on, Anton was busy scrolling through the pictures on his phone, until he came to the one he would always remember. It was a shot of Shannon, wearing the tiny bikini in which she had been kidnapped back in the Bahamas during the search for the submarine, and taken while she was climbing the aft stairway on 'Shillelagh'. He turned the phone and showed the photo to Tammy. "Is that you or is it your twin?"

He heard a sharp intake of breath, and turned to look at her face. Her eyes were wide, questioning and confused. "That's not me, I would never wear a bikini that small, and so it stands to reason that it must be my twin."

"Or at least, a doppelganger."

"Exactly."

"Now you can understand my confusion when you approached me and you didn't even acknowledge my presence, can't you?"

"Yes, I certainly can."

"So, Tammy. Now that we have been properly introduced, why don't you slide over one seat here next to me and allow me to buy you a drink?"

"I still don't know your name."

"That's easily remedied. I am Anton Kohl, and I am here on vacation from Dresden, Germany, at your service." He bowed slightly, and she giggled, a sweet melodic sound.

"Now you can get me a Dark and Stormy. It is…"

"I know what a Dark and Stormy is. It is one of my favorites, also. But, more important, the barman knows them, too." He signaled the man over and placed his order while Tammy slid over one seat, much to the disgust of all the other males in the bar. No one challenged him, since he looked more than capable of looking after himself. He was astounded by the resemblance that Tammy had to Shannon, and intrigued by the possibilities of this chance meeting.

When their drinks arrived, they raised their glasses and saluted and sipped. "So, Tammy, why are you here in the BVIs? You sound American to me."

"Yes, well, at the risk of sounding crass, I am here looking for a relationship. At this point in time, any kind of relationship would do."

He was shocked but intrigued. "That sounds very definitive, but kind of surprising. Forgive me for asking, but I'm sure there is a story behind it."

"Just the usual bullshit. My ex-fiancé and I were childhood sweethearts, destined to be married and have umpteen kids, and we even got as far as the church. On the steps, I had an epiphany. I suddenly realized that this was not what I wanted, and so I ran from the church, and I have been running ever since. He wants me back, but I ain't going. This is but the last stop so far."

He sat silent for a moment, thinking about how to put it. "Well, Tammy. See that boat out there? The big Sunseeker with the blue hull and the white cabin? Well, that's my boat, and I am on it all by myself, all alone and lonely. Now, I am not going to suggest that you join me on my boat; that would be too vulgar. However, if you were to invite yourself onto the boat, I would have no objections to that."

She sat still for a second, her mouth open and amusement lighting up her face, "Now that has to be the best pick-up line I have ever heard in my life."

"I do have my moments," he said.

She took another sip of her drink, this one a little larger than before. "So, do you have room for another suitcase on that boat? That's all I have with me at the hostel up the road, where I'm staying at the moment."

"I'm sure we can find room for one suitcase, as long as it isn't too big. Space is limited on a boat, you know what I mean?"

"So, why don't we finish our drinks, then go and look at my suitcase, and you can decide if it's too big for your boat?"

"That sounds like a plan to me."

She joined him on the boat that afternoon, and that night, after the suitable wooing period, they made sweet, mutually acceptable, love. Each for their own reasons but each feeling the other's anguish and anxiety. Tammy for the journey she had so impulsively taken all the way from the steps of the church, and Anton for the desire he felt for Shannon, which he now realized came from the time when he had seen her in that tiny bikini, her almost perfect body so close to being fully on display, and his desire to see the rest.

The next morning they awoke, sated and spent, for it had been a marathon session, but for Anton, it was a revelation for once again he had slept without the nightmare. It seemed to him that sex was the answer to driving the devils out. He vowed that, if it was indeed the answer, he would never have a problem with that.

The next week went by like a roller coaster, many highs and lows as they ran the boat up and down the Sir Francis Drake Passage between the islands of the BVIs, visiting all the places Captain Elaine had mentioned and lots of others. Tammy grew less and less inhibited as time went on, luxuriating in the fresh air and sunshine, at first going topless and finally naked, much to Anton's surprise and delight, as they ran the passages between islands. Since it was during the working week for mere working class humans, boats were few and far between, but towards the end of the week she seemed almost to exalt in the exhibition of her naked body, leaving her clothes off until the last moment before entering the harbors they visited. It was a worrying trend for Anton, for he was trying, for obvious reasons, to keep a low profile. Despite the fact that they were on a multi-million dollar yacht, the sight of a naked lady on said yacht was sure to raise eyebrows and comments that he didn't wish to deal with.

About midweek, January the tenth in fact, feeling satisfied and self assured, he made what was to be his first major mistake since his miraculous escape from the helicopter.

He felt sure that Jack was fully aware that he was still alive and could not help himself from gloating to his nemesis that that was in fact the case. He still had Jack's cell phone number in his own phone, and when they were in the marina on Virgin Gorda, he found himself with cell service for the first time during their tour among the islands. He could not resist sending Jack a zinger, and texted him, 'I hear the weather in Tortola is nice, Horst'. He never received a reply, nor did he expect to, but he felt sure that Jack would get the message.

Since they were cruising near Road Town, by mutual agreement they decided to extend their cruising for another month, until the end of February. That's when he made his second mistake. He docked the boat at the marina where Sunshine Charters had their home base and the agent came hurrying out in alarm.

"Captain Kohl, welcome back. There isn't a problem, I hope." he said as he rushed up to the yacht, taking extremely obvious notice of the young, beautiful, scantily clad woman accompanying his client.

"No, no, no problems at all. In fact, we are enjoying ourselves so much that we want to extend our charter until the end of February, and, seeing we were nearby, we decided to come in and pay for the extension in full. There won't be a problem with that, will there?"

"No, of course not. Just come into the office and we'll fill out the paperwork. It shouldn't take more than a few minutes." The agent was relieved and anxious to get Anton's signature on the contract, and could clearly see why the man wanted this extension.

As they walked to the office, Anton asked, "Just how far am I allowed to take the boat, anyway?"

"Well, we normally restrict our charterers to BVI waters, but in your case, since you have international experience, we will allow you to go as far as Puerto Rico in the west and as far as St. Martin in the east. We do recommend not going to St. Croix or Antigua, since there have been reports of violence and robberies against tourists in both of those places."

"So can we write into the contract a line that allows me to go to those islands you mentioned, if I choose to venture off the beaten path, so to speak?"

"Yes, of course. That would not be a problem."

Paperwork completed and cash having changed hands, Anton strolled back to the boat in no hurry as they would be spending the night at this marina. Meantime, behind Anton's back, the agent immediately began phoning his boss and all the other agents about their extraordinary stroke of luck finding this rich man who paid cash for everything. It was something that would stick in everyone's mind later on.

Back aboard the boat, Anton and Tammy settled down at the dining room table with the nautical charts and the first of their Dark and Stormies, planning where to go on their extended vacation.

Chapter 8

As with all things mechanical, this one broke down just when it was most needed. Jack cursed out aloud, something he was hesitant to do even at the worst of times. But this one might prove their undoing. Just as they were about to leave Nassau after their meeting with the Bahamian officials, for their trip to the Caribbean, the boat's air-conditioning unit gave a last gasp and expired. This necessitated returning to Ft. Lauderdale for a few days in the repair yard at Bradford's to put in a new unit, because, where they were headed, air-conditioning was as necessary as food and water.

The day after the wedding, Jack had spoken with Charlie Palmer, and forwarded the text message Horst had sent to him. Charlie had immediately enlisted the help of the CIA and FBI, and the State Department had asked the officials in the BVIs for their cooperation in finding Horst Keller, for Charlie wanted this guy apprehended as badly as Jack did. But even after a week, so far there had been no results.

They had been ready to head to the Caribbean when the A/C went down, so they were forced to spend a few days at Sean's house, chafing at the bit. Jack had the keys to Sean's house, just as Sean had the keys to Jack's boat, and since Sean and Katie were in Europe on their honeymoon, the house was standing empty anyway.

Sean and Jack had spoken several times, mostly about the fact that the Brady Bunch had been wrapping up their lives in Ireland in preparation for moving to the States, specifically Ft. Lauderdale. Helped through the paperwork and the formalities by Sean and Charlie Palmer, they were all making plans to emigrate. For some peculiar reason, Jack was looking forward to seeing them all again, but especially Erin. His thoughts strayed to her from time to time, and he had to consider the fact that maybe he did have a very vivid imagination, as he had always claimed. He still had fond memories of Haulover Beach. With all due respect to Shannon, we guys still have those somewhat inappropriate thoughts sometimes.

At Jack's prodding and after payment of a considerable premium, the work on the boat seemed to fly along, and soon it was ready to go. The money that the government had paid them, for recovering and turning over the gold from the sunken submarine to the rightful owners, allowed them to pay the hefty expenses they incurred. Before they knew it the boat was fixed and they were ready to go.

They left midweek, the week after the wedding. With her newly added fuel capacity, Jack saw no need to conserve fuel, so he cranked the speed of 'Final Option' to twenty-five knots, and soon outran the big cruise liners which used the Old Bahamas Channel as they were doing. Their two-day run to their first destination, Charlotte Amalie, on the island of St. Thomas in the U.S. Virgin Islands, simply flew by.

The weather cooperated as well, making for a smooth, uneventful passage.

The day on the beach at Haulover must have affected Shannon as well as Jack, for as soon as she saw no contacts on the forty mile radar, she walked up to Jack sitting in the helm seat on the flybridge and caught his attention. Making sure that he was watching and fully attentive, she slowly and seductively removed her bikini top and threw it at him. After a short pause, she hooked her thumbs into the top of her bikini bottoms and, excruciatingly slowly, slid them to the ground. Naked, she leaned against the consol, glaring at Jack, silently daring him to follow her example. His huge grin signaled his approval and acceptance of the situation, and his board shorts landed on top of her bikini shortly thereafter.

"You know, they *can* see us." Jack said, nonchalantly.

"Who?" she asked as she looked quickly around.

"Up there in the sky, NASA, NRO, NSA, CIA, FBI, who knows? If they can read the number on a license plate on a truck in Moscow, they can certainly pick up your delectable figure."

"Well, I hope they have a heart attack staring at something they can't have." This was followed by a heartfelt one finger salute to the spies in the skies. Then she softly giggled and folded herself into his arms.

They spent the rest of the trip naked except for one occasion when a west bound cruise ship passed their east bound course within a mile and Jack felt it prudent to slip on his shorts, but Shannon just slid a sheer cover-up over her naked body. Although to Jack, standing a few feet away, it was obvious that she was naked, to the cruise ship passengers a mile away it probably looked like she was wearing a dress. Besides, what did it matter? Giving the old farts one more look, and a premium look at that, before they popped off was a blessing for them!

They passed by San Juan on the last night, all lit up and brilliant in the wee hours of the a.m., still highly visible even from five miles out to sea, and reached the island of St. Thomas at dawn. Coming in from the west, Jack decided to use the West Gregerie Channel between Water Island and the Sub Base, rather than fighting his way through the half dozen cruise ships he saw making their way through the main channel toward the West Indian Dock at Havensight. He did, of course, make sure that his beautiful girl was all covered up before making the turn toward civilization.

As they made their way past all the boats, old cruising sailboats and smartly presented powerboats, a collection of houseboats, and some barely floating wrecks which were anchored beside Water Island, Jack noticed that another cruise ship had entered the channel behind them, probably intending to dock at the Sub Base. They continued through Crown Bay, and past Sandy Point into the Haulover Cut, between Hassel Island and Careen Hill which would take them to a point where they could cross the main harbor to their marina in Long Bay.

Emerging from Haulover Cut, they watched fascinated as a small commercial seaplane aligned itself into the wind and with a roar of powerful engines, sped across the harbor and lifted itself gracefully off the water, bound for St. Croix. Not since the disastrous crash of one of the Chalk's seaplanes taking off in Miami many years ago, and the company's subsequent demise, had Jack seen a passenger seaplane take off. He admitted to himself that he found that sight stirring and wished that he had continued with his flying past the point of solo and cross country. Unfortunately, his love of boats had taken precedent and left no spare time for any other distractions. After a stop at the ferry dock to clear customs and immigration, for Jack had become adamant about complying with the authorities and the proper procedures after their close call with the authorities in the Bahamas, they crossed the harbor to their pre-arranged berth at the Yacht Haven Grande marina, located at the foot of the West Indian Dock, and just a short walk to either the Havensight shops, or, in the other direction, the downtown area of Charlotte Amalie. It seemed the ideal place to hang out for a few days to a week before beginning their island hopping in earnest.

By the time they had washed the salt off the boat and themselves, and changed into shorts and T-shirts, sport socks and sneakers, it was almost lunchtime, so they decided to take the short walk into town. Their destination for lunch was Cuzzin's restaurant, a place of which Jack had fond memories. He had been there on a previous visit, when he and his now-deceased wife had played tourists and had taken a 7-day cruise of the Eastern Caribbean. They walked down the harbor side drive, past Fort Christian; the oldest structure on the island, dating from the 1600's and built by the Danish, who owned these islands until they were sold to the U.S. becoming the U.S. Virgin Islands. They spent a few minutes browsing through the Vendors' Market, before getting directions to Cuzzin's.

After a short search, because the restaurant was located one street back, on Back Street, of course, from Main Street, Jack and Shannon entered the smallish place, and, confronted with a fifteen-minute wait for a table, chose to have their lunch at the bar as others were doing. This naturally was no problem for the servers, who were friendly and helpful, taking the time to explain the many local dishes for those who were unfamiliar with Caribbean cuisine. Jack ordered salt fish and fungi, while Shannon wanted the curried shrimp and conch. Sipping their Blackbeard Ale from the bottle, they took the time to admire their surroundings. The old brick walls of the place were interspersed with coral rock, old ballast stones and other unidentifiable pieces of masonry layered together with a crème colored concrete which looked centuries old. Artwork hung in various places on the walls and it all looked local and original, and was a perfect contrast to the rough walls. A few pieces of commercial advertising were also included, especially for Cruzan Rum, for the distillery was on the island of St. Croix. It should have added a jarring note, but somehow it all blended in harmoniously.

The food arrived shortly thereafter and the huge portions looked much too big to finish, but it was hot and so good they both finished every bite, washed down by a second Blackbeard Ale each. Reluctantly, they both managed to haul their now heavier bodies off their barstools at the end of the meal and Jack left a large cash tip on the counter along with the cost of the meal, which was surprisingly reasonable considering the quality and quantity of the food, and the laid back atmosphere of the place. They both promised to return, soon.

They spent the afternoon browsing and shopping on Main Street, visiting Diamonds International, Little Switzerland, and Omni Jewelers in search of the perfect wedding band set. They also quenched their thirst at the Hard Rock Café, even if it was a cliché to say you'd been there.

Late in the afternoon, they climbed the ninety nine steps and eventually ended up at Blackbeard's Castle, where they enjoyed a sumptuous meal watching the sunset from the open patio before catching a taxi back to their marina. By ten p.m., they both agreed that it was time for bed, together. Because of the necessity of keeping a night watch during the passage from Ft. Lauderdale, it had been several days since they had last slept in each other's arms. That was a situation that they had promised each other to remedy tonight.

The next few days were spent exploring the ins and outs of St. Thomas. Days were for swimming, snorkeling and scuba diving using the Novurania tender. This method of transportation was the ideal vehicle to take them to Morningstar Beach, Coki Beach, and even Magens Bay on the north side of the island. The day they went scuba diving, they discovered the wreck of the Cartanza Sr, a tramp steamer from WWI in a cove off Buck Island, an island which was only a fifteen-minute boat ride from Charlotte Amalie. It was in only thirty five feet of water so it was an easy dive, but a rewarding one since the coral encrusted wreck was far superior to what was off the Florida coast. They even managed a swim with the sea lions at Coral World Marine Park.

Evenings were for food, fun and drinks, and pleasant times were had amongst the yacht crews that hung out at Mojo's and Rock'n Robin, but they felt especially at home at the Shipwreck Tavern. One enjoyable evening was spent at Senor Frog's; taking money at the pool table from crew who thought themselves pool players and who thought Jack was a lightweight. Sean's lessons and aggressive play at home surely came in handy, much to the dismay of some people who found their wallets a little lighter.

By Wednesday, they felt that they had sampled all that was unique on St. Thomas and decided to move to neighboring St. John. They would be missed by the staff and crews of the multitude of private yachts in the marina, many of who had become friends, and who all promised to keep in touch until next time they met. When they left at noontime, there were many willing hands on the dock to help see them off in admirable fashion.

Jack exited St. Thomas harbor and an hour's slow cruise amongst the many scattered islands brought them to Cruz Bay, the biggest metropolis on St. John and its port of entry. It turned out to be a sleepy little hamlet of maybe several thousand inhabitants, most of whom worked for the Park Service, for two thirds of the island was a National Park courtesy of Laurance Rockefeller, who donated the land, or for the tourist and hospitality industries. They followed the ferry from St. Thomas into the bay, but turned off and waited when the ferry headed for its dock. Since the harbor was small and quite congested, they had to wait outside the harbor for the exit of a 120-foot Westport named 'Island Escape' and when they finally went inside the harbor, the man on the dock from which the Westport had exited waved them over.

As they drew close to the dock, Jack was maneuvering the boat with the remote control, while Shannon was rigging the fenders and the docking lines into their correct places. Two feet from the dock, the man deftly caught all the lines Shannon threw to him and quickly made them fast to the dock.

He smiled a gap toothed grin at them. "Welcome to St. John. I'm sure you saw that Westport 'Island Escape' leaving? Well, she leases this slip year round and I know for a fact that she ain't coming back for at least a week, 'cause I'm the dockmaster here. I can rent you this slip for that week or any portion of it, if we can come to some kind of an arrangement,"

Jack smiled back at him, thanking the stars for his good fortune, for slips were difficult if not impossible to find during the season in a small place like Cruz Bay. He had already resigned himself to anchoring out, which was a pain in the neck, or paying for a mooring. He was delighted to be offered this slip.

"I'm sure we can work something out," he said, knowing full well that the fee for the slip had to be cash, and that it would inadvertently slip into this man's back pocket. That's just how things worked in these islands, but he knew a deal when he saw one.

Jack invited the dockmaster aboard and paid him cash for five days out of the ship's safe, and the man walked away whistling a happy tune, the money already filling the lower recesses of his back pocket.

They spent the rest of the day aboard the boat, and after washing the salt off the boat, relaxed in the sunshine attempting to recover from the last several days of activity and partying. At dusk, Shannon prepared a simple meal which they ate on the flybridge with drinks, watching as the daytime activities slowly wound down, the tourists catching the last ferry back to St. Thomas, and the somewhat subdued festivities of the small town starting up. To be honest, if they had been inside the boat, there wouldn't have been enough noise to keep them awake; but the music drifted

157

across the water with just enough volume to be able to recognize the songs without the annoyance of having to raise their voices.

In fact, it was peaceful enough that several times Jack noticed himself on the verge of nodding off. When Shannon finally leaned against him, her head on his chest, and started breathing in that regular, rhythmic fashion which indicated sleep, he decided enough was enough and lifted her slight body and carried her down two flights of stairs to their stateroom and laid her on the bed. He then went back up to the flybridge, checked that everything was secured, checked all the lines to the dock and all the electrical connections, re-entered the main salon and locked the doors, setting the alarm as the last action before turning in. When he entered their stateroom, he noticed that she had awoken for a while, undressed and thrown the covers on the floor and was laying naked on her back, sound asleep. He sighed, got undressed and joined her, falling asleep as soon as his head hit the pillow, lying on his stomach, one arm draped across her waist.

The next morning, after locking up the boat, they went to breakfast at a quaint little spot called the Deli Grotto in Mongoose Junction, which was an arcade of unique stores selling eclectic wares for wide ranging tastes. Alongside the usual touristy T-shirt and beach ware shops was located a jewelry store which had been voted the best in St. John. As Shannon found out immediately after the breakfast, the gold and silver jewelry that was offered for sale at Caravan Gallery was exquisite. The problem they encountered was not in not being able to find something suitable, as in St. Thomas, but in trying to decide which of the many ring sets that they adored was the right one.

It took most of the morning, but eventually they ended up with exactly the design they wanted, a beautiful elfin design in yellow gold and woven platinum and silver which looked inspired by the 'Lord of the Rings' movies, and which complemented

Shannon's engagement ring, the one designed by Jack, perfectly. Jack also felt extremely lucky to walk out of there only fifteen thousand dollars poorer for the matched set. Naturally, their purchase required a quick trip back to the boat to deposit their symbols of unity into the ship's safe.

A little after noon it was time to visit a collection of shops they had heard about in cruising guides, on the internet and by word of mouth. Their expectations were not only met but exceeded when they arrived at Wharfside Village. This was the place to find anything from a dream home on St. John to a different kind of mood ring. The food in this mecca also ranged from haute cuisine to hot dogs and fries. They ducked in and out of many stores on a whim, sometimes buying, sometimes not, and carrying something alcoholic around with them at all times. They ate dinner at Rumbalaya Caribbean Bar and Grill, on the open air deck with an expansive view of the harbor and the beach. It was a good thing that they were walking and not driving for they arrived back at the boat in the later-than-normal hours of the night, quite inebriated.

The next morning, they rented a Jeep for the day and drove around the island stopping at all the tourist sites that had been mentioned by the various shopkeepers and drinking companions the day before. Naturally, since it covered two thirds of the island, most of the time they drove through the mostly unspoiled wilderness of the Virgin Islands National Park, which was being allowed to return to its natural state. Only St. Lucia and Dominica, further down the Antilles island chain, could claim the title of 'greenest island' and possibly wrestle it away from St. John. They concentrated mainly on destinations that lay inland, away from the beaches, stopping for a while to admire the ruins of Annaberg Plantation, a Danish sugar cane estate from the 1800's. Soon they were on the road again, climbing ever upward and eventually found themselves arriving at the top of the mountain in the center of the island.

The extravagant vistas demanded that they stop and break out the picnic basket they had acquired along with the Jeep that morning. Jack found a small lookout just off the road, with a table and a couple of seats which had obviously been constructed for the express purpose of viewing the magnificent, wild terrain stretching out below them. He commandeered the table and soon they were enjoying the picnic lunch and admiring the view. It was extremely quiet up this high and the road had very little traffic with a car or Jeep or minibus loaded with tourists, passing only every ten or fifteen minutes or so. Most of the time the only sounds they heard were the soft whistling of the gentle breezes through the trees below them and the quiet calls of birds in those trees.

As they watched, and talked, and pointed out places to each other, Jack noticed an almost imperceptible mist gathering over the steep slopes of the trees down in the valleys below. The changeable weather of the winter season was upon them and, shifting his gaze to the south east, Jack was not surprised to find storm clouds gathering, and gathering quickly and roaring down upon them.

"Time to go," he said, pointing out the clouds. "Unless you fancy a second shower today."

Shannon was still packing up the picnic basket and Jack was struggling to put up the weather curtains on their open air Jeep when the first squall hit, and hit with a vengeance. All thought of staying dry went out the window in the first ten seconds of the deluge which hit the top of the mountain, and the best they could do was to huddle together under the top Jack had managed to raise before the inundation. Suddenly, water was pouring from every pore and crevice on that mountain top.

"Now you know why everything around here is so green," Jack shouted, barely able to make himself heard over the tumult.

"Never questioned it for a second," Shannon shouted back, grinning from ear to ear. Truth was she loved storms and always had. One of her favorite childhood memories was of being curled up against the bay window panes of the living room in her parents' old farmhouse in Ireland, and watching as a ferocious winter storm came streaming inland from Dingle Bay to inundate the landscape and assist in the age old process of keeping Ireland green. Now, of course, both her parents and the farmhouse were distant memories, ever since the accident that killed them both during her early teens.

She was wrenched out of her reverie by a brilliant flash of lightning and a simultaneous clap of thunder, so close together that they both jumped. They didn't see where it had hit but they knew that it had to be close.

"We have to get off this mountain top," shouted Jack, as he started the engine and slipped the Jeep into drive. Ever so slowly, he eased the vehicle away from the edge of the cliff where they had been parked, crept across the turn out, found the road in the blinding downpour and started their descent into, hopefully, a safer place. The road steepened dramatically on the side of the mountain leading back to Cruz Bay, and the sheer volume of water flowing down and across the road several times threatened to pick up and float their four-wheel drive Jeep right off the side of the narrow road, which was unfenced and not barricaded for the most part, on the steep downhill side. A plunge over the side would have been unpleasant at best, deadly at worst.

'I hope I haven't made a mistake, trying to drive down through all of this,' Jack thought, gritting his teeth as for the umpteenth time, he wrestled with the steering and brakes trying to keep the vehicle from committing suicide. He was having visions of Dennis Weaver's antagonist in 'Duel'.

Eventually, the road started flattening out and as the possibility of an off-road excursion diminished, they both started to breathe easier and Jack was able to maintain a safe speed the rest of the way. The rain was still coming down in torrents when they finally rolled slowly into Cruz Bay, and parked in front of the rental place. The agent in the office was asleep behind his desk, assuming correctly that nobody in their right mind would want to be renting out a vehicle in this deluge. He seemed quite surprised when Jack and Shannon virtually 'swam' into his office, bringing the wind and the rain in with them.

"I believe we wish to return the Jeep at this time," began Jack, grinning, "And, I think we should be given a discount since we washed it for you before bringing it back."

Seeing the grin, the agent laughed uproariously, and said, "no discount, but I can offer you a warm up."

From his desk drawer, he produced an open bottle of Jameson's and, rising from his seat, he walked to the back room and returned with three glasses filled with rocks. While this seemed to be a common practice for him, Jack had to wonder just how many people had been caught unawares up on that mountain over the years. With an elegant flourish, the agent poured a goodly measure in each glass and passed them out.

"To your very good health, sir and…miss." He had glanced at Shannon's ring finger and found nothing there, for she did not normally wear jewelry, and had made the correct assumption in that they weren't married, at least not yet.

Jack and Shannon took seats, plastic as it turned out, and spent a pleasant hour with the agent talking about the town, the people and the island as the rain outside bucketed down. After three Jameson's apiece, the rain showing no sign of letting up, they decided to take their leave, braving the downpour to return to 'Final Option' looking, and feeling, like a pair of drowned rats.

"Let's try not to do that again, shall we?" Shannon asked as she went below to get a hot shower, having stripped off most of her saturated clothing on the aft deck and looking forward to slipping into something dry, but she was smiling when she said it.

Once again Jack was full of admiration for this woman he loved with all his heart. Most women would have been angry, or at the very least upset at this unforseen and unfortunate event, but she was, as usual, cool, calm, and collected. It seemed that she exercised a very firm control over her emotions, as seen by her reactions to the many situations they had faced together over the past year.

That evening, they discussed the possibility and wisdom of going over to Tortola. Horst Keller was still at large and the authorities had no clue where he was, but Jack was convinced that he would not have exposed his location that blatantly unless he had a good reason for it. But, try as he might, Jack could not fathom any possible reason other than to lure them there. But even that did not make sense, because Horst had to know that Jack's first action would have been to call the authorities as he did. The man was probably in Trinidad, or Europe, or Australia, for all they knew. They didn't even know for certain if the person who had sent the text was actually Horst, or an imposter with inside information.

As they continued their exploration of St. John the next day, this time by water, they again discussed the possibilities of going to the BVIs. Their first stop of the day was Trunk Bay, where the Park Service had laid out a spectacular snorkeling trail through the colorful reef, which they both enjoyed immensely.

They had decided to take the tender and make a circumnavigation of St. John, so they headed east through the Narrows. At a position just north of Haulover Bay, Jack pointed north to a large island a few miles away, "That's Tortola," he said to Shannon. "About forty five minutes away."

"So close? Well, it certainly doesn't seem any more dangerous than these islands, does it?"

"That has been my main argument all along. If Horst lured us down here, for whatever reason, he could get to us here just as easily as over there."

She was silent for a few moments, weighing the possibilities, and then said, "In that case, let's go there tomorrow, if you still want to."

They completed their circumference of the island, stopping at various bays along the way to swim and snorkel, and by nightfall were pulling into Cruz Bay and alongside the 'Final Option'.

After a great deal of serious discussion during their excursion, they had decided to take the bull by the horns and take the boat over to Tortola the next morning.

Chapter 9

The sun was just one hour above the eastern horizon when 'Final Option' rounded the final headland and entered Road Harbour on the island of Tortola, BVI. Anchoring just off the town pier, they took the Novurania tender in to clear customs, a procedure which was accomplished with a minimum of fuss and time. They returned to the boat and proceeded around to Village Cay Marina, where telephone reservations had been made the night before for a one-week stay. They were fortunate that, because of the size of their boat, they were given an outside slip at the end of 'A' dock, which was normally occupied by the Westport 'Island Escape', but she was not due back for at least two weeks, being on extended charter. The slip was also the easiest one to get in and out of due to its positioning and distance from the shore. "What a pretty little town," said Shannon as she admired the quaint town encircled by the green hills which rose above it. The busy waterfront area was a sea of colors and the vendors' market by the cruise ship dock was busy with newly arriving tourists from the huge cruise ship which was still discharging passengers who were coming and going throughout the area.

Jack maneuvered the big boat deftly alongside the dock with the remote control, and as they tied up and prepared to go ashore, the fifty foot Sunseeker with the blue hull and white cabin directly across the dock from them didn't even register on their radar. They failed to notice the surreptitious movement of the blinds as the occupant of that boat surveyed them from within. *'Damn, damn, damn. It is too soon. Who would have thought that they'd get here so soon? This has to go down tonight.'* Horst/Anton thought to himself.

He watched them leave the boat and walk down the dock toward the shore. He watched Jack as he entered the dockmaster's office to pay for their stay while Shannon stayed outside to drink in the atmosphere of the new town they were in. He continued to watch even as Jack came out of the dockmaster's office and they turned and walked toward the town and were soon lost from his view in the crowds of tourists who were busy shopping in the vendors' market.

He stopped and quickly formulated a new plan; one he thought had a good chance of working with just a smidgen of luck. He was glad that he had had the forethought of contacting an old friend of his who knew him as Horst during the times he was here on the Senator's yacht, 'Shillelagh'. This friend was the one who had supplied him with the Glock and the silencer he now had stashed away. Problem number one was out of the way. Problem number two was sleeping below in the master cabin. Tammy. Somehow he had to keep her away from Jack and Shannon's sight; if they saw her the whole plan would go to hell.

Prisoner! The word entered his mind involuntarily and his consciousness quickly seized on it. He went to the engine room and filled his pockets with wire ties, the kind the police use now instead of handcuffs. He also grabbed a new box of shop towels. He tried to think of anything else he needed for the job at hand but was unable to think of anything. He hurried down below to the master cabin, and as he hoped, Tammy was still asleep in their bed. She stirred as he straddled her but put up no resistance as he wire tied one of her hands to the headboard, and then when he did the other one in the same manner, she finally came awake.

She asked him in a sleepy but husky voice, "So, is this a new game you want to play?"

"Sorry, Tammy." he said with some regret as he grabbed two shop towels, stuffing one into her mouth and tying the other around her head to keep it in, leaving her to breathe through her nose. With both hands tied above her head and him sitting on her stomach, there was little she could do to resist, but he could see the beginnings of fear combined with resistance in her eyes as she suddenly realized that something was seriously wrong. He jumped off her unexpectedly and lay on one leg while tying the other one to the footboard. Then he repeated the procedure with the other leg, and she was immobilized. She had been sleeping naked and the sheet had been thrown onto the floor during the brief struggle. He picked it up and gently covered her naked body, saying, "I'm sorry, but something unexpected has come up and I can't let you be seen outside the boat. I would have asked you nicely, but then you would have demanded an explanation, and I just can't give you one right now. I just want you to lie here still and quiet until this situation resolves itself, and it will; then tonight I'll tell you all about it, and tomorrow we will both laugh about it."

He could see tears forming in her eyes, and he felt unable to deal with that, so he left her alone and took the stairs to the main salon, grabbing the silenced Glock from the safe before he went. The miniblinds were still closed and the cabin was dark and gloomy even in the bright sunshine of the day. He opened the smallest section of blinds facing the shore just enough and positioned himself in such a way that he could see out, but nobody could see in, and then he waited. And still he waited, and then waited some more. And while he waited, he thought about his plan, which even he admitted to himself was becoming more and more diabolical by the minute.

Meanwhile, Jack and Shannon had wandered through the vendors' market, and having exhausted all the stands they had visited without buying anything except a coverup for Shannon since they had not realized there was a strict, local dress code, which prohibits swimwear, brief attire and shirtless men in town.

Apparently the bikini top Shannon had chosen to wear was considered too brief for the locals' taste, and one little old lady at their first stand had taken the trouble to point this out, in a nice way, of course. She had made a sale for her trouble and beamed at Shannon in her new, colorful island shirt buttoned all the way to the neck.

Since they had decided on lunch in Road Town, and after the two top buttons on Shannon's shirt had been undone, an arrangement that suited everyone, they walked around like lost tourists until some kind soul pointed them in the right direction toward Main Street. They settled on Pusser's Company Store and Pub, since Jack had heard about it and its famous Painkiller rum drink even back in Ft. Lauderdale. They had beers and sandwiches for lunch, the Painkiller having been put off 'til evening and then spent some time in the Virgin Islands Folk Museum. They wandered along Main Street and Waterfront Drive in the afternoon, looking into the stores and window shopping along the way.

As darkness fell, they found themselves at the Ft. Burt Marina, at the other end of the harbor from where their boat was. There they found, what else, the Pub, and since dinner and a drink were definitely called for after all the walking they had done during the day, their plan came together and they stayed.

They were quite surprised to find that all the big screen TVs in the place were tuned to American NFL football, and, since the Seahawks were playing the Packers, they settled in with dinner and drinks and watched the game. They left at nine when the Seahawks won the game in the final seconds and walked to Pusser's for their anticipated Painkiller, and they were definitely not disappointed. At ten p.m., utterly exhausted and slightly inebriated, they left Pusser's and walked back to their boat.

Horst spotted them the minute they stepped onto the dock and, grabbing the Glock, quickly and quietly crossed the dock and boarded 'Final Option', secreting himself behind the bulkhead on the far side of the boat and waited for the couple to arrive.

When Jack and Shannon arrived at the boat a few minutes later, laughing softly and speaking quietly out of deference to the people sleeping on their own boats, Jack did the gentlemanly thing and preceded Shannon through the gate in the side railing of the boat and then he turned and gave her his hand to help her board. They walked down the side deck Indian file to the aft deck where Jack disarmed the alarm with his key fob and unlocked the door. Horst chose this moment to quickly emerge from his hiding place, and he threw a massive arm around Shannon's neck and stuck the Glock into her back between the shoulder blades.

"Jack," he said quietly, "Don't try anything stupid. I've got a Glock aimed at Shannon's heart and I'd hate to see her die right here and now."

Everyone instantly froze. "Horst Keller!" Jack exclaimed, thoroughly disgusted and pissed off at himself for allowing his enemy to make such an easy capture.

Horst smiled, "Just open the door and go inside. Don't turn on any lights, and don't be a hero. Walk through to the dining table and stop there."

Without any choice in the matter, Jack did as ordered, and Horst and Shannon followed. Horst slid the salon door closed with his foot, then proceeded over to where Jack was standing.

"Down the stairs and into your cabin, and not too fast, Jack. Shannon and I will be right behind you."

When they were all assembled in the master stateroom, Horst released Shannon and allowed her to stand by Jack, covering both of them with the Glock. He reached into his pocket and pulled a number of wire ties out of it and tossed them to Jack. "Tie Shannon's hands to the headboard with these, not too tight and not too loose, I'll be checking them. Then tie her feet to the footboard. Do it now," he growled, but softly.

Again, with no choice at all, Jack did as he was commanded, tightening the ties enough so that she could not get out of them but not tight enough to cut off her circulation.

"Very good, Jack. Now you can open the safe, and then stand back over there."

"So you're going to rob us, too?"

"Not at all, Jack. In fact, there is only one thing I want from the safe. Shannon's passport."

"It isn't in there. I left it in the pilothouse after we cleared customs this morning."

"Oh, c'mon, Jack. I know how paranoid you are with security. That passport was back in the safe before you started the engines to come over here this morning. I guarantee it. Now, the safe, open it!"

Again, no options presented themselves. Jack went to the safe and opened it. "Very good, now take out Shannon's passport and close the safe again." He did as he was told. The passport was right on top of his, and he opened it to be sure he had the right one. He did, and showed it to his captor, who produced a plastic, ziplock bag from his pocket.

"Excellent, now drop it in this bag. And also take your wallet, and everything else, out of your pockets and drop them in the bag, too" After Jack had complied with the latest order, Horst zipped up the top of the bag and placed it into an inner pocket of the jacket he was wearing. Incongruously, he was also wearing a pair of lightweight sailing gloves.

"Great, now we're cooking with gas. I'm sorry to leave you in such an uncomfortable and compromising position, Shannon, but Jack and I have business to take care of up above. In the interest of your comfort, I am not going to gag you because you know what would happen to you and Jack if you were to try to raise the alarm. I want you just to lie there nice and quietly until Jack and I have finished our business, O.K?"

Shannon agreed to his orders with a nod of her head.

"Jack, you will go up the stairs to the salon and if you try anything, I'll shoot you and then come down and shoot Shannon. Am I being quite clear on that?"

Jack looked at him for a second with hatred in his eyes, but gave a shallow nod of the head and, turning around, climbed the stairs to the salon, with Horst following a safe distance behind.

"All right, Jack, let me tell you what I want you to do. You will start the engines, turn on the navigation lights, and then go ashore and release all the lines to the boat. You will use that cute little wireless remote you've got to get us out of the harbor to that flashing green buoy out by the entrance and then set a course of 090 degrees Magnetic. If you speak to anyone, or try to run, or do anything I don't like, I will shoot you and then shoot Shannon. Look closely into my eyes, Jack; I swear to you I am deadly serious about this."

As Horst moved closer and aimed the silenced Glock directly at Jack's face, Jack looked into those eyes by the reflected light from the dock and he saw murder, mayhem and madness in them. Without any other choice, Jack walked over to the pilothouse, started both engines and the generator, and turned on the navigation lights and the radar.

It took but a few minutes for the engines to warm up, and Jack grabbed the remote from its hook and walked out the salon door. "Don't forget, Jack. I *am* serious! I *will* kill Shannon!" Horst called softly after him.

Jumping to the dock, Jack disconnected the shorepower connection, allowing the Cablemaster to coil the electrical line inside the boat, and then untied the bow, stern and spring lines from the dock and threw them aboard, before he boarded the boat again and guided it away from the dock with the remote control. He then walked back to the pilothouse and steered for the buoy. When he reached it, he set the autopilot to 090 degrees Magnetic, and turned to Horst, "What now? Where are we going?"

"Patience, Jack. You *will* find out, but all in good time."

Down below, Shannon felt the boat moving, and a wave of apprehension washed over her. In the dark with nothing to provide a distraction, the physical exercise of the day and the alcohol she had consumed, combined with the gentle motion of the moving boat, conspired to send her off into a deep sleep, despite the discomfort of her restraints and the fact that she fought it intensely with great desperation.

Keeping Jack, who was standing at the helm, in sight at all times, Horst went to the bar and returned with an unopened bottle of Jack Daniel's and one rocks glass.

"Sit down at the pilothouse lounge and slide all the way around the table, Jack."

Jack obeyed and was soon positioned six feet away from Horst with the table between them. Horst placed the bottle and glass on the table. "Now open the bottle and pour out a full measure."

Once again Jack obeyed. "Now drink it all down." Horst said, grinning.

"I actually prefer it on the rocks." Jack had a suspicion that he was not going to like tonight's party.

"Just drink it! Now!" Horst waved the Glock in Jack's direction quite forcefully.

Jack took the glass, and slowly sipped at the contents. "Shoot it or I'll shoot you, understand?"

No choice, so Jack downed it. "I really prefer Jameson's, if I'm going to drink it straight."

"If you are still conscious after that bottle is gone, I'll give you your Jameson's. How's that? Now pour yourself another, Jack, to the rim this time."

Jack reluctantly complied, and several more times the routine was repeated. Horst, now standing by the helm, glanced at the radar screen and with grim satisfaction, noted that there were no other boats anywhere near them. He also was pleased to see that they were almost in the position he had determined suited his purposes the best, midway down the Sir Francis Drake Passage, and halfway between the islands on either side of the passage.

Horst had now only to glance in his direction to induce Jack to, once again, fill his glass and drink it all down. Well over half the bottle had already been consumed.

"By the way, I understand that your little Christmas party ended up one guest short." Horst was actually smirking when he introduced this piece of information, causing Jack to hesitate in mid-swallow.

"What do you mean?" He asked after swallowing.

"I was there, Jack, ready to finally finish our little business dealings. You cost me a lot of money, you know, and you caused me to lose face in front of my crew. This could have been settled right then and there if that drunken bitch hadn't interfered. I had to keep her quiet, you understand?"

Jack was halfway out of his seat, hands going for Horst's throat before he was stopped by the table and the sight of the business end of the Glock. "You stinking, rotten bastard!" he shouted, "You killed my ex-wife!"

Horst seemed genuinely shocked but recovered instantly, "Shut up and sit down, Jack!" he shouted back, and then continued quietly, "I didn't know she was your ex-wife, she was just a drunken bitch who needed to be quieted down. I didn't even mean to kill her, but she hit her head on the seawall going into the canal. I looked for her but couldn't find her in the dark."

Both men were quiet for a few minutes, glaring at each other across the table.

"But enough pleasantries, take another drink, Jack. Now!"

As they drew close to midway, Horst slowed the boat down to ten knots and induced Jack to take yet another drink. He had barely finished that last drink, when he suddenly cried, "I'm going to be sick!" and desperately tried to slide out from behind the table.

"Quick, Jack, onto the swim platform," cried Horst. He followed behind as Jack made a hurried escape from the cabin, onto the aft deck and down the stairs to the swim platform, where, hanging on to the railing, he performed a less-than-graceful Technicolor yawn and emptied his evening meal into the dark water.

He had no time to recover; and only a microsecond to react when he felt Horst's presence behind him and felt the soft rush of air as the gun barrel headed for his skull. He ducked and suffered only a glancing blow, but that, combined with Horst's foot in his backside, was enough to propel him head first into the water. He thought he heard Horst shout a curse, "Damn it!" as his head disappeared under the churning water of the prop wash from the boat. He felt like a load of laundry in a washing machine and struggled to find 'up' in the darkness.

He *actually had* heard Horst yell, "Damn it!" when he suddenly realized that he had left the remote control in the pilothouse and the boat was still operating on autopilot. He rushed into the boat through the salon to the pilothouse, knocked off the autopilot and put the boat into a hard turn trying to get back to where Jack had gone overboard. Naturally, in the dark, he knew that he had little hope of finding Jack; for he was certain that Jack would do everything he could to prevent that. Unlike survivors of a shipwreck, who would do anything to be found, all Jack had to do was stay underwater or down behind any wave he could find. After thirty minutes of circling and trying to locate Jack with the spotlight, Horst gave up and headed back toward the harbor.

When he finally surfaced at the end of his oxygen supply, Jack felt completely disoriented. Turning a full circle, very slowly because of the lack of equilibrium he felt due to the alcohol he'd consumed, he was already being careful whenever he moved, he watched as the stern light on his boat was rapidly disappearing into the darkness. For one full second, he wished he was back on the boat, before he realized the consequences of such a wish. Unbelievably, at that exact moment, the boat was put into a hard turn and started back toward him. He felt a moment of panic, glancing left and right, and even behind, before spotting the bulk of an island off to his left in the direction of the boat but a little to its right. He started swimming awkwardly, for he still had no coordination in his movements, toward the island. He had not gained much distance before the boat was upon him, searchlight beaming across a wide swath of water.

He treaded water, watching as the boat and the beams of light came toward him, and he was able to determine that the boat would miss him if he could stay out of the spotlight's beam. The light came close, but missed him, and soon the boat swept past his position and he resumed his slow struggle toward the island. Behind him he sensed that the boat was turning again, the sounds of its engines transmitting clearly through the placid water. It passed his position once again, but further away now and he didn't have to duck any lights this time, as he still struggled slowly toward the island.

Half an hour passed, with the boat getting further and further away but by only small increments. Then suddenly it turned and headed away, presumably toward the harbor and he was left alone, a speck in the middle of the water. He felt partly relieved, partly anxious, for the prospects of him making landfall were not in his favor. He was, however, determined to try, and slowly he swam toward the island, which now seemed marginally closer. At least, that was what he chose to tell himself.

He had no idea how long he swam; he had always been a good swimmer, his favorite stroke being the Australian crawl, but after a while, his alcohol addled brain refused to send the correct signals to his muscles and coordination broke down. The mere thought of expending the energy to lift his arms clear of the water became an exercise in futility, and he soon settled, frustratingly, for the slow but steady pace of the breaststroke.

As often as was necessary, and the rest breaks were coming closer and closer together each time, he would slowly roll over on his back for a while and just drift to conserve energy, but unfortunately, the calm, placid and surprisingly warm water would try its hardest to lull him off to sleep. Several times during that long night he would awaken suddenly, spluttering and coughing salt water from his mouth and lungs.

The last time he rested, he noticed a definite lightening in the eastern sky which signaled that dawn was close, a revelation which was suddenly snuffed out by a huge rock that blocked out his view of the horizon. He was so startled by this vision that he rolled back onto his stomach only to have a small wave breaking on the beach knock him ass over teakettle, and cause him to swallow a large quantity of salt water on his way to being unceremoniously deposited on the beach like a piece of driftwood. He shook his head, and spluttering seawater, he used his remaining strength to haul himself further up the beach. He tried to stand but only succeeded in forcing his stomach to rebel against his efforts, and he threw up again. His last reserves expended, he collapsed into his own vomit and passed out.

As Road Harbour came into sight, Horst throttled back to idle, because at around midnight, it was not in his plan for anyone to notice his comings and goings. The first part of his plan had worked, if not perfectly, at least well enough that he now felt that his enemy, Jack Elliott, was dead, drowned out in the middle of the passage between the islands. Whether his body would be found or not, he was not concerned about, since there would be nobody left to point the finger at him once the second part of the plan had been completed.

Fully utilizing that wonderful remote control that Jack had so conveniently installed on the boat, Horst had no trouble docking the boat in the exact position that it had occupied before they left. He tied the boat to the dock, connected the shore power, and shut down the engines and the generator, turned off the navigation lights and the radar, and mixed himself a drink, the last of the Jack Daniel's and Coke, before continuing with phase two of his plan. He went below, carrying his drink to check up on Shannon, only to find her fast asleep.

'So much the better,' he thought. 'I really have to agree with Jack's assessment, though, Jameson's is so much better than this crap.'

He sat quietly for a good ten minutes, checking the marina, which at this time of the night, was quiet as a graveyard. He put the glass in the dishwasher, locked the boat on his way out and crossed to his own boat on the other side of the dock. He went aboard and then down below and found Tammy where he had left her, still wide awake. Her eyes widened in fear when she spotted the silenced Glock he had so haphazardly stuck in the waistband of his shorts.

"Tammy, I have good news. The situation that I told you about this morning has been totally cleared up, and I want to show you the results."

He reached into his pocket and brought out a switchblade knife and opened it. It was razor sharp and with it he deftly sliced through the wire ties holding her legs to the footboard. She moved her legs, not kicking out at him as he had expected, but bent her knees and placed her feet under her, leaning to one side away from him, curling into a fetal position as much as possible.

He moved to the side of the bed, leaned over her and sliced through the wire tie holding her left hand to the headboard. He had expected her to lash out at him, but she just lay there, looking into his eyes. With a flick of the wrist he parted the last wire tie, and she brought her hands down, rolled onto her left side, away from him and curled into a full fetal position. He untied the shop towel behind her neck and she spit out the other one from her mouth.

"Tammy, I need you to get up and get dressed."

"Why?"

"Because we are going for a walk and I don't want anyone to see you naked. I need to show you why you've been tied up all day and night."

"I need to pee first, and I want something to eat. I'm starving."

"OK, we can do that."

She got up slowly from the bed, on the opposite side from him, and walked slowly to the bathroom. It only took her a few minutes, and after the flush, the door opened tentatively. She peeked out, saw him still sitting on the bed and walked over to the drawers. She chose a pair of panties and a bra and put them on.

"I think jeans and that nice, wine colored shirt would be appropriate, and wear your boat shoes."

She noticed that everything he had suggested was dark colored, but chose not to comment on it. She simply went to the closet, found the items and put them on. He led her up the stairs and into the galley where she quickly put together two ham and cheese sandwiches and grabbed two bottles of Red Stripe from the fridge. Their after-midnight snack was surprisingly satisfying; and the mood lightened considerably.

They left the boat shortly before one in the morning and walked up the long dock toward shore. Horst was careful to keep a firm arm around her shoulders, but she seemed unusually calm, considering the ordeal she had been through that day. He thought that maybe his powers of persuasion were better than he had counted on, or maybe she was still suspicious, but was just waiting to see how it was all going to play out.

As they passed the dockmaster's office and turned onto the street past the closed stores, the almost muted sounds of an NFL football game came through the windows of the office.

'He must be watching the late game from the West Coast,' thought Horst, as he noted with grim satisfaction that nobody had seen them leave.

They walked past the closed stores and soon came to the vendors' market, also closed and shuttered tight for the night. They kept going until, about halfway to the cruise ship pier, Horst grabbed Tammy's arm and dragged her behind one of the deserted stands and pushed her up against the rear wall.

Tears were rolling down her cheeks, her body giving him no resistance, when she asked, already knowing the answer, "You're going to kill me, aren't you?"

As his big hands encircled her delicate throat, his thumbs finding the soft center above her clavicle, he began squeezing hard, and the last words she heard were, "Yes, I'm afraid so. I have to." Then she blacked out.

He stood there for quite a while, holding her dead body up by the neck long after she was dead, his face a mask of pain and regret. Finally he lowered her to the ground, and checked for a pulse or breath. Since neither one of those options was present, he felt a few tears escape his eyes. Once again, he had let his rage overcome his better judgment with predictable results, and the regret he felt threatened to overwhelm him.

He shook those thoughts out of his head and finished what he came to do. Taking great care not to smudge Jack's fingerprints on it, he placed Shannon's Passport into Tammy's back pocket, took Tammy's ID and put it in his pocket, and placed Jack's wallet on the ground, rolling Tammy's limp body on top of it.

He quickly scanned the area, first from behind the stand, then moving up the alleyway, and conducted a slow, meticulous scan of the whole area. He saw nobody and heard nothing out of the ordinary. He then walked quickly back towards the marina, sticking to the shadows as much as possible, and paused when he heard the muffled sounds coming from the dockmaster's office. The game was still on and from the excitement in the voices he heard, it must have been drawing to a conclusion. He slipped past the office unseen and walked quickly down the dock to 'Final Option'. He swung aboard, unlocked the door, and then locked it securely once inside. He stopped to listen, but heard nothing; no warning, and no challenge.

He went below and into the master stateroom, lingering awhile over the sight of Shannon, still fast asleep on her back despite the bonds holding her in place, which must have been extremely uncomfortable. He once again produced his switchblade, which he opened, and sat down on the bed next to Shannon.

She came awake with a start as his weight settled on the bed, and fear crept into her eyes at the sight of the knife he held before her. She stifled a little cry and looked into Horst's face. She felt immensely sad when she saw his broad smile of triumph, knowing that he, at least, felt that he had won.

"Shannon, my dear, I'm going to explain what is going to happen here so you will understand the consequences if you don't do exactly what I tell you to do. In a second or two, I am going to cut all the wire ties holding you down. I want you to get up, walk up the stairs with me and go across the dock to my boat, the Sunseeker with the blue hull. Now, I think that is a quite simple thing to do. Do you think you could do that without any fuss?"

"It appears that I don't have much choice, doesn't it?"

"That's the spirit. And just remember, I have this silenced Glock. It doesn't make any more noise than a loud fart, so no one will come to your rescue, and you'll be dead. Now, I don't want that to happen, and neither does Jack. I'm sure you don't want that, either, so please just do as you're told, OK?"

He received a hesitant nod to his question, and it appeared she was considering the consequences.

He went to the closet and pulled one of Shannon's voluminous shopping bags out and began filling it with a varied assortment of Shannon's clothes. Everything from bras and panties, swimsuits and cover ups, shorts and tops to jeans and shoes went into the bag, and then he placed it on the floor by the door.

He walked over to her and looking down at her, his knife in one hand and his other hand on the Glock in his waistband, he sliced through the ties that held her feet. Then he proceeded to her hands, the left first as it was furthest away, and then the right. He stepped back, but was surprised to find that her reaction was even more subdued than Tammy's had been. She just lay there as if she was still restrained to the bed. He was a little unnerved by her lack of fear and concern. But then he remembered her showing the same control when she had been kidnapped by him for the Senator during the debacle in the Bahamas.

"Now then, Shannon, if you will get up and pick up your bag, we will go up the stairs and across to my boat. And, please, no tricks; I am a very good shot and you would not stand a chance. Understand me?"

"Yes," she said as she seemed to struggle a little bit to stand on her very shaky legs.

She walked slowly over to the bag, holding onto various objects for support, and picked it up. She then turned and headed up the stairs, with Horst behind her. As she got to the top she hesitated, looked around and suddenly asked, "Where is Jack?"

Pointing to the empty Jack Daniel's bottle, he said, "Sleeping off last night's drunken session in the forward cabin." He did not realize how close his lie would eventually come to the truth, except for Jack's actual location.

She looked at him strangely, but shrugged her shoulders and continued through the salon to the aft deck, with Horst close behind. He locked up and alarmed the boat and placed the key and fob on its hook inside the locker below the sink on the port side of the aft deck.

After a careful survey of the dock, the pair crossed to the Sunseeker and Horst led her below to his cabin and proceeded to wire tie her to his bed. Her bag was deposited in the forward cabin. The good thing about charter boats was that every cabin needed to be able to be locked both from the inside or the outside with a key in order to preserve the intimate privacy of the individual guests.

"Shannon," he said to her as he was closing and locking his stateroom door. "Get yourself some sleep, and I'll see you in the morning."

He then went back to the pilothouse and started the engines and generator, and while they were warming up, went ashore to disconnect the shorepower and the lines holding the boat to the dock. He turned on the navigation lights and the radar and slowly and carefully backed the boat out of its slip and then went forward into the harbor. As he idled down the harbor toward the open ocean, he was whistling a happy tune.

To anyone watching, but unfortunately no one was, they would only have guessed that his was just another pleasure boat getting an early start to the adventure of a lifetime.

Chapter 10

Present Day

Chief Inspector Ian Cavendish arrived at his office in the Police Annex of the Government Buildings at precisely 7 a.m., as he had for his entire career, for he felt it extremely important to be prompt. Before he had even had the chance to take off his coat, or sit down, the phone on his desk started ringing.

'Oh, bother,' he thought, *'I haven't even had my tea yet.'*

Nevertheless, he answered it on the second ring. "Cavendish." he spoke softly into the instrument.

"Chief, this is Andrew, in Dispatch. We have got a murder over at the vendors' market and the Commissioner wants you to handle it personally." This did not surprise him since he was the one person in the department who seemed to handle murder cases in the most efficient way, even though very few murders were committed on the islands.

"Do you have any details?"

"Yes, sir. A young white woman, late twenties or so found strangled to death behind one of the stalls in the vendors' market. Our guys and the medics are already on scene and the area is cordoned off; the coroner is on his way."

"Then I'd better be on my way, too. Thank you, Andrew."

Since it was only a five minute walk to the market, C.I. Cavendish did exactly that, feeling that the need to take a car was unnecessary. When he arrived he was immediately welcomed by two police constables.

"Good morning, Chief Inspector, sir. PC Wilkins and this is PC trainee Williams." Wilkins was a tall, stout black man and he

184

indicated a slim, pretty young black woman who seemed to swim in her uniform.

"Ah, Wilkins and Williams, I've heard good things about you two."

The big man positively beamed, "Why, thank you, sir, much appreciated."

"Well, then, what's the story here?"

Wilkins consulted his notebook. "We received a call at 6.30 this morning about a dead woman behind this stall from a Joe James, who owns the stall. We arrived on scene at 6.38, and secured the scene after we determined that the woman was dead. The medics arrived at 6.42 and confirmed. We have cordoned off the area between the stalls and the seawall to the bay, and we have Mr. James in his stall ready to take his statement."

Just then the coroner arrived in his vehicle, and stepped out to greet the Chief Inspector, "Cavendish, I see you beat me again. Funny how you always manage to do that."

"Dr. Barrett, you are just in time, we were about to examine the body. Shall we?"

"By all means, lead the way."

They started down the alleyway between the stalls as Wilkins and Williams went to question Joe James. They found the dead body lying on her back in the weeds at the back of the stall. The police photographer was just finishing up taking his photos and stepped back. Following procedures, both men produced disposable gloves and put them on and Cavendish knelt down beside her body and felt for a pulse.

"She hasn't been dead for long," he observed, "The body is still warmish."

"Let's see how accurate you are," the coroner said as he knelt down beside him. He produced a thermometer and placed it in her mouth, holding it under her tongue, and then pointed to the obvious ligature marks on her wrists. "Looks like someone kept her prisoner for a while. And it must have been a man with big hands because the bruising on her throat goes all the way around her neck, even while his thumbs crushed her larynx. The lividity in her finger tips shows me he must have held her up against the wall for a while before he dropped her here."

"Nasty business," said Cavendish. No matter how long he had been a policeman, a senseless loss of life such as this had always been difficult for him to take. A beautiful young woman, for that much he could see despite the anguished look on her face, cut down in the best years of her life.

Removing the thermometer from the victim's mouth, Dr. Barrett remarked, "92 degrees Fahrenheit would indicate that she has been dead approximately four hours."

"Help me roll her over; I want to see if we have any other damage to her body." As they rolled her onto her side, Cavendish said, "Stop!"

With Barrett holding the body steady, Cavendish extracted from her back pocket a U.S. Passport, and with great care, dropped it into an evidence baggie. That's when he saw a man's wallet which had been hidden by her body lying on the ground. That too went into an evidence baggie.

The photographer snapped away as this procedure was accomplished, and finished up as Cavendish waved him away. He checked his digital photos to be sure he had everything necessary.

"That is convenient, I would say. One piece of evidence to tell us who she was and one to tell us who killed her?" Barrett asked, somewhat skeptically.

"A little too convenient, I'm thinking, but we shall see. What about time of death?" Cavendish asked.

"According to the reading on the thermometer, I'd say sometime between midnight and 3 am this morning. I'll be more precise when I have her liver temperature. The lack of rigor mortise would tend to point to this time frame too."

Barrett and Cavendish both stood up at the same time, and the doctor signaled the medics to bag the body and place it in the ambulance. "I'll be able to tell you more back at the lab."

Barrett followed the ambulance out of the market as Cavendish walked to the front of the stall and entered. He spoke directly to Joe James, an older black man who had owned that particular stall for as long as anyone could remember. "What can you tell me?" he asked.

"I arrived at six this morning, as I usually do, despite the fact that I stayed 'til midnight last night cleaning up the stall so it would be ready for this morning. It'll be busy today since we will have two cruise ships in port. It wasn't until I felt the need for a smoke that I came back here and found the body, poor thing." To Cavendish, the man seemed genuinely distressed, perhaps more than one would normally expect.

"Did you touch the body?"

"Only to feel for a pulse. Those marks on her neck pretty much told me I wouldn't find one."

"Do you know who she is?"

"I've seen her around the market a few times but I've never spoken to her."

"So you couldn't tell us where she came from?"

"No, sir. But I think I saw her on one of those boats over in the marina, sir."

"Which one?"

"I don't remember, but it was at least a week ago."

"Did you see or hear anything unusual last night or this morning?"

"No, sir. Everything is as it should be, and there wasn't a soul around last night, as far as I could tell."

"All right, Mr. James, you finish up with the Constables and if I have any more questions….."

"I'm here all day, every day, sir. A man has to make a living, you know.

"Of course you do, and I won't keep you any longer. Wilkins and Williams, I want you to scour this area and bag anything unusual that you find."

"Yes, sir." said Wilkins.

Cavendish walked back to his office, carrying the two baggies of evidence, and upon arrival, turned them over to the forensics department.

"Dust these for fingerprints, then photocopy everything, and have it on my desk in an hour. Also, that's an American passport. I want to know when it entered the BVIs. Smartly now."

"Yes, sir," was aimed at his back as he turned and walked away.

Cavendish sat in his office until after lunchtime, receiving phone calls from the coroner and forensics, and a package from the latter containing the photocopies he had requested. He was trying to make sense of the contradictory evidence with which he had been presented. Joe James had said that he had seen her for the past week, but the customs office said she had arrived only yesterday. The man's wallet contained a Florida Driver's License, cash and a few credit cards, as well as a photograph of the woman with the man whose picture was on the driver's license. Customs officials said that this man had also entered the BVIs yesterday, in the company of the murder victim, on a private yacht.

Cavendish decided to have his lunch at the marina restaurant, right after he questioned the dockmaster, Tommy Fisher, who he knew very well because his father was a sergeant on the police force. He entered the office and found the man at his desk with the remains of his lunch still spread out before him.

"Good afternoon, I am Chief Inspector Ian Cavendish, and I would like a word with you."

"I know who you are, Chief Inspector. How may I help you?"

Cavendish pulled from his inside coat pocket, the photocopy of the passport picture, folded to hide the name and details, and asked, "Do you know this woman?"

"Yes, sir, I do. Her name is Tammy Bishop and she is the girlfriend of the man who has chartered the blue and white Sunseeker from us."

Now Cavendish was totally confused. "And what would his name be?"

"His name is Anton Kohl, and he is a sales rep. from Germany over here on vacation."

A slight hesitation before the next question, "Do you know the name Shannon O'Loughlin?"

"Yes, sir, she is the fiancée of Jack Elliott, who owns the big Neptunus at the end of 'A' dock."

"How long have they been here?"

"They, who?"

"All of them!"

"Anton and Tammy have been here about a week, Jack and Shannon arrived yesterday, why?" He suddenly sat bolt upright, "Oh, my God, Tammy isn't the girl who was murdered last night over at the market, is she?"

"How did you know about that?"

"News travels fast in this small community, you know that, especially something like this."

"Yes, of course. No, it was not Tammy who got murdered, but Shannon."

"Then why show me Tammy's photo?"

"This photo is from Shannon's passport."

"But they're identical, unless they are both one and the same person."

"You know, I've been thinking the same thing, but the timeline is all screwed up. Tammy's been here a week and customs tells me Shannon arrived only yesterday. So which is it?"

"And we have two different boats involved."

"Speaking of boats, I think I need to have a word with these two gentlemen. Can you take the time to show me the two boats which are involved?"

"Yes, of course. I want to get to the bottom of this, too. Right this way, Inspector."

The two of them left the office and walked down 'A' dock, and when they got to the end, Tommy scratched his head and said, "The Sunseeker is gone. It was right here yesterday when I went home at 5:30 p.m. They must have left late last night or early this morning. But the Neptunus is still here," he said, indicating 'Final Option' still sitting serenely in its berth.

Cavendish pulled the photocopy of Jack's driver's license from his pocket, and said, "Now you are going to tell me that this is Mr. Anton Kohl, right?"

"No, sir. That is Mr. Jack Elliott, just as it says on the license." Tommy confirmed.

"Well, thank God, someone is exactly who they say they are."

Cavendish balled his fist and banged loudly on the hull. A minute passed without result, before he stepped aboard and banged loudly against the bulkhead by the salon door, again without any result.

"I've got a key to the boat in my office. It's a requirement that the key is left at the office, in case of emergency. I think this qualifies as an emergency, don't you?"

"I do indeed. Good man. Go and get the key, and I'll take a look around while you're gone."

As soon as Tommy left, Cavendish slipped off his brogues and walked in stocking clad feet around the main deck and then climbed to the flybridge, constantly scanning for something out of the ordinary. He had found nothing by the time Tommy arrived back with the two keys and the alarm fob.

Cavendish disabled the alarm and unlocked the salon door, and with Tommy standing guard, went in.

He quickly, but thoroughly, searched every cabin and any space which was large enough to warrant attention, but apart from a couple of glasses in the dishwasher, and an empty bottle of Jack Daniel's on the pilothouse table, nothing seemed amiss in this clean and well kept yacht. He exited the yacht and locked the salon door, walked down to the swim platform and used the second key to unlock the door to the crew quarters. He searched them thoroughly as he did the engine room which accessed off the crew quarters. Again he found nothing out of the ordinary. He then locked the crew quarters door and together they left the boat. Inadvertently they forgot to rearm the alarm system, a mistake that Jack would notice upon his return.

They walked slowly up 'A' dock to the office, Cavendish deep in thought. He grabbed a chair, sat down and Tommy mirrored his move.

"Tommy, I want you to keep an eagle eye on that yacht. Whatever else you need to do today, delegate it. I want to know the second that Jack Elliott returns, and I don't want him to know that I need to speak to him. And I want to know when that Sunseeker comes back, because I need to speak to this Mr. Kohl, too. Can you do that for me, with the greatest discretion, of course?"

"Of course I can, Inspector. You can count on me."

"Your father will be proud of you." Cavendish placed his card front and center on the desk.

"That works for me, too."

Cavendish left the dockmaster's office, still mildly confused, but confident that he at least had a decent start on the investigation. Now it was just a matter of finding the people involved and questioning them. Something was sure to turn up to explain this convoluted mess, and someone was sure to slip up under questioning. He felt sure of it.

He went next to the coroner's office and walked into the autopsy room unannounced.

"Dr. Barrett, what surprises do you have for me today?"

"No surprises today. Unfortunately, this young lady died just the way I surmised. Strangulation. Although, I can't say at the moment whether it was lack of oxygen to the brain or the crushed larynx that actually killed her. Either way, the person responsible is one and the same."

"Time of death?"

"Probable no later than three and closer to midnight. Why, is that important?"

"It might possibly be. You never know. Right now, I have a lot of loose ends and some confusing issues that don't seem to make any sense, and the more information I can find, the closer I'll be to solving it."

The rumbling in his stomach reminded him that, here in the middle of the afternoon, he had not yet had lunch, something that he was determined to alleviate. For whatever reason, he decided that a nice piece of fish at the marina restaurant was in order and he walked back to the Village Cay Dockside Restaurant where he had an enjoyable, if late, lunch. He had barely finished when his cell phone rang.

"Cavendish," he answered, noting that his heartbeat had jumped slightly.

"Tommy here, sir. Jack Elliott has just come back to the boat and he has people with him."

"I'll be right there." He threw a couple of twenties on the table and rushed out.

Sixty seconds later, he was standing beside Tommy watching Jack and a young couple with a kid walking down the dock toward his boat. He decided to wait to see if Jack's guests were going to leave before confronting him.

"What did you do, fly?" Tommy wanted to know.

Cavendish laughed gently at Tommy's consternation, "I was actually having lunch, next door. So, now we wait."

An hour later, he watched as the guests left the boat, which was his signal to start down the dock. He saw Jack look at him in a curious way, as if anticipating a confrontation, but didn't know what to make of that. When he introduced himself, the younger man showed no sign of stress, in fact, showed more friendliness than anything else, even joking about his appearance. So it was with a small amount of trepidation that he started his questioning and was surprised at the candidness that Jack showed, right up to the point when he told him about Shannon.

Chapter 11

BAM!!!!!!

SHANNON!!! Her name hit him like a shockwave and all his memories abruptly flooded back into his brain. **Last night! Damn Horst Keller!** He felt dizzy, he felt sick and disoriented. He lowered his head into his hands, which he suddenly found slippery and wet with his tears. He started shaking uncontrollably when he recalled the Inspector's words, *'arrest you for the murder of your fiancée'* and he started sobbing.

"He killed her; that stupid, rotten, murdering, slimy kraut, son-of-a-bitch asshole killed her! WHY! I'm gonna find him and tear that block of stone he calls a heart right out of his chest with my bare hands! **Bastard!!**" He was muttering to himself, with all the emotion and grief he felt. His sense of desolation and loss brought his tirade to a slow close, and he felt a determination and a resolve come over him. He would find Keller and kill him, very slowly and excruciatingly painfully.

He was surprised to find an arm around his shoulders, and the Chief Inspector sitting close to him, supporting him. "Get a hold of yourself, young man. I know you're grieving but we have to find out what happened. And the only way that's going to happen is for you to pull yourself together and tell me the whole story."

Jack took several deep breaths and slowly straightened up in his seat on the couch. Cavendish moved back to his chair as Jack valiantly tried to compose himself.

"Tell me what happened; start at the beginning and don't leave anything out. You never know which detail might help us solve this murder."

"Am I under arrest?"

Cavendish hesitated for a moment, and then said, "Not at this time, I want to hear what you have to say."

Jack began, "We, Shannon and I, arrived here yesterday morning from Cruz Bay and went through customs. We registered at this marina, then went for a tour of the town which turned out to be an all day and most of the night excursion. When we returned after ten to the boat, we were attacked by Horst Keller and forced inside the boat and down below, where he made me tie Shannon to the bed. He made me open the safe and take out Shannon's passport and he took everything I had in my pockets, including my wallet, and put them in a plastic bag. He then made me start the boat and leave the harbor and sail close to Virgin Gorda, plying me with liquor the whole time. I must have had a full bottle of Jack Daniel's, and I was about to be sick, so he took me to the swim platform, hit me over the head with his gun, and threw me overboard. It was a miracle I was able to get to shore, but I made it and collapsed. I have spent all day today trying to get back here, and trying to regain my memory, which only occurred when you mentioned Shannon's name."

"And who is this Horst Keller?"

"He is my arch enemy, a nightmare who has haunted Shannon and me for almost a year now."

"Why?"

"He was the captain on the yacht of Senator Shamus O'Malley, and he was supposedly killed in the helicopter crash in which the Senator died. Somehow he survived and out of spite, I guess, sent me a text from this island. There was a State Department bulletin sent to all the islands in the Caribbean asking for information regarding his whereabouts."

"Now that you mention it, I do remember that request, if only because it was so unusual. But I had forgotten the name. So you say he is here now?"

"He was last night."

Retrieving the photocopy of Shannon's passport photo, he passed it over and asked Jack, "This is your fiancée, Shannon, right?"

Jack nodded and numbly replied, "Yes."

Cavendish sat deep in thought, his chin resting on the knuckles of the intertwined fingers. After several minutes, he dialed a number on his cell phone.

"Tommy, Ian Cavendish here. Do you have time to come to Mr. Elliott's boat on 'A' dock?"

"Sure, sir. But I'm off duty and at home. It'll take me about five minutes to get back there."

"That's fine; take your time. We are in no hurry."

Cavendish ended the call and he and Jack sat in silence until Tommy arrived. Jack's mind was reeling with remorse and regret and once again the tears threatened to come. He shook himself mentally, admonishing himself that he had to keep a clear, uncluttered mind if he was to catch Horst Keller.

A polite knock on the hull and Cavendish's "come in," announced Tommy's arrival. He entered and stood there in the salon in his 'civvies', T-shirt, shorts, and flip-flops, as opposed to the smartly dressed young man who was the dockmaster. "Evening, Mr. Elliott, Chief Inspector." he said, nodding his head at both of them.

"Jack, you wouldn't happen to have a picture of Horst Keller, would you?"

Thinking back to the time at Pier 66 when Horst and the Senator were breaking into his boat in search of Capt'n Pete, Jack replied, "I do believe I do."

He got his laptop out of the entertainment center drawer, and started it up. After a few moments, he was able to pull up his photo files and chose a photo, which when double clicked, opened up in Photoshop, his photo editing program. The photo showed Horst Keller, full face, looking around to make sure nobody was watching. He swung the computer around toward Tommy and Cavendish.

"See anyone you recognize, Tommy?"

"Yes sir. That is Mr. Anton Kohl, different hairstyle, but no doubt, it is him."

"I suspected as much. But Mr. Elliott says that his name is Horst Keller, and he is wanted for attempted murder. So now, we have several mysteries. We have a man with two names; we have two women with different names, one of whom is lying on a slab in the morgue, and the other who is missing. Both of you recognize the woman on the photo I have, but each of you thinks it is the other woman. Curious, isn't it?"

"Wait," said Jack, spinning the laptop back around to face him. He went back into the photo files and pulled up several shots of Shannon, wearing several different outfits and one with her hair up, put them side by side on the screen and swung the laptop around. "Do you recognize this woman, Tommy?" he asked.

"Yes, that is Tammy Bishop, Anton Kohl's girlfriend. Her hair is different but that's definitely her."

"Sorry, Tommy, you are wrong. Those are all photos of my fiancée, Shannon. You should know, you saw her the day we arrived and came into the office to register."

"No, Mr. Elliott, you came in by yourself. She must have waited outside, because I never saw her. If I had, I would have inquired about Mr. Kohl, for he is the one she had been with for the past week."

"You know, I think you are right. I remember looking for her when I came out of the office and found her looking at the menu for the restaurant."

Cavendish, who had been sitting silent throughout this whole exchange, finally spoke up. "I think the best thing we can do right now, is to go over to the morgue, determine exactly who is dead and formulate a plan for finding the other one. Tommy, Mr. Elliott, do either one of you have any objections to accompanying me over to the morgue for a positive identification?"

"No," they both answered at the same time.

Cavendish got up, followed by Jack and joined Tommy, who was still standing, and together they walked down the dock, after carefully locking and alarming the boat. After a two minute stop at Tommy's house, to allow him to slip into jeans, a shirt and boat shoes, for it would be cold inside, they continued on their way to the morgue. For Jack, he was beginning to see a small glimmer of hope, a tiny pinprick of light at the end of a long, dark tunnel, but he would not allow himself too much hope in case they were dashed against the wall.

When they entered the morgue, they were surprised to find Dr. Barrett still there despite the lateness of the hour. "Inspector, how may I help you?" he said.

"We've come to make a positive identification on our market victim."

"But I thought you had her passport."

"Yes, well, like I said at the time, maybe it seemed a little *too* convenient."

"Very well, she is right over here." He walked over to the six slot freezer unit and opened the one at table height. The white sheet clad body was obviously one of a slim, shapely woman, and Jack's heart skipped a beat or two when he realized that he had seen that form before, in his bed. Tears started tickling at his eyes, and he cursed himself for thinking that there was any hope that it wasn't Shannon. When the coroner folded the sheet back from the face and shoulders, and Jack recognized the face before him, the tears started in earnest, rolling down his cheeks and wetting his shirt, and he just stood and stared, making no attempt to hide his sorrow. He looked across the table at the Chief Inspector, who was looking down at his shoes, embarrassed, and at Tommy beside him, who was matching his tears, drop for drop. Somehow this incongruity didn't seem right.

"It's Tammy, without a doubt" said Tommy, in a sad voice, "I remember the day when she got that little butterfly tattoo on her shoulder last week; she was so proud of it, and she ran around showing everyone."

"What!!" whispered Jack, not believing his ears? "Shannon didn't have a tattoo anywhere on her body." He moved around the table, wiping tears from his eyes and upon seeing the tattoo, tears of relief flooded his eyes. He felt a great weight lift from his shoulders and his heart soared. Relief flowed into his mind, followed a split second later by feelings of utter remorse. This young woman had died simply because she looked like Shannon, and he felt ashamed at the joy he was feeling that it was not Shannon.

"I have to be certain," he said, "Shannon has a small sickle shaped birthmark just below the nipple on her left breast. We used to joke all the time that it was the only flaw on her perfect body. Will you check for me, Doctor?"

Dr. Barrett came over and folded the sheet down a little more, revealing the left breast and the clear patch of skin below the nipple. There was no birthmark. Jack let out the breath he hadn't realized he was holding and turning, found a chair by the wall. Sitting down heavily, he put his head into his hands and cried.

"Now all we have to do is find Mr. Kohl or Keller, whatever he calls himself, and find out where Shannon is." Cavendish walked toward the door, indicating for Tommy to follow, and grabbing Jack by the shoulder on his way out. They hadn't even reached the outside door before Jack asked where they were bound.

"My office, I need to return to you your wallet and Shannon's passport. Until we find out different, we have to assume that she's alive, and so she will need her passport sooner or later. I have to formulate a plan to find where this Horst Keller has taken the boat. He could be anywhere between Puerto Rico and St. Martin, and that's a huge area to cover given our limited resources."

They entered the office, and Cavendish immediately went to the drawers where the evidence was locked away, opened one and handed Jack his wallet and Shannon's passport. Tommy, who had been unusually quiet on the short walk over to the office, undoubtedly thinking of the consequences of what he was about to reveal. He might well get into trouble with his boss, but decided to go ahead with it out of respect for Tammy. He suddenly piped up with, "You know, Inspector, I can locate this Horst Keller for you, assuming he is still on the boat. I can at least tell you where the boat is."

"How might you be able to do that?"

"When we first got into business, we 'lost' a few boats to theft, so we decided to do something about it. Very few people know about it, and definitely none of the charterers do, but we have installed a hidden GPS transponder in every boat we charter. It sends out a location every minute and we have software that tracks where that particular boat is every minute of the day. Unless you know that it is on board, and search very hard, it is almost impossible to find it. Mr. Kohl has his Captain's License, so it is possible that he knows about the transponders, but only if he has been in this area lately since the practice has not been in place for very long. Even if he does know about them, the place that we mount them is impossible to get to unless the boat is out of the water. I will be able to tell you where the boat is with an accuracy of ten meters or so, and onboard we'll find Horst and hopefully, Shannon, too. "

Jack dared not hope it was going to be that easy, but he was willing to try anything at this point. Cavendish was also skeptical, but Tommy seemed to know what he was talking about, and with nothing to lose, he suggested that they go down to the marina office right away.

They found the night manager on duty in the dockmaster's office when they got there, and after expressing surprise at seeing them at that late hour, he was more than helpful. Tommy got to work on the computer, looking into the records for the chartering of the blue and white Sunseeker, finding the name and registration number, and with that information looking up the transponder code for that particular vessel. He then brought up an electronic navigation chart of the area and, on the appropriate screen, plugged in the transponder code. After a few seconds, the computer decided to give up its information and a flashing red circle appeared on the screen along with a track leading away from Road Harbour, and a box with the required navigational coordinates in it.

Tommy grinned broadly, for the system had worked perfectly. "The boat is presently anchored in Kelly's Cove on Norman Island and, according to the figures, has been there for about eighteen hours. He left here about four in the morning yesterday."

"Which would have given him plenty of time to commit the murder before he left, if he did indeed do it." Cavendish observed, looking straight at Jack. "You, on the other hand, were on Virgin Gorda at the time, and you didn't know Tammy Bishop, so therefore you would have had no reason to kill her."

"Thank you for that, Chief Inspector, I appreciate your logic. That poor woman; her only crime was that she looked so much like Shannon even I was fooled, and she lost her life because of it." Once again, Jack's joy at finding the boat so fast was tempered by the remorse he felt for the dead woman.

Cavendish picked up the office phone and punched in a number from memory, then put on the speaker.

"Virgin Islands Search and Rescue, what is your problem?" asked the voice on the other end of the line.

"This is Chief Inspector Ian Cavendish of the British Virgin Islands Police Force. I need to speak to the duty officer most urgently."

"Yes, sir, I'll transfer you right now."

There was a series of clicks as the transfer was made, and ten seconds later a strong male voice came from the speaker. "Good morning, Chief Inspector, Captain Tony Attwater, duty officer, VISAR here. How can I be of service this morning?"

Jack's mouth was hanging open at the fact that such manners and courtesies were displayed at two in the morning, but to Tommy and Cavendish everything seemed normal and in order.

"Good morning, Captain. I apologize for the early hour, but I find myself in a rather urgent and precarious position here."

"How can I help?" was the immediate response.

"I need a helicopter and two patrol boats to carry out a rescue operation on a suspect boat anchored in Kelly's Cove at dawn today. It's a hostage situation involving an American woman, I'm afraid, and we don't have much time. Are you able to help me, Captain?"

"I'm certainly going to give it my best shot, sir. Give me your number; I'll get back to you shortly."

Cavendish reeled off the numbers for his cellphone and the marina office and hung up. Jack sat stunned at all that had happened. "Do you really think they can get a helicopter and two gunboats at this time of the morning and at such short notice?" he asked.

"They haven't let me down yet." said Cavendish, a smirk on his face.

It took thirty excruciatingly long minutes for the phone to ring, during which time they were all left with their own thoughts. Jack was already studying the marine charts on the computer screen, working out courses and distances, and calculating time of travel in the 'Final Option'. Cavendish watched him intently, already guessing what he had in mind, and Tommy sat there eyeing the locked cabinet where they kept the two shotguns, just in case of trouble, of course.

When the phone did come to life, Cavendish answered on the first ring and put it on speaker.

"Chief Inspector, Attwater here. It appears that I will be able to help you, after all. We have one patrol craft here in Road Harbour and another coming over from St. Thomas. They were very happy to help when they learned an American woman was involved. The helicopter is an Air/Sea Rescue unit inbound from St. Croix. All the participants should be here by five and you can give them a briefing at that time. Is there anything else you can think of that you might need?"

"Not at this time, thank you, Attwater. Might I ask that you also attend the meeting here at the marina in case we do need additional assets from you?"

"I wouldn't miss it for the world, sir. I'll see you at five."

They hung up and Cavendish turned to Jack. "I know what you're thinking of doing, lad, but I must advise you that you are being foolish if you think you can participate in this plan."

"Chief Inspector, if you think you can stop me, you had better be prepared to arrest me, chain me to the wall in your deepest cell, and prepare to face the consequences of your actions, because I'm going with or without your consent or blessing. That is my fiancée over there, and she is everything to me. I would rather die trying to rescue her than to sit here waiting for a report and helpless to do anything about the situation."

Cavendish was not surprised at the determination Jack was displaying, and made a split second decision, "I still think you are foolish, lad, but if you are going, you'd better take me and Tommy and a few constables with you."

"I am going; I know this man, I know his tactics and what he is capable of, but I'd be honored to have you and Tommy with me, and your constables, if you think that's necessary."

"Good, then let's put our heads together and come up with a plan that'll work."

By five a.m., all the participants had gathered in the dockmaster's office. Cavendish introduced himself and Jack to the crowd, then outlined the plan.

"We have gained an extra vessel, the seventy foot yacht belonging to Jack. It is his fiancée who is being held hostage, so I advise everyone to be careful using your firearms, or you will answer to Jack."

Everybody looked at Jack, who, compared to the agents around him, was not that much of a physical specimen, but they all acknowledged that if Shannon came to any harm at their hands, there would be hell to pay. They say a woman scorned is deadly, but a man trying to protect his true love is a man possessed.

"Here is the plan, plain and simple. The subject vessel is a fifty foot, blue and white Sunseeker. The three boats will proceed to a position three miles north of Water Point marked WP1 on your charts. The two patrol craft will tie to the swim platform of the yacht, stop their engines and allow the yacht to tow them into Kelly's Cove. The yacht has been specially modified with sound proofing and underwater exhausts to be almost totally silent at idle.

In this way we hope to be alongside the Sunseeker before they even know we are coming. The helicopter in this scenario is strictly backup. If they manage to see us too soon and slip their anchor, and get up and running, the boats will give chase. The helicopter will be the boat's shadow and will carry two snipers who can be deployed if they have a clear target. At all times, remember to shoot only if you have a clear target. There is a hostage aboard, one who we want to survive. We hit them at first light, good luck to all."

As Jack walked purposefully back to his boat, he was joined by Cavendish and Tommy, PC Wilkins and PC trainee Williams, all carrying sniper rifles with scopes. When Jack raised his eyebrows at the young female trainee, PC Wilkins caught his eye and said, "She has the best score with a sniper rifle we have had at the Academy for the past fifteen years."

At fifteen minutes past five, the three vessels exited Road Harbour, and they were soon joined by the helicopter.

Chapter 12

Almost to the minute, twenty-five hours before, Horst had started the passage in his Sunseeker that Jack was only just beginning in his Neptunus. It had been a pleasant moonlit night and Horst had felt quite comfortable navigating in these waters, having commanded the Senator's yacht 'Shillelagh' here in the Sir Francis Drake Passage many times in the past. From the charts he carried in his head, as well as the electronic ones on the boat, he knew where all the dangers lay and he knew of many bays and anchorages hidden away from the beaten path. As a captain with many years experience, he felt comfortable running this boat by himself, and since Shannon was still wire tied to his berth in the master cabin, he felt comfortably at ease, despite the fact that he knew that he would soon be hunted by the law. Without a doubt in his mind, he was certain that, sooner or later, someone would put two and two together and come up with the correct answer about what had been happening in Tortola. He only hoped that it would take them a period of time to figure it all out, long enough to allow him to reach his private island in the Grenadines, where they would never find him.

After about thirty minutes of running, having left Peter Island to port and Pelican Island to starboard, he spotted Water Point dead ahead. He swung out just a couple of points on the compass to give the fringing reef at the Point a wide berth and made the long smooth turn to port into Kelly's Cove. He was thanking his lucky stars for it appeared that the cove was deserted, and so he was able to select the mooring buoy furthest from the beach on which to tie up to, since he didn't want to give Shannon any hope of trying to escape by swimming from the boat to the shore before she could be caught.

Once secured to the mooring buoy, he shut down the engines, but left the muffled generator running, finally being able to sit back and enjoy the quiet of the early morning for another thirty minutes. He put on coffee to brew and went below to awaken Shannon, for there were details to be worked out before they went much further on their journey. He entered the master cabin and noticed that she was, naturally, lying in the same place since she was tied there. He also noticed that she was awake and if looks really could kill, he would have gone up like a nuclear explosion at the glare she gave him. He walked over to the bed and sat down on the bed quite close to her, a lot closer that she would have preferred. But since she had no choice in the matter, she chose not to say anything.

"Good morning, Shannon. I sincerely hope you managed to get some sleep, despite your rather uncomfortable position. Coffee is brewing, but I just wanted to come down so we can get a few things straight. The way I see it we can do this one of two ways. Firstly, you are going to come with me one way or the other. Now we can do that the easy way or the hard way. The easy way is that you give me your solemn promise not to try to escape, nor harm me in any way, nor try to damage or impede the boat in any way, and not to try to use the radio or warn anybody who comes within hailing distance. In return, I will cut those ties off your hands and feet and will allow you to have the run of the boat, except for when we are both sleeping, when you will be locked into the forward cabin, without restraints. Don't even think of trying to outwit me, or overpower me. I have this silenced Glock, and I am an excellent shot; I also have a switchblade and I've been taught knife fighting on the street, and I am much larger and stronger than you, and although I would hate to do it after all the trouble I've gone through to get you here, I *will* kill you if I have to. If you try and are unsuccessful, there will be consequences. The hard way is that

I wire tie you to the bed inside the forward cabin and gag you until we reach our destination. That would be very uncomfortable for you because we still have a good ways to go, but I'm sure you would survive it."

He stopped talking and watched with great interest as her expression changed from pure hatred to enlightened realization and finally to resignation as she wrestled with the problem and finally resigned herself to the fact that she had absolutely no choice in the matter. "OK, we'll do it the easy way." she managed to get out.

"Your solemn promise?"

"My solemn promise, on my honor as a former girl scout."

"Really?"

"No, not really, but it sounded good." She gave a crooked half smile, but it was forced.

"I'm going to get the coffee, how do you take yours?"

"Black...please."

He nodded his head, acknowledging the compromise she had made, and went to the galley, marveling at how much difference a simple word of politeness could change the dynamics of the situation. He poured the coffee into two large mugs and brought them back to the master cabin, setting hers on the bedside table and his on the dresser. He then leaned across her body, and with his switchblade, cut first one wrist free and then the other. She reached out and picked up the mug of coffee and took a healthy slug, then put it back.

"Please, Horst. I have got to go."

"Forgive me, of course you do." He checked the bathroom for potential weapons, then walked over and cut the ankle restraints with his knife. She stumbled a little as she put her weight on one foot which had fallen asleep, but hurried as well as she could into the bathroom and locked the door behind her.

He heard the muffled sound of a small engine close by seconds before a discreet knocking on the hull alerted him to the presence of another person close by.

He moved to the bathroom door, and whispered, "Shannon, remember your promise," before making his way topside. There he found a small well-used runabout with a single occupant, smiling up at him.

"Good morning to you, sir. You *do* have to pay for these moorings, sir. Unless you want to anchor out."

Putting on his brightest smile, Horst said, "Of course I do. Just like the last time I was here. How much will that be?"

"One night or more, sir?"

"I'll pay for two nights, after that, we'll see."

"Very good; sir. Fifty feet, I'm guessing. That'll be twenty six dollars total, sir."

Horst peeled a bill off his roll and handed the man the fifty and told him, "For your trouble having to come all the way out here, keep the change for yourself."

The man beamed like a beacon and smiled from ear to ear, "why, thank you very much, sir." He put his little boat in gear and slipped away before Horst could change his mind. With a sense of mild relief, Horst watched him go. *'So far so good,'* he thought. There had been not a sound out of Shannon, and even if she had chosen to shout, she would probably not have been heard above the noisy outboard engine on the runabout. She probably realized that it would have meant two dead bodies floating in the cove. He hoped so, anyway.

He went back down below, and found Shannon sitting on the bed, drinking the remains of her coffee. "Who was that?" she asked. She seemed relaxed and unconcerned, much to his surprise.

"The man collecting the rent for this mooring," he replied nonchalantly.

"Oh. Well, I kept my end of the bargain; I kept quiet. Can I go out on deck now?"

"Yes, of course. What would you like for breakfast?" For a change, he seemed a perfect gentleman.

"Just because we have struck a bargain, don't you think for one second that we are going to act like a couple, Horst Keller. That ain't gonna happen."

"Of course not, but you do have to eat. You are quite welcome to cook it yourself."

With that he turned and went up the stairs, leaving her dumbfounded and unsure of what to do next. Moments later she smelled the delicious odor of bacon frying and her salivary glands betrayed her resolve. She took the stairs two at a time and arrived at the galley in time to see him about to put the bacon back into the fridge. "Two rashers for me and two eggs, sunny side up.....please. Is there any coffee left?"

For the first time since Shannon had known him, and for the first time in too many years, Horst threw his head back and laughed heartily. It was a deep rumbling sound, almost like an earthquake from a distance away, but, at least to Shannon, it sounded quite pleasant. A moment of embarrassment passed between them, and then he threw her bacon into the skillet and broke four eggs into a second pan. He pointed to the automatic coffee maker, still more than half full, and she helped herself to more coffee. She did notice that he kept the gun in his waistband, even while cooking, before she took her coffee out to the aft deck and sat down at the dining table that some thoughtful naval architect had placed there.

While the food was still cooking, he brought out knives and forks, napkins, salt and pepper shakers and butter and marmalade along with the placemats, and left her to distribute the items to their proper places. When he brought out the eggs and bacon, with a slice of toast, he placed one in front of her and sat down on the opposite side of the table. They both started in on their breakfasts and both found that they were famished.

"Horst, where is Jack?" Shannon, quite unladylike, spoke with a mouthful of eggs.

"As far as I know, still sleeping off his hangover in the forward cabin," lied Horst, with conviction.

"He will come after me; I'm sure you realize that."

"Yes, I know, but where we are going, he has a snowball's chance in hell of finding us."

"Where are we going?"

He hesitated in a moment of indecision, "Oh, what the hell, I don't suppose there is any harm in telling you, since you won't be able to pass the information along. We are going down to the southern end of the Lesser Antilles to my own small private island in the Grenadines. With the help of the Senator, I bought it many years ago, by passing my ownership through an untraceable shell corporation. It is just big enough for one house and a boat shed, and is far enough away from any other island that you could swear you were alone in the middle of the ocean. Nobody ever goes there and the police don't go to that part of the Grenadines because all the other private owners don't want them there. It is the ideal place to disappear for as long as is necessary."

"Sooner or later, Jack will find you. It will only be a matter of time. You know he has plenty of money from all that gold in the submarine, so he will spend whatever it takes to find me."

He was silent for a few minutes, debating about how much to reveal to her at this point in time, and finishing his breakfast at the same time. He finally decided that nothing was the best thing to tell her, so, having finished his breakfast, he stood and collected the plates and silverware and walked them into the galley and placed them into the dishwasher, leaving her to clean up the rest.

"So what happens now?" she asked him when he returned.

"Well, we are going to stay here for the rest of the day and tonight, and leave early in the morning. I am going to sunbathe and listen to some music, eat, drink and get an early night tonight so I'll be fresh in the morning. We have a long way to go tomorrow. You do whatever you like, as long as it's on this boat."

"Computer?"

"Really, Shannon. How stupid do you think I am? The computer is password encrypted, and your cell phone is, unfortunately, still on Jack's boat."

"I guess I'll sunbathe, too, then. I don't suppose you have any music that's to my taste?"

"You are welcome to look through the boat's music list; there is a CD player in there, too, if your music is not in the digital library. And if you are going to sunbathe, I'd like you to wear that tiny bikini you wore the first time I kidnapped you. In fact, I insist on it; we'll make it your uniform from now on, since I took the time to select it especially when I was packing your bag. And speaking of bag, go down now and move your bag to the forward cabin, and get changed in there; it'll be your cabin from now on. Meantime, I'll try to guess what kind of music you like."

She shook her head to clear it, for she had no idea where the sudden change in his temperament had come from, and whether or not she was responsible for it. She cleared the table and walked the items to the galley, thinking on what she had learned in the last few minutes. One, she was given her own cabin, which meant he didn't intend to force her to sleep with him, at least, not for the moment. Two, he still seemed to trust her, for she was in the galley alone, with all the potential weapons that represented: carving knives, meat tenderizer, fire extinguisher, seemed the list was endless. Three, he still, obviously, cared about how she felt, because he was trying so hard to make sure the commands he gave her came across as requests, rather than orders.

"How about listening to some some Enya and some U2?" His voice came from the salon where he was obviously going through the music CDs in the ship's library.

"Yes to both of them," she called back, before heading below. She went to the master cabin and grabbed her bag and made her way to the forward cabin. On the way she noticed that the key to the door into the midship cabin was still in the door, and on impulse, she grabbed it. When she entered the forward cabin, the first thing she noticed was that the key to her cabin was missing. She tried the stolen key in the lock, but although in went into the hole, it wouldn't turn. It seemed to be one of those old fashioned keys. Not the Kwikset type where you can have a key in both sides of the lock and both sides will work, but one of the castle gate type of key where if there is a key in one side you cannot insert a key from the other side. She didn't know how, yet, but she felt it might become important in the future, so she secreted the key away under the corner of the mattress.

She went into the bathroom, the lock still worked on that door, and undressed quickly. She impulsively decided to take a shower and to take her time about it. Screw him, let him wait. It's not like she was looking forward to anything that awaited her on the upper decks. *'He can bloody well wait,'* she thought.

She took over an hour to get ready, showered for a long time, shaved carefully, moisturized her skin and blow dried her hair just so, and put on some subtle, but not sexy, makeup. She then slipped into her tiny black bikini. Hah! Bikini they called it; basically a G-string bottom and you wouldn't believe the top; if you took a number ten envelope and cut it diagonally lengthwise and attached to those two pieces of material to a number of thin pieces of twine; it would still be bigger than the suit she now wore,

213

and had paid over a hundred dollars for. She had never considered herself voluptuous, but these tiny pieces of material barely covered not even half of what she did have. She idly wondered why she had bought it in the first place at such an exorbitant price, but then remembered the look on Jack's face the first time he had seen her wearing it, and immediately knew why.

Although she looked around for something else to delay her departure, she could find nothing which would have sounded plausible. She walked hesitantly down the passageway and up the stairs to the salon. Horst was nowhere to be seen, so she stepped out of the salon onto the aft deck. Still no sign of him, but as she glanced around the anchorage, she noticed that, despite it being close to noontime, there were no other boats in the cove, for which she was thankful. She moved, a little self-conscientiously, out onto the side deck and walked a circuit of the boat but saw no sign of Horst. *'Maybe I've gotten lucky, and he's fallen overboard.'* she thought hopefully.

Back on the aft deck, she slowly climbed the stairs to the flybridge. There, unfortunately, she found Horst, lying on a large sun lounge at the rear of the flybridge, listening through earphones to some music, and watching her body intently as she climbed the last few steps up to his deck. He was wearing only board shorts, and this was the first time she had seen him without a shirt. She even had to admit to herself, his physique was spectacular.

"Ah, there you are. I was beginning to think you had melted and flushed down the drain. But never mind; here you are now, and look at you, all dolled up just for me. You know you don't have to go to so much trouble for me; I'll love you any way you come."

She stood before him in total shock, "what did you just say??"

He hesitated for a fraction of a second, just long enough to make it a lie, "What I said is I love you, Shannon. Is that so hard to understand? Tammy was nice, but she wasn't you." He stopped suddenly, realizing his mistake.

"Who is Tammy?"

"Just an old girlfriend from way back. She is of no consequence anymore."

"I highly doubt that; that you could have a girlfriend, I mean. You are much too self-centered for that."

"Now don't go making me mad with your critical remarks. You still have to realize that you only have the freedom which I allow you; you could still spend the voyage to my island tied to the bed, if I so desired."

She said nothing, just stood before him, openly defiant, her eyes flashing hatred. He caught the look and decided it was about time for an object lesson.

"As small as that bikini is, I believe it would still leave some very disturbing, and undesirable tan lines, so I want you to take it all off." he said, a leer growing on his face, despite his flint hard eyes glaring at her.

Her mouth dropped open, and she stood there dumbfounded.

Unfolding his switchblade, he said, "Now, Shannon, or I'll just come over there and cut it off."

She recognized instantly the menace in his voice and hesitantly put her hands behind her back. She gained a little moral courage when she thought to herself, *'just pretend that this is Haulover Beach'*. Her hands found the bow which was tied in the strings of her bikini top and reluctantly untied it, allowing the strings to drop away from her sides. The weight of those strings was insufficient to drag the heavier material from her breasts, so she raised her arms, untied the bow behind her neck, and let the top fall to the deck.

She heard Horst's sudden sharp intake of breath and thought, *'oh, what the hell'*, quickly grasped the bows on either side of her bikini bottom, untied them and allowed that scrap of material to fall to the deck to join her top. She then placed her clenched fists on her waist and stood before him, naked and totally unembarrassed.

"Wow. Now I see what Jack sees in you." Horst whispered in awe.

"No, you don't, Horst. All you see is skin; you have no idea what is in here," she said, touching her heart, "what Jack sees in my heart, all the love and trust I have for him and he has for me is something you would not have a clue about. With that block of ice that you call a heart, you could not even begin to comprehend what Jack sees in me. All you can think about is yourself."

Horst raised himself up from the sun lounge, onto his elbows. He could feel the rage returning, being fanned into full blaze by her words; the rage that had been with him since boyhood; the rage he had tried unsuccessfully to keep under control all his life. He tamped it down viciously, and succeeded in tempering it, although he could still feel it burning in the pit of his stomach like he had swallowed a beaker of acid.

"That's enough!" he shouted and she took an involuntary step backward at the sudden change in his demeanor. He pointed to the sun lounge opposite him, and yelled, "Lie down there, on your back. Now!"

He stood up as she reluctantly backed over to the indicated sun lounge, sat down and finally lay down on her back as ordered. He walked the few steps over to her, knelt down on one knee and placed his left hand gently on her stomach. His right hand still held the open, razor sharp switchblade, and she shuddered and tried to

216

cringe away from his touch. He gazed down at her naked body and smiled.

"Remember your solemn promise? How I mentioned consequences? Well, for the upset you have caused me just now, the consequences of that will be that your birthday suit will be your new uniform. You are not to wear one stitch of clothing, unless I tell you to. Do you understand me?"

Fully aware of how far she had pushed the limit and how close she had come to crossing that line, she reluctantly nodded her head slowly and whispered, "Yes."

He felt his breathing slowing down to a comfortable rate, and the acid slowly dissipating in his stomach, and he realized that the rage had somehow been returned to its box. He gave her stomach a tiny squeeze and stood up, closed the switchblade and returned it to his pocket. He indicated with his head the CD player and a number of CDs on the table beside her. "I brought you your music," he said, sitting down in his own sun lounge and putting on his earphones. Even though muted through the earphones, she heard the sounds of heavy metal bands at full volume emanated from his headset. She shook her head and thought, *White Snake, or maybe even, Megadeath, I'm not quite sure which. Anyway, definitely not my kind of music, but how appropriate'.*

It didn't take more than five minutes for her to completely forget that she was lying totally naked not three feet from her avowed enemy. She put an Enya CD into the player and was soon relaxing to the sweet, soft sounds of 'Caribbean Blue', one of her favorites. She closed her eyes and drifted into a relaxing semi-sleep, and stayed that way until the last song on the CD had wound to a close. She lay in the silence until she noticed that the sun, while not broiling hot as it would be during the summer, was nonetheless causing her to sweat a little; or as the Australians so colorfully put it, glisten. With just a small effort, she remembered that she had seen a tube of sunscreen in the galley, and besides, she could use a drink.

She opened her eyes and glanced over at Horst, expecting to find him watching her, but his eyes were closed and he appeared asleep. She quietly swung her legs over the side of the lounge away from him, and stood up. She walked stealthily, not quite on tiptoe, over to the staircase, and started down.

"If you're going to the galley, could you bring me back a Red Stripe, thanks?" Horst asked.

She turned and saw him watching her, a smile on his face, and she mumbled, "Sure."

She walked quickly down the stairs and through the salon, grabbing a bottle of Gosling's rum along the way. Once in the galley, she filled a glass with ice, poured in a measure of the rum, topping it with ginger beer to make a Dark and Stormy. She grabbed a Red Stripe as she returned the ginger beer to the fridge, rummaged through a drawer to find an opener, and popped the top. She grabbed the sunscreen off the window ledge and turned to put away the Gosling's, and ran breast first into Horst, who had followed her down and snuck up behind her. He grabbed both her wrists and held them out away from her body, the bottle in one of her hands and the sunscreen in the other. Since he was almost a foot taller than she was, he looked down onto her face, and then lowered his gaze to her breasts, and finally even lower. She felt herself grow cold and weak inside and closed her eyes, feeling tears prickling at the edges. Surprisingly, he stepped back from her and took the bottle from her hand, and then muttered, "Sorry that I frightened you, I thought you knew I was here."

He returned the bottle to the bar, picked up the Red Stripe and went up the stairs to the flybridge, leaving her shaking inside and silently cursing him, and also herself for being so weak. Taking a deep breath, she picked up her drink and along with the sunscreen, climbed up to the upper deck. By the time she arrived, he already had his earphones on and was sitting back, drinking his beer, and listening to his music, which she noticed had been turned down from deafening to merely loud. She put down her drink, and sat down facing away from him. She opened the sunscreen and started applying it to her face and neck, her arms and torso and finally her legs in a light rubbing motion. She was aware that it was so much easier to put on sunscreen without the strings and material getting in the way, and she appreciated the long smooth strokes she could make on her body.

She was suddenly aware that he had been surreptitiously watching her when he said, "I could do your back, if you wish."

"Thank you but no thank you, I'll just lie on my back; that way it won't get sunburned." she answered primly, belatedly realizing that it meant that she wouldn't be able to prevent his scrutiny of her body.

She was surprised when he just nodded, leaned back and closed his eyes, listening to his music, sipping his beer and making no further comment. She put into the player another Enya CD and relaxed with her own drink, listening to the soft strains of masterfully performed music whispering into her ears.

The afternoon passed quietly, until the setting sun forced from her a slight shiver. Even in the islands, wintertime can cause a dramatic shift in temperature with the setting of the sun. She looked around for her cover up but once again the situation hit her in the face. She was naked, she didn't have a cover up and she was not allowed to put it on even if she had had one.

"I'm getting cold. I'm going down below," she said as she rose, collecting her things.

"OK." he stirred, but did not get up.

She went below into the salon, thankful that the heat of the day still lingered in that enclosed space. For want of anything better to do, she picked the TV remote from the coffee table and turned on the TV. The satellite feed from the States was showing an episode of Judge Judy, and she ignored it.

She went to the galley to refresh her drink and did not notice him as he slipped into the salon. When she returned, and noticed him sitting on the couch, gazing intently at the screen, she deliberately chose one of the club chairs across the table from where he was sitting. Once more she chose sight of her naked body over proximity to him. She took a sip of her drink, placed it on the table, folded her arms across her breasts and crossed her legs in self defense, although it was far too late for that, and said, "Can we talk?"

He looked up at her, smiled, placed the TV on mute and said, "Sure, what about?"

She took a deep breath, for she was not sure how this was going to work out. "About you."

"Me?"

"Yes, you. What happened to you? Why are you like you are?"

"What do you mean?"

"Horst, you are a handsome, attractive man, with a great physique, obviously educated, accomplished, and a catch for most women. But you have a devil inside you that won't let you go. What happened to you?"

He sat up, suddenly very tense, narrowed his eyes at her, and growled, "Be very careful, Shannon, remember the consequences."

"Horst, you have already taken my happiness, my hope, and," she spread her arms and legs wide to reveal everything to his view, "my dignity and my self-esteem. The only thing that 'consequences' could mean at this moment would be either a severe beating, you raping me or my murder, and, quite frankly, while I would fight you every inch of the way, that would be a relief from not knowing what was to happen in the future. Probably all three, sooner or later, because I am not going to roll over and be what you want me to be any time in your lifetime nor mine. Coercion only goes so far."

His eyes grew larger and larger as she spoke and he leaned back into the backrest of the couch, his smile growing broader as she continued her speech. He finally held up his hands in an attempt to stem the tide.

"OK, ok. Relax. What do you want to know?"

"Everything, Horst, from the day you were born to now. I mean, I'm not a psychiatrist or even a psychologist, but I might be able to help you get rid of that monster inside you."

With highly skeptical eyes, he looked at her, and said, "Too late for that. But if you really want to know…"

"I do." she said, and left it at that.

"OK. I was born in Dresden, Germany and my earliest childhood memories were of being beaten on a daily basis by my drunken father. He would come home from work and start beating away at my mother and me, right up until the day I took a hammer and beat his head to a pulp, while he was beating my mother. I was twelve at the time, and I was locked away until I was eighteen for that murder. That was when the rage started, and ever since then, every time I am placed under extreme stress, the rage escapes the box I've placed it in and I do something I can't control. You came close this afternoon, but I managed to control it."

"But surely there is treatment or medication for what you're going through."

"I don't know if there is. I've never tried to find out." Horst looked sad because of that revelation.

"OK. Perhaps that is something you might want to investigate after this little situation is over; I am assuming that it will be over at some point, one way or the other. But, please, don't let me stop you. Go on."

"I don't know if you are aware of the fact that Hans Kessler, the SS officer on the submarine you found in the Bahamas was my uncle."

"Yes, the Senator filled us in on that."

"Well, because of that, when I had to get out of Germany because nobody wanted to hire a murderer, my mother arranged for the Senator to find me and set me up with employment. He did a great job, the first time anyone had ever shown any interest in my welfare, and sent me, at his expense, to maritime school. I had never even been on a boat before, but I found, to my and everyone else's surprise, that I liked it and got good at it. He hired me on to one of his boats as a deckhand after I graduated, and I rose steadily in the ranks until he fired Capt'n Pete and I became captain of the 'Shillelagh'. You surely cannot blame me for holding him in the greatest respect considering what he had done for me."

"Of course not, but there is still the matter of, what do you call it, your 'rage'. You did some pretty despicable things in Florida and the Bahamas."

Surprisingly, he lowered his head and his voice, too. "Yes," he said, barely audibly. "And, unfortunately, I continued to do them after I left the Bahamas. I am not going to confess anything to you, but I did do things that I now regret, because I simply couldn't control the rage."

They sat in silence for a long time, each with their own thoughts. The salon grew steadily colder, an indication of the weather conditions and not the revelations between them. As she had on the flybridge, she felt a slight shiver and wrapped her arms around her body.

Breaking the silence, she asked, "So, no additional 'consequences'?"

He looked up from his dazed state, "No, not today."

He got up and walked toward his cabin. He paused at the top of the stairs, turned and said, "It seems like it is going to get cold tonight; if you want to put on shorts and a T-shirt, that'll be OK."

She was shocked, but replied, "No, I am going to put on the heat in the boat; I have gotten used to going 'au natural' and I kind of like it." She felt that she had won some kind of psychological victory.

"Whatever," was his only reply, as he disappeared down the stairs to the lower deck.

She went to the temperature control panel, switched it from cool to heat and entered 75 degrees, a compromise between day and night, and a comfortable sleeping temperature.

Her stomach suddenly growled, reminding her that she hadn't eaten since breakfast. As she opened the freezer, the cold air spilled out and she shivered again, this time more violently. She grabbed the first thing that came to hand, a chicken pot pie, and slammed the freezer shut. She read the instructions and set the stove to 350 degrees, and waited for the chime. Still taking advantage of the truce she seemed to have established, she went to the top of the stairs, and called down, "I'm putting a chicken pot pie in the oven. Do you want one?"

There was a long period of silence, and then finally his voice answered, "Yes ... please."

She retrieved another pot pie from the freezer, this time standing to one side to allow the frigid air to flow past her, and closed the freezer just as the chime sounded. She opened the oven, luxuriating in the warmth flowing over her and put in the two pot pies.

He emerged from below a half hour later, looking somewhat subdued, and sat down at the dining table she had set.

He had obviously showered and changed into shorts and a T-shirt, but was still barefoot.

Trying once again to push the boundaries, she observed, "You were gone for quite a while; weren't you concerned that I would simply dive overboard and swim to shore? I'm sure that there are people on this island who would have helped me."

He looked up at her from his seated position, "I guess that I was counting on the fact that you are a woman of your word. You gave me your solemn promise that you would not try to escape, I believed you, and here you are, still aboard. Funny how that works, when you are an honest person. Unlike me; I would have been long gone by now."

A ding from the galley announced that dinner was ready. "I also made a salad, if you want some."

"Without sounding like a married couple; yes, please. Blue cheese dressing for me."

"For me, too." she said, somewhat disconcerted at how similar their tastes were.

They ate, mostly in silence, except for the few requests for condiments, and then, during the cleanup phase, a few compliments. He seemed somewhat ill at ease, but then, he was dressed and she was naked, so that may have been the explanation. He seemed distracted, unsure of himself when, the chores finished, he took her hands in his and said, "Shannon, you are the most beautiful, and definitely the most desirable woman I have ever met in my life. I had hoped to get to know you better, but from the guts, poise and determination you have shown me today, I feel I know you, probably better than you know yourself. Despite what you said before, I can definitely see what Jack sees in you, in your heart and in your soul. My only wish is that it had been directed at me instead of him. So, although you have proven that you will keep your word, as per our agreement, I now have to lock you in the forward cabin. We will be leaving very early in the morning, so I suggest you get a good night's sleep, because we have a long way to go tomorrow."

He took her by the hand, led her down the stairs and along the passageway to the forward cabin and opened the door for her, as a proper gentleman would do. She slipped inside the cabin, but at the last second, felt the hand of the man behind her deliver a soft slap to her right buttock.

She turned to glare at him, with her 'oh, really' face already in place, only to be confronted by a boyish grin, and his smartass remark.

"Hey, sometimes desire and opportunity will win over common sense."

She just shook her head as she closed the door, and stood there waiting as the expected locking of the door occurred. She waited until he had withdrawn his key and retired to his cabin. Despite her earlier apprehension, she decided that, because of the way the day had gone, she was not going to jam the door with the other key hidden under the mattress, saving it for another time when she might need to jam it into the lock, preventing him from entering, even if he so desired.

As she stepped into the shower to wash the sweat and sunscreen off her body, she felt proud of herself for handling what was a delicate but dangerous situation the way she had. She had gained some insight into his demeanor which might come in handy later on. She was still determined to get away from him, despite what he said, and despite what she had promised.

Chapter 13

Just before six in the morning, Jack brought 'Final Option' to a standstill one mile short of their destination. The two gunboats closed on the stationary yacht from the stern and when they were close enough, threw lines to Tommy, who was standing on the swim platform. He tied on each boat in turn, one to each side of the platform and they both stopped their engines. The powerful outboards on the gunboats were much too noisy if they hoped to catch Horst by surprise. The sound-proofed engine room of the Neptunus was almost silent when running at idle. When Jack received word that the two gunboats were secured, he bumped the transmissions on both engines into forward and the yacht continued on its way at a steady three knots.

Jack checked his laptop again, as he had done every five minutes on the journey over from Road Town, and was once again pleased to see that Horst's Sunseeker had not changed position. They continued on their slow, but quiet, course until they were past the reef stretching out from Water Point. They could now see into Kelly's Cove, and the only boat in the cove was the blue and white Sunseeker Horst had chartered, sitting serenely at the last buoy in the mooring field.

Jack's elation at finding their enemy so quickly suddenly turned sour when, with a roar of its engines, the Sunseeker accelerated away from them at a quickly rising rate of speed. They had been caught flatfooted and they knew it as the speeding Sunseeker literally flew out of the cove toward Treasure Point. In seconds, it was at forty knots and accelerating fast.

That morning, Horst woke at a few minutes before the alarm went off at five. He punched the alarm button, preventing it from sounding and went to the galley for coffee. The automatic drip coffee maker was still set for 6 am; he had forgotten to reset the time the night before, so he started it manually. While waiting for the coffee to brew, he unlocked the salon door and took a walk around the deck of the boat. The full moon illuminated the cove and allowed him to scan the area for anything unusual. He saw nothing that wasn't expected, but he also noticed the lightening of the sky to the east and knew dawn would not be far off.

Inspection finished, he walked back to the galley and poured two mugs of freshly brewed coffee and went below. Unlocking the forward cabin door, he knocked loudly, announcing, "Wake up time, sleepyhead, I have coffee for you."

At her invitation, he opened the door to find her already up, and standing naked by the foot of the bed.

"I woke up when the elephant stomped by on the deck above my head," she said primly, accepting her mug of coffee.

"Damn, even first thing in the morning? You are not only beautiful, but smart and witty, too" Horst could not tear his eyes away from her, and had to remind himself that he was not on his island yet.

"Are we leaving?" she asked.

"Yes, I want to be out of this cove before sun-up, so we need to start now. Do you want breakfast, or shall we have it as we are running along?"

"I'll make some breakfast while you are preparing the boat. Bacon and eggs?" she said, surprising him further with acceptance of the situation and the circumstances.

"OK. Hop to it." He reached out and gave her bare bottom a playful slap as she passed him on her way to the galley, and got an angry glare and a raised middle finger in return. He answered her with a mischievous grin.

As she scurried up the stairs, he held back, thinking. *'What's going on here? Is she trying to pull a fast one on me? Or is this a classic case of Stockholm syndrome?'* Although people in general dismissed Horst's intellectual capabilities as nonexistent, he was, in fact, quite well read and cunningly smart. It was only during, and because of, the rage that he appeared at times to be out of control and lacking any redeeming qualities.

After climbing the stairs and passing the galley, he saw that the bacon was already frying and the eggs were being scrambled. He went to the pilothouse and started the engines, to allow them to warm up to operation temperature. He was about to go forward to release the mooring rope when she called, "Breakfast."

He quickly thought, *'eat first, and then we'll go,'* as he slid into a chair at the dining table. Settings were already on the table, and after placing the plates on the table, she seated herself across the table from him.

"So where are we going today?" she asked.

"After a refueling stop in St. Martin, we will run overnight to my island in the Grenadines. We should be there by this time tomorrow."

"And if someone, like the authorities, in St. Martin or the Grenadines asks for our passports, what are you going to tell them?"

"Oh, I have passports for both of us in the safe. Not in our real names, of course, but real passports."

"How can you possibly have a passport for me, especially one in an assumed name?"

"It is a genuine passport belonging to a friend of mine who looks exactly like you; her hair is a bit shorter in the photo but otherwise, you two could be twins. Your new name, by the way, should anyone ask, is Tammy Bishop."

"Tammy, as in your ex-girlfriend?"

"Correct. I only started going out with her because she looked so much like you, it was uncanny."

"And you don't think she will report her passport missing to the authorities?"

"She won't because she can't. I made sure she was dead." He realized his mistake the split second it was out, and he felt the rage returning with renewed energy.

He stood up from the table, knocking over his chair, and stormed from the salon. She sat there in a daze, feeling herself tearing up. *'Dead, killed, by Horst?'* she thought. Her whole world had just been turned upside down and her carefully thought out plans from the night before now lay in ruins. With this revelation, how could she now convince him that she was going along with his plan, and even accepted him until he let down his guard and she had the opportunity to escape. For the first time, she started to believe that she might not come out of this alive. She was suddenly scared, more scared than she had ever been before in her life.

Horst burst from the salon, the rage pulsating at full force now and started toward the bow of the boat. He stopped suddenly, staring out to sea to where 'Final Option' was just clearing Water Point, towing the two gunboats. "Shit!" he yelled, "They've found me." He ran to the bow and untied the mooring line and let it slip off the boat before sprinting back inside. As he ran his ears picked up the unmistakable 'whop, whop, whop,' of a helicopter, and he glanced inland to see it just clearing the ridge.

He ran full speed through the salon, past the dining table where Shannon sat; her tear filled eyes glazed over and he threw himself into the captain's chair. One hand on the wheel and the other on the throttles, he firewalled both throttles while hauling the wheel to starboard, sending the plates on the table flying and smashing on the floor. Shannon's chair tipped over, sending her to the floor, too, fortunately without injury.

After completing about 85 degrees of the turn, Horst hauled the boat onto an even keel and trimmed the boat for maximum speed. The rev counters were almost in the red as the Sunseeker continued to pick up speed, but they were almost at maximum speed already. He finally looked up at the horizon, adjusted his course slightly to avoid running into the reef at Treasure Point and finally looked backward at the rapidly disappearing mooring field, and at his adversary in 'Final Option'. Horst knew that he only had to run a few miles into U.S. territorial waters before the British gunboats would be forced to turn back, since they could not operate in foreign waters. This made him smile and for a precious few minutes, the rage subsided.

Jack had not anticipated the sudden, unexpected departure of the Sunseeker and was scrambling to get the two gunboats untied and their engines started so they could give chase to the fleeing criminal. As soon as they were clear and on their way, he had also firewalled both throttles, as Horst had done minutes before, but without any hope of catching up. His bigger boat simply didn't have the speed that the smaller, lighter Sunseeker had and he knew that without the advantage of the GPS tracker, it was a lost cause. Maybe he couldn't get there as fast, but he would always know where Horst was. Or at the very least, where the Sunseeker was.

Shannon picked herself up off the floor and moved to the pilothouse where Horst was sitting gazing intently at the electronic chartplotter, watching the icon which indicated the Sunseeker move rapidly toward the line on the chart which was the dividing line between the U.S. and the British Virgin Islands.

He looked behind him once again, judging the distance between the two gunboats and his boat and calculating his chances of making it into U.S. territory before they caught up.

They were gaining, their engines being able to crank a few more knots out of their lighter boats than he could out of his, but it seemed to him that he was going to make it. He allowed himself a small smile as he glanced back at Shannon, who had remained a short distance away from him. He was almost starting to relax a little, when the sudden appearance of the helicopter directly astern jolted him out of his complacency. He switched on the autopilot, grabbed his Glock from his waistband, shoved Shannon aside and walked through the salon to the aft deck.

The chopper was directly behind the boat, close enough that he could see the two sniper rifles poking out the doors on either side of it. In a display of bravado that he really didn't feel, he stepped onto the sun cushion at the back of the aft deck, braced himself on the overhead, brought his Glock to bear on the pilot of the helicopter and let go two rounds. The silenced Glock made two rude farting sounds, and he saw the glass of the helicopter's front window craze and spider web, and it banked suddenly to the left, with Horst following it with his Glock. Both snipers in the chopper were now unsighted, one looking into an empty sky, the other at the water rushing by a few feet below them. Horst prepared to put a few more rounds into the belly of the helicopter.

Shannon, who had followed Horst out onto the aft deck, gave a small cry which was lost in the noise of the helicopter's rotors and engines, and launched herself at Horst. She hit him with her shoulder and side of her head right on the butt and propelled him up and over the side of the boat. The Glock escaped from his hands by the unexpected blow and flew through the air to land on the cushion of the sunpad. Miraculously, due not only to fast reflexes and superb training, but also to no small measure of luck,

Horst was able to twist in mid air and grab the low railing which surrounded the sunpad and so was able to prevent himself from going all the way overboard, although his body still dangled from his hands and his feet were dragging in the water rushing past the boat. Shannon, from the recoil of her body hitting his, wound up on all fours at the edge of the sunpad, where she started to crawl toward the discarded Glock. She had almost made up the distance when she found that her progress was suddenly impeded by the strong hand of Horst grabbing her ankle tightly. He pulled her bodily toward the edge of the sunpad and he was only stymied in his attempt to throw her overboard when she thrust out her other foot and placed it on the rail, directly on top of his other hand which was hanging onto the rail for dear life. It was a Mexican standoff; he couldn't drag her any further and couldn't free his other hand, she couldn't get away from his ankle hold nor could she allow him to free his other hand. They looked into each other's eyes for several seconds, and then, unbelievably, she heard him shout over the roar of the engines at full throttle, "Remember your solemn promise, Shannon?"

"I don't keep my solemn promises to murderers, scumbag!" she yelled back at him.

She suddenly thrust out the leg on the rail, straightening it out and rolling onto her stomach, her hands reaching out as far as her body could stretch to try to get the Glock. She could feel Horst trying desperately to haul her back toward him, but she thrust again and again trying to close the three-foot gap to the gun, but it remained tantalizingly out of reach.

"Dammit!" she yelled in total frustration, slamming her closed fist into the cushion. The Glock jumped about a foot into the air and dropped a couple of inches closer to her outstretched hand. Her eyes grew wide and she stared uncomprehendingly at the gun for just a micro second, and then immediately started pounding the cushion unmercifully, each blow moving it closer to her hand. Horst almost grinned, sensing her frustration, but having no way of knowing exactly what she was trying to achieve, he still felt, with his superior strength, that he was winning. Shannon gave a final decisive blow which brought the Glock to her hand, and she grabbed it and turned it in her hand, checking the safety, which was off since Horst had been shooting at the helicopter.

She rolled once more onto her back, spread her legs and carefully aimed the Glock right between Horst's eyes.

"Let go of my ankle!" she growled at him, taking extra special care in her aim at his head.

He was suddenly still; looking down the barrel of your own gun does have a tendency of making you think about the consequences. After a few seconds hesitation, he shrugged and released her ankle, placing his hand back on the railing.

She scrambled backward a few feet, out of his reach, being very careful not to waiver in her aim for the center of his face. He smiled suddenly, saying, "If this is to be the last sight I see in this world, I have to say it's a good one." Something caught his eye and he suddenly looked forward. Because of the abruptly startled expression on his face, Shannon involuntarily looked that way, too. The sight which greeted her eyes was disturbing, to say the least. They were rushing toward a beach at top speed, and by the time she looked back again, he was gone. He had walked his feet up the side of the boat, hanging on by his hands alone, and then used his powerful legs to propel himself away from the side of the boat, letting go with both hands as he pushed. She looked back in time to see his body cartwheeling across the water at fifty miles per hour, skipping like a thrown stone across the concrete-hard water. Only seconds later, he disappeared below the surface.

She could spare no time to see if he resurfaced, and broke into an all out sprint in a desperate scramble to stop the boat before it hit the beach. She reached the pilothouse, hit the autopilot off and yanked the wheel hard to starboard. The input from the rudders heeled the boat over almost onto its rails and started a high G-force turn that pinned her to the helm seat hanging on to the steering wheel with all her strength, and the whole world tilted at a crazy angle. More by sheer luck rather than judgment, she managed to miss the beach by fifty feet, but the rocks at the end of the beach by mere inches. As they flew by, she let out a deep breath that she hadn't realized she was holding, and was in the process of straightening out the boat into its normal running position when it finished its 180 degree turn, hit its own wake and flew like a seaplane from the surface of the water and into the air.

Both engines redlined, having no water to push against, and the torturous scream from the engine compartment foretold of imminent destruction. She yanked the throttles down to their off position, and silenced the screaming, but the boat was still flying, tail down because of the weight of the engines. Because she had not had time to finish straightening out the boat, it started an excruciatingly slow roll to starboard. Time stood still; the few seconds of flight seemed like an eternity, and she gripped the wheel with all her strength, involuntarily closing her eyes against what she knew was coming. But when finally the tail of the boat hit the surface of the water, the whole boat tripped and came crashing down, partially on its side, with a sickening crunch that sounded like every bone in a body fallen from ten stories had broken at once. She lost her grip on the wheel and was thrown like a rag doll across the cabin, under the dining table and against the wall where she hit the back of her head and lost consciousness.

It was barely three minutes later when the two gunboats, having observed the erratic course the boat had taken, the flight and crash of the Sunseeker, arrived on the scene. They circled the now stationary, damaged boat warily, guns aimed at the points of the boat from which they expected trouble, but no movement was observed. Finally, since they had crossed into the territorial waters of the U.S. Virgin Islands, the helmsman on the American gunboat from St. Thomas, assuming jurisdiction, switched on his loudhailer, and yelled, "Sunseeker, you are surrounded and covered by weapons. All persons aboard are to step out onto the aft deck with their hands raised above their heads. Do it now!" There was no response and they were contemplating a boarding when 'Final Option' finally arrived a few minutes later.

Jack wasted no time on formalities, bringing his boat alongside the now stationary Sunseeker. He left Tommy in charge of the Neptunus with instructions to raft the two boats together, and jumped down to the side deck of the smaller boat.

He had his own Glock in his hand, safety off, as he landed and immediately started for the aft deck.

A couple of quick looks past the bulkhead assured him that it was clear and he walked, crouched down, through the salon door. He saw Shannon immediately upon entering, lying under the dining table, naked, and maybe hurt, but he still took the time to clear the rest of the boat before tending to her.

By the time he got back, she was stirring.

She sat up slowly, fingering the tender spot on the back of her head, and wondering where the goose egg had come from. She couldn't remember where she was or what had happened. She looked down and found she was naked, but couldn't remember why. She jumped when the soft touch caressed her shoulder, but relaxed when she recognized his familiar voice which simply asked, "Shannon, are you all right?"

She turned and looked into his concerned face and, with an award-winning smile plastered upon her face, answered with conviction, "I am now."

Chapter 14

Jack ran to the aft deck, and yelled to Cavendish. "Horst is not on the boat. Radio the gunboats and the helicopter to search for him." The Chief Inspector ran to the pilothouse and relayed the instructions to his fleet, which started an immediate search.

Jack then helped Shannon down the stairs, and she directed him to the forward cabin, where he assisted her in getting dressed in a bra and panties, shorts and a T-shirt. She cleaned up in the bathroom and took some aspirin for her headache, which was mild but disconcerting. She stuffed everything of hers into the bag that Horst had brought and announced that she was more than ready to go home.

She had by now recovered sufficiently from her ordeal to make her own way up the stairs, out onto the deck and across the small gap between the boats. Once back aboard 'Final Option', she breathed a huge sigh of relief. She was only slightly startled by the appearance of the four strangers who came out of the salon to greet her, but it was only because Jack was right beside her, his arm around her shoulders.

"Shannon, this is Chief Inspector Cavendish, and the harbormaster, Tommy. And our two heavily armed police escorts are PC Wilkins and PC trainee Williams. Gentlemen, this is Shannon, my fiancée. Alive, thank God, as you can clearly see."

Cavendish put out his hand, somewhat disconcerted. "It is my real pleasure to meet you; here on the boat, alive and not in my morgue, which is where your look-alike ended up. I'm sorry to have to tell you that."

"Thank you, nice to meet you. Horst confessed to having murdered Tammy. I don't think he meant to confess, but it just slipped out." She was still a little hesitant, not yet up to speed on

236

what had actually happened while she had been held prisoner by Horst.

"By the way, you can add one more charge of murder to the growing list against Horst. He confessed to me that it was he that killed Rain on Christmas Eve in Ft. Lauderdale." Jack went on to give the details of Rain's demise to the Chief Inspector, and then turned and asked, "Tommy, can you get the Sunseeker back to harbor with the help of Wilkins and Williams? I want to get Shannon to a hospital as soon as possible for a check-up, just in case."

"Of course, Mr. Elliott. Not a problem."

"From now on, Tommy, it's Jack. And thank you for all your help today."

"You are very welcome, Jack." Tommy turned and jumped aboard the other boat, followed by the two PCs, started the engines again and untied it from the raft-up. He pushed off and started for Road Harbour at a reasonable speed since nobody knew how badly the boat had been damaged after such a cursory check. Best news was that it didn't seem to be shipping any water.

Jack went and coiled the lines and flipped the fenders inboard, while Cavendish led Shannon into the pilothouse, and sat her down in a seat at the booth. Jack came in soon after, fired up the engines and set a course following the Sunseeker back to Road Harbour.

The two gunboats were searching the area for Horst or his body, and the helicopter was searching not only the water, but the shoreline as well. Unfortunately, the helicopter soon had to leave due to lack of fuel, and although they searched until nightfall, the two gunboats found nothing and returned to base unsuccessful in their mission.

With Jack steering the boat, following the Sunseeker, Cavendish seated himself in the booth across from Shannon, and asked, "Do you feel up to giving me an account of what happened to you?"

Hesitant at having to recall her ordeal, she nevertheless nodded and described in detail what she knew. She left nothing out, including how she had been forced to prance about nude in front of her hated enemy. She also gave as much detail as she could about Horst's island in the Grenadines, and her conviction that it was the place he would go if he was still alive. She seemed concerned about her culpability in causing bodily harm to Horst, but Cavendish assured her that there would be no charges coming her way. After that, she brightened up considerably, until she saw the worried look on Jack's face.

"What's wrong?" she asked him.

"He didn't....?" She could tell that Jack was almost in tears, and she suddenly realized what his concern was. She stood up and came over to him, wrapping her arms around him and holding him tight.

"No, Jack, he didn't rape me. In fact, he didn't even touch me, except for a gentle slap on my bare ass." She stood on tip toes and kissed him, soothing his worries, and luxuriating in the strong arms he wrapped around her, laying her head against his chest. Cavendish coughed loudly, reminding them that he was still there.

"Mr. Elliott, Ms. O'Loughlin, I am so glad this has worked out so well for you, given the circumstances. I just hope that you don't think that this kind of situation is the normal thing here in the islands."

"Firstly, it is Jack and Shannon, and I just want to say thank you for being there for us. This could have had a totally different outcome if you hadn't been the person you are." Shannon was gushing, finally realizing how lucky they were to have had this man investigating instead of some by-the-book guy.

"In that case, you may call me Ian. Just not around my men, you understand." Cavendish smiled for the first time since this whole episode had begun, confident that he had made two new friends.

Horst surfaced in great pain. His left shoulder was agonizing and his left knee wouldn't bend properly and every time he moved it he heard crunching noises. He was also bitterly disappointed when he saw that, somehow, Shannon had managed to miss not only the beach but the rocks as well, although by the slimmest of margins, and manage to bring the boat to a standstill, wallowing in its own wake. He cursed inwardly, but still had enough admiration for her skill to allow himself a small smile. While he watched, the two gunboats closed on the Sunseeker and the helicopter reappeared, damaged but still flying.

He began the agonizingly slow but reasonably short swim to the rocks on the south side of the beach, and when he reached them, he turned and saw 'Final Option' approaching and rafting-up to his boat. He knew he didn't have much time, because as soon as it became apparent that he wasn't aboard, a full scale search would start, looking for him. He stumbled over the rocks toward the tree line behind the beach. A walk up the beach would have been easier, but would have left obvious marks anyone could have followed. He was counting on the sun to dry the rocks he was scrambling on before anyone came looking for him.

He made it to the tree line just as the gunboats roared away from the two rafted-up yachts, and came barreling toward the beach and the helicopter made a spectacular turn, heading inland. He had only a few seconds to locate and roll under a large bougainvillea bush before the chopper came roaring over, not twenty feet above the trees. It flew the length of the beach, hovered for a while over the rocks and reefs on the north side of the beach, before slipping a short distance inland to look for any obvious recent disturbance in the sand. It came back to the south side of the beach, its scrutiny enhanced by the two snipers Horst could see hanging out of the doors on either side of the chopper in their harnesses. He hugged the main trunk of the thirty foot bougainvillea above him, trying to blend into the deep shadows under the flowering bush which sheltered him.

He heard the distinctive whopping of the rotor blades directly above him and felt the bush moving aggressively as the downward force of the blades kicked up the sand around him. For what felt like many minutes, but was only in reality a few seconds, the whirlwind continued, sending grit into his eyes, ears and nose because he did not dare to move a muscle for fear of being spotted.

The chopper moved inland again, every pair of eyes aboard looking for something that was out of the ordinary, something that was not supposed to be there, but finding nothing to raise suspicions. The pilot finally circled out over the bay once more, to where the gunboats were searching for a swimmer or a body. It didn't matter which, as long as it was a definite conclusion. But, like the helicopter, they had found nothing.

Horst lay still under that bush for what seemed like hours, until finally he realized that the helicopter had left. He turned his head slowly, looking seaward, and spotted the two gunboats still searching. They were further away from his position, one to the north of him and one to the south. He hesitantly moved slightly, again feeling the sharp stab of pain in both his left shoulder and left knee from being slammed into the concrete-hard water. He tried tentatively to sit up and found that the new position eased the pain slightly. Grasping one of the branches of the bougainvillea with his right hand, he managed to regain his feet, and hopped away from the bush on one foot. Keeping the bush between him and the shoreline, he stumbled his way slowly inland.

He had gone only a short distance, when he spied a broken branch lying on the ground beneath a tree. It was thick enough to take his weight, but a little too long to use as a crutch. He picked it up, inserted it into the V of the tree's branches, and, using his body weight, broke it off into a useable length. Using his right hand, he gently lifted his left arm into the V of the tree, and manipulating his shoulder while slowly increasing the pressure on the joint, he popped the ball back into the socket. The pain was intense, and he saw stars, but almost as soon as his bones were aligned correctly, the pain started to diminish. Still, it was not a procedure he would recommend for anyone.

After a few minutes of much needed rest, sitting on the ground, he began digging into the ground beneath the tree. He quickly came upon the spider roots of the tree, and dug several useable lengths out of the ground. Utilizing the shorter of the two pieces of the branch as a brace for his damaged knee, he straightened the knee, in great pain, and tied the branch on with the spider roots. With his knee somewhat immobilized, and using the longer piece of the branch as a crutch, he found that he could stand and move about a lot easier than before. He used his new-found mobility to move away from the beach at a faster pace.

He had hobbled about a half mile when he encountered a road. Well, a track, at least, it being simply two wheel ruts leading further inland. Since the ruts were headed in the right direction, and since it was considerably easier to navigate the ruts than the open field, he decided to follow them. Fortunately, they led him to a proper road which he recognized from his numerous trips into the Virgin Islands National Park over the years working for the Senator. Despite the heat and lack of water, he continued his now single-minded journey throughout the afternoon, stopping to rest whenever he felt he could go no further. The road was eerily deserted, being a dead end a few miles on. The few vehicles that he heard coming allowed him to hide before they saw him, for he had no wish to be discovered now.

His destination was the home of an old friend, Desmond Bailey, who lived, or at least used to live, in Coral Bay. They had not seen each other for several years, but the old man was an eccentric ex-cruising sailor who had settled in town after his cruising days were over. Unless he had died in the meantime, unfortunately a distinct possibility, Horst felt he was still there, and would help if asked.

He reached the outskirts of Coral Bay just after nightfall, and slowly made his way, by a circuitous route, and avoiding anyone he saw, to the home of his friend. It was well after nine when he finally knocked on the front door, which was answered after an interminable amount of time, by his frail friend, Desmond.

"As I live and breathe, Horst Keller, my old friend," the old man could barely believe his eyes, but suddenly noticed the leg brace and the crude crutch which kept Horst barely standing at his doorstep. He cried out in alarm, "but what happened to you? Are you all right?"

"Wa… water!" Horst managed to get out before falling at the door, thoroughly dehydrated and utterly spent. He dragged himself into the room and collapsed on the floor, while Desmond rushed to the 'fridge and came back with several bottles of water, one of which he opened on the way back. Horst weakly grabbed the opened bottle and drank deeply in several great gulps, his mind telling him that this was better than the finest whiskey he had ever had. He finished the second bottle more slowly, but with the same enthusiasm as before, until he finally found the strength to drag himself onto the couch, aided by Desmond.

"Is Doc Ramsey still around?" inquired Horst.

"Yes, he is. If you are OK, I will go and fetch him. What should I tell him is wrong with you?"

"Dehydration, dislocated shoulder and wrenched knee, and tell him to be discrete, I don't want anyone to know that I am here, understand?" Horst looked Desmond right in the eyes as he spoke, making sure the old man knew that, as in times past, this meeting was not strictly on the up-and-up, and needed to be kept quiet.

The old man nodded once, stood and turned, and hurried out the front door. Horst, who was already feeling a little better and becoming more aware of his surroundings, noticed that the TV was on, with the sound muted. A serious looking, but quite attractive young lady was reading the news, the caption reading 'Survivor Sought'. He toggled on the sound with the remote and heard. "This morning, a combined police and air/sea rescue chase across the international border from the BVIs to St. John failed to find any sign of the man police are seeking in connection with the gruesome strangulation death of a young woman in Tortola. The man is identified as Horst Keller, also known as Anton Kohl, and this is his photo," Anton's passport photo flashed onto the screen. "Police ask anyone with any knowledge of this man's whereabouts, to call them with the information." He turned the TV off, and thought, *'Damn, damn, damn, they've identified me already. They are a lot quicker off the mark than they used to be.'*

Horst jumped when the front door was suddenly thrown open and two men quickly entered, but relaxed as soon as he saw their familiar faces.

"So, you bloody old pirate, what trouble have you gotten yourself into this time? The last time I saw you was, let me see, oh, yes, when you busted up old man Kelsey's bar." The man speaking was about Horst's size although he had gone a little to flab from the relaxed island living.

243

Unable to contain himself, Horst grinned and said, "Hi, Doc, good to see you, too. Even though I still maintain that I only busted up the people who were busting up the bar."

The Doc put down and opened his bag, and gave Horst a quick but thorough examination. Then, he sat back and announced his findings. "Dehydrated, without a doubt, but not too badly. Drink water and GatorAde until you start pissing, you'll be all right. Shoulder, you seem to have fixed that yourself; I see a little swelling, but if you just apply some ice to it, you'll be fine. As for the knee, you have wrenched it badly, but I can't find anything broken, so you might have gotten lucky. I'm going to put this air cast on it and give you pain meds and come and re-evaluate in the morning. You want to tell me what is going on, or should I guess?"

"Better for all concerned if you don't know, Doc."

"You *are* the subject of a manhunt, you know?" Doc Ramsey didn't like not knowing what was going on, especially since there was a good possibility that what he was doing was illegal, immoral or fattening.

"Yeah, I saw the news. I swear to both of you that I had nothing to do with any of this. So far, only you two know I'm here and I would like to keep it that way. There will be a big payday coming your way if you keep it our secret." Horst hated to lie to his friends, but he couldn't take the time or effort to explain to them his heartfelt obsession for Shannon. He almost couldn't explain it to himself.

Both men were nodding their heads, and Doc spoke for them both. "For old times' sake, we will do this for you, but the money would also come in handy for a pair of washed-up old sailors. Am I right, Desmond?"

"Yeah, Doc." Neither man was broke, and they were both living the life they had chosen, but Horst knew that a little nest egg would be appreciated.

Doc stood up, collected his bag and said as he walked out the door, "I'll see you in the morning. In the meantime, get some rest and stay off that leg."

Desmond fetched another bottle of water and two bottles of GatorAde and forced Horst to drink all of them, along with taking his pain meds. Desmond threw a frozen pizza into the oven, which they ate as they sat and talked about the good old days. Horst was not surprised to find himself famished, since he had not eaten all day. When he finally felt the urge to go, Horst hobbled to the bathroom, and then into the bedroom. He called good night to Desmond, who was already bunking down on the living room sofa, and then performed the second most important operation of the day, after surviving. From the buttoned front pocket of his cargo shorts, he extracted his carefully waterproofed cell phone, locked into a commercially available product that was a precaution most prudent sailors take when they venture out on the water, and with his fingers crossed, powered it up. With immense satisfaction he watched the start up screen actually start up, and after providing the password, scrolled quickly to the meticulously copied Swiss and Cayman Island account numbers and passwords. His heart beat a little faster when he saw that they were all intact. His list of contacts was also all there, and he now realized that, although battered, bruised and almost broken, at least for the moment, he was not out of the game just yet.

If he had been a religious man, he would have thanked God that he had had the foresight to deposit his laptop and other documentation into a safe deposit box at a small bank in Road Town, during one of his many excursions into town with Tammy. He reminded himself to get Desmond to collect it for him later.

It was with obvious relief that he turned off the phone, rewrapped it in the plastic, waterproofed bag and hid it under his pillow, then stripped off all his clothes. Although sweaty, sandy and salt encrusted, he was so exhausted that he decided to forgo a shower until morning and lay down between the sheets. He fell into a deep and dreamless sleep the second his head hit the pillow, and he didn't stir until ten a.m. the next morning.

Chapter 15

Chief Inspector Cavendish was on his cell phone to headquarters in Tortola, and on the radio talking to the gunboats and the helicopter at the same time. He was attempting to coordinate the search and gain information on the subject as quickly as possible, so that if a land search was called for, the necessary resources would be in place with the minimum of delay. He had already had a frustrating talk with his boss, the police commissioner, who, when informed that the person they were chasing was the same man who the U.S. State Department wanted to talk to in connection with the death of Senator Shamus O'Malley, had abruptly told him to find him and apprehend him immediately without offering any suggestions as to how this might be accomplished. His attempt to recruit the local police at Cruz Bay in St. John to start a search for the man had been equally frustrating; since the policeman on the desk seemed to think that he shouldn't be taking orders from a Brit and preferred to wait until orders came from his own headquarters. Even the fact that Horst was wanted by the U. S. State Department didn't move the man to action. *'Not all policemen are cut from the same cloth,'* thought Cavendish as he fumed over the delay. *'Nor do they have the same dedication, determination, or even ability to want to catch the criminals, the way I do'.*

His frustration was further enhanced at lunchtime when the helicopter reported that it was low on fuel and had to go to Charlotte Amalie to refuel. This slight delay of an hour or so had suddenly turned into an all afternoon delay since a report of a sinking vessel required the helicopter to fulfill its primary mission, that of air/sea rescue. The two gunboats were conducting a typical search pattern but had so far not turned up anything. Because of the dangerous reefs close to shore on this end of the island, they could not risk getting too close and therefore could not say for certain whether or not a body, or a fugitive, was hidden in the rocks close to shore. They were both moving in opposite directions along the shore, and away from the point where they assumed the man had fallen into the water for no one had seen him go overboard. The few clumps of seaweed and floating debris that were spotted and investigated from time to time were only adding to everyone's frustration.

Unable to pursue any other course without further information, Cavendish asked Shannon to walk him through the whole scenario again from the time Horst had appeared on 'Final Option' until the time they had arrived on the scene after Horst had gone overboard. This she did slowly and carefully, aware that the minutest detail might be the one that gave that vital clue that would lead to the apprehension of the criminal. She even gave as much detail as she could remember about Horst's island in the Grenadines, thinking perhaps that a physical description might be the clue as to where he might be hiding, if he was still alive. As Jack followed the Sunseeker on its slow cruise back to Tortola, 'Final Option's satellite phone started ringing. It was such an unusual ring tone and only occasional happening that for a few seconds, no one moved. Jack finally realized what it was and grabbed the receiver.

"Jack Elliott," he said into the instrument.

"Jack, this is Sean, in Ireland."

Seeing that Cavendish was off his cell phone for the moment, Jack reached over and put on the speaker for the sat-phone. "Hi, buddy. How's married life treating you?"

"Oh, just great. Katie is here with me. How is your life going?"

"Just fine, now. Why?"

"Because we are getting news reports over here that you have been arrested for murdering Shannon. What the hell is going on, Jack?"

"Oh, God. Sorry, Sean, but it's just that the media getting the story all wrong, again. Shannon is right here with me and she is just fine."

From beside him, Shannon spoke into the phone, "I'm fine, Sean. Thanks for your concern, but all I have is a bump on the head and a slight headache."

"Thank the stars for that. The reports had me so worried. I know the two of you and I know Jack wouldn't do that to you and I know you wouldn't let him."

"Sean, you're rambling," Jack said with a smile at Shannon.

"Yeah, I know. So tell me what happened?"

"It was Horst Keller. Somehow he survived the helicopter crash in the Bahamas, and wound up here in the British Virgin Islands. Apparently, he murdered a young woman who looked enough like Shannon to fool even me, left Shannon's passport and my wallet by the body and tried to frame me for the murder. He then kidnapped Shannon, again, and took her for a wild ride all over hell and creation, until we caught up with him and Shannon had the opportunity to kick his ass overboard at fifty miles per hour."

"Now who's rambling? But, congratulations, Shannon, I always told you that you could look after yourself. Anyway, I'm glad to see it all worked out."

"It's not over yet. We are still searching for Horst, or his body, and this time I'm not going to be sure whether he is dead or not until I see his body."

"Call your mother. She is bound to have heard about this and is probably worried sick."

"You are right, Sean. I promise I will call her. Thanks. We'll talk to you soon."

Cavendish's cell phone started ringing and Jack quickly signed off so the search could continue.

Jack placed a call back to the States and talked to both his parents, assuring them that his and Shannon's state of health was as good as could be expected under the circumstances.

It was early afternoon before the two yachts finally made it back to Road Harbour, and tied into their respective berths. Shannon was quickly escorted to the hospital, while Tommy organized a crew of dayworkers to check and clean the two boats. She was given a thorough exam at the insistence of Cavendish, who threatened severe reprisals on anyone who didn't cooperate. X-rays were taken and a cat scan was performed, and finally she was given a clean bill of health, some pain medication, and was sent home to recuperate.

At nightfall, back onboard 'Final Option', Cavendish reluctantly said good bye, with a promise to keep them updated on developments. Since the gunboats had come up empty and had been sent home, the truth was, that no one expected any further action, at least not until the next day. The Cruz Bay Police Department, who had finally agreed to carry out a search for the missing fugitive, would be starting that search in the morning. Jack and Shannon sat together in each other's arms at the flybridge table in total silence, an adult beverage before each of them, each organizing their own thoughts about what had happened.

They were about to leave for dinner at the marina restaurant, when the sat phone rang for the second time that day. Thinking it was Sean calling back again, Jack put it on speaker phone.

"Jack Elliott here."

"Jack, it's good to hear your voice again. This is Sam Katzman, in Monaco."

"Sam, it's so good to hear from you. How can I help you?" Jack automatically went into his stock broker mode whenever a former client called him, and Sam had been an exceptional client.

"No, Jack, this time it's what I can do for you. I know your plans for coming to Europe fell through last year, but are you planning to come this year?"

"That is what we are planning."

"Good, because I just happen to have a slip next to me for the Monaco Grand Prix, and I would love to have you come and use it. I had planned to have two yachts here, but my plans for the second yacht fell through, and, since it's already paid for, I would like you to have the spot, free of charge."

"Well, Sam. I appreciate you thinking of me, but those spots are like hen's teeth. You could probably make a tidy profit selling it to someone else."

"Yes, I could. But I want you to have it. Call it a bonus for all the profit you have made for me over all these years. I could send you a check but I thought a gift which is almost impossible to get would be more welcome, especially since I know how much you like Formula 1 racing."

"Sam, I can't tell you how happy this has made me feel. I accept, with good feelings from the bottom of my heart. When is the race?"

"May 26th. But the spot is open from May 20th until May 29th, over the Memorial Day weekend."

"All right, we will be there with bells on. Thanks, Sam."

"My pleasure. I'll email you later with the details. Good night to you."

"Goodnight, Sam." Jack and Sam hung up at the same time and Jack shook his fist in the air, his excitement somehow dissipating the events of the day. "Yes," he shouted.

"Guess we are going to Europe this year," observed Shannon sarcastically.

Horst woke suddenly, the sun bright in his eyes, wondering where he was. As he turned over in the bed, the twinge of pain from his knee brought reality crashing back at him. Fortunately, the air cast had absorbed most of the turning forces and only that first twinge was the result of his move. He lay still, but no sound came from within the house. Moving carefully, he crawled out of bed and put on his shorts and hobbled down the hall to the living room. He found no one there although the blanket and pillow were still on the couch, and moved to the kitchen. He opened the 'fridge, found it near empty, but grabbed a bottle of water.

Just as he closed the 'fridge, he heard the front door open, and he looked around desperately for a place to hide. He was still looking when Desmond walked in bearing an armload of groceries, which he placed on the table. "Oh, good, you're up. Doc said he'd be by around noontime and to wake you if you weren't up by then. Had to go to the grocery store, figured with that knee, you'd be staying a couple of weeks, and I had no supplies. Had to go to several different places, I didn't want to raise any suspicions that I was shopping for more than one person."

"Thanks for putting me up, Des. I'll make it up to you."

The old man just shrugged, and let it go at that.

"Could you go to the store for me this afternoon?"

"Sure."

"Obviously, I can't go out since my picture is plastered all over the news. But I need you to get me two pairs of shorts, a pair of jeans, underwear, boat shoes, two T-shirts, a button down shirt and a ball cap. Also get a light jacket, a cheap suitcase, a charger for an HTC 1, and a rechargeable shaver." He patted his back pocket, giving thanks for button down pockets, withdrew his wallet and handed Desmond a couple of still slightly damp hundred dollar bills.

"OK. If you want to put the groceries away, I'll go right now."

As soon as Desmond left, he put the groceries away, and then went through his wallet; sorting through the cash and credit cards for the ones he could no longer use. Except for the cash, there was not much left, but that was a situation he would remedy shortly. All the cards he had on him were in the name of Anton Kohl, and he knew the first time he used one, they would not only know he was alive, but have an idea of where he was. With all the outlet stores and restaurants in the Virgin Islands, security was tight and very sophisticated.

He moved to the living room, and switched on the TV, muting the sound for he didn't want anyone wondering why the TV was on while Desmond wasn't home. He saw the same news anchor from the night before on the screen and risked turning on the sound, but very low.

She informed him, "The search for the missing sailor, Anton Kohl, resumed this morning at first light, with air/sea rescue boats from both the British and the U.S. Virgin Islands taking part. A land search is also taking place and all persons are asked to give their cooperation and any information to the police officers taking part in this operation. Again here is the photo of the man police wish to question." His photo popped up on screen. "He goes by the name Anton Kohl, but might also be calling himself Horst Keller.

Police ask that if you see him, do not approach him but call the nearest police station. And now to international news....."

Horst felt depressed, but worse yet, he could feel the beginnings of the rage building inside him. He tried hard to suppress it but it was gaining the upper hand. He decided that work was the answer he was looking for, and he found pencil and paper and set to work with his cell phone. He again felt fortunate for the foresight he had had back in Florida, when he purchased this particular cell phone and set it up in an untraceable account.

His phone calls were all international. First, a call went to Miami in order to set up a new bank account; one which could not be traced back to him. The lady at the bank turned out to be very helpful when she was informed about the amount of money that was being transferred.

The next call went to the Cayman Islands, to a bank with numbered accounts, where he requesting the transfer of funds from one of the late Senator's numbered accounts to his new untraceable Florida bank account.

Then, another call to Florida, to a man who could and would, for a price, provide him with complete sets of papers, including passports, for four new identities. There would be one Swiss, one German, one Austrian and one U.S. and with all the ancillary documents to go with them. This was the same man who had provided the Anton Kohl identity. He already had several sets of pictures of Horst, including one with a beard, which is what he was instructed to use for two of the four new passports, all in different names which he had made up on the spur of the moment. The next call was to a different Cayman Islands bank transferring the agreed-upon amount to the man's provided account number.

He made another call to a different Miami number, engaging the services of a woman whose specialty was tracking down boats and ships for the fraud department of a worldwide maritime insurance company. He gave her the name, hailing port and registration number of 'Final Option', its current location, and told her to track Jack's boat wherever it went.

His final call was to an old friend who was given the number of Horst's new Miami account and instructed to withdraw three bundles of one hundred thousand dollars each and the addresses of where to mail them. The man worked for a ten percent fee, so he was well compensated for a day's work.

Feeling satisfied with his accomplishments, he was just finishing up when Desmond returned with his purchases. Horst was very pleased with the chosen clothes, for Desmond had used common sense in his choices. There were dark and light pairs of khaki shorts, nicely cut blue jeans, a flamboyant T-shirt and a very subdued one, a light blue, classic cut, short sleeve button down shirt, and a dark blue waterproof jacket with a built in hood. A grey baseball cap completed his new wardrobe and everything fit into the light grey suitcase with room to spare. Horst even noticed that Desmond had bought, not a brand new suitcase, but a slightly battered one from a pawn shop. "Less conspicuous," he said. Horst unpacked and plugged his phone into the outlet with his new charger, but decided against shaving.

At Desmond's suggestion, they each had three fingers of Jameson's over ice and settled down to reminisce about days gone by. Despite the dull, throbbing pain in his knee, Horst felt confident about his ability to slip through the cordon laid down by the law, and to continue as he always had, looking out for number one. He also savored the thought that, with his new identities, and his ability to track 'Final Option' anywhere she went, and with the infusion of plenty of cash from the Senator's numbered accounts, he might yet extract his retribution on Jack and finally have his way with Shannon, with or without her consent or approval.

This was, after all, the second time that Jack had managed to thwart his plans, and Horst was determined that it wouldn't happen a third time.

Chapter 16

All morning of the following day, Jack also spent his time on the phone calling internationally. He used his satellite phone, mainly because it was more reliable than his cell, but also because it was encrypted.

His first call was to Sean and Katie in Ireland, where he caught them just finishing lunch.

"Morning, Sean, it's Jack. Oh, wait, I guess it's afternoon over there."

"Hi, Jack. Yes, we've just finished lunch. What's up?"

"How's the honeymoon going?"

"We are having a ball. If I had known that Europe was going to be this much fun, I'd have come years ago. But I have to tell you, I'm rather looking forward to going home, and so is Katie."

"Would you and Katie be able to meet us at the boat on the New River in four days' time?"

"Sure, we can do that. But why?"

"Shannon and I will probably be taking the boat to the Mediterranean this summer, and I would like to get all our friends together in one place to explain exactly what happened to us here in Tortola, so there are no misunderstandings."

"Sounds like a great idea to me; Birdman and Moses coming, too?"

"Yes, of course. If it hadn't been for Birdman's helicopter and the diary Moses held on to, we might not have found anything at all. Of course, Capt'n Pete, Courtland and Janine will probably be there; I haven't talked to them yet; and I want to invite Charlie Palmer."

"I agree; they are all our friends."

257

"Anyway, I'll leave you to make your own arrangements, just be at the boat in four days' time, okay?"

"We'll be there."

Jack's second call was to Capt'n Pete in Florida, who was just starting his breakfast aboard his newly acquired yacht, the old 'Shillelagh', now renamed 'Triumph', which the old man planned to charter out to various affluent parties. After the usual pleasantries, Jack asked Capt'n Pete to join them on the boat, four days hence. The answer was an enthusiastic, "Yes, I'll be there." Although the Capt'n was not much for TV or the radio, he nonetheless had heard the news reports of Shannon's murder and Jack's arrest for the crime. He told them that he was looking forward to hearing all about it.

Jack's next call was to Courtland, and he was pleasantly surprised to find that Janine was also there for he had interrupted their morning workout at the gym. They were pleased to hear from him but he sensed a slight hesitancy in their voices, due, he supposed, to the news reports which he imagined they had heard. With Shannon also on the line, he quickly reassured them that the media had gotten the story wrong again, as they so often did. Shannon's was the calming voice that convinced them that everything was all right.

Once the atmosphere had settled, they listened carefully to Jack's plan and readily agreed to be at the boat in four days. The mood was much lighter when they finally finished their conversation.

Jack then called Birdman. He was pleased to find that he and Moses were out in their hangar behind the new house Birdman had purchased at an air park/residential community in far western Palm Beach County, and they had been busy preflighting Birdman's Rotorway Exec 162 helicopter for a hop over to Marco Island. Both had heard and discounted the sensationalized news reports of the incident in the British Virgin Islands, but were glad to get confirmation of their disdain for the local news outlets. They both happily agreed to be at the boat four days later, and looked forward to seeing Jack and Shannon, as well as the rest of the crew.

The next call went to C. Bryant Palmer, who was already going over briefs for an upcoming meeting, but when informed about who was calling, was more than happy to take their call. Of all the people Jack had spoken to that morning, Charlie was the only one who was privy to the full story of the incident, having been kept up to date by the BVI police of the outcome, which was still somewhat up in the air. The searchers had still not found Horst Keller, either alive or any evidence of his body, and everyone was at a loss about how to proceed from this point. When informed about the plan to meet at the boat, Charlie quickly checked his calendar, and informed them that, unless WWIII started, he would be able to attend. Before hanging up, he expressed his relief that both of them had come out of this sticky situation intact in mind, body and spirit.

Jack and Shannon again spoke to Jack's mother and father via speaker phone, reassuring them that they were both OK and that they were preparing to come home. They just had to tie up a few loose ends before leaving in the morning.

Jack's final call of the morning was to the Ft. Lauderdale dockmaster, reserving the slip they were used to on the New River for the boat. Since Jack had been to that slip many times before with the boat, and he knew the dockmaster very well, he was assured that the slip would be waiting for him in four days' time.

Shannon and Jack went to lunch at the marina restaurant, which they had learned to enjoy due to its diversity of fare and the friendly staff. Once more the lunch was delicious and filling, and, being stuffed to the gills, they walked slowly over to the police station, basking in the sunlight along the way.

Almost before they asked, they were being hustled into the office of Chief Inspector Ian Cavendish, who rose and greeted them warmly, especially Shannon, who got a hug.

"I am so glad to see you both, looking so fit and healthy. Come in and sit down." He seemed to genuinely appreciate their arrival. "I am afraid that I don't have any good news for you. The man seems to have vanished off the face of the planet." Ian walked back around the desk and sat down in his chair.

Jack's face showed a momentary flash of annoyance, quickly replaced with a mask of inevitable acceptance. "If he is still alive, he has had plenty of time now to hunker down in one of his friends' houses, and I'm afraid we will never find him. He has been a captain in these waters for many years, and I'm sure he has hundreds, if not thousands, of places staked out that he could hide for as long as necessary. I hate to be cruel, but the best we can hope for is that the jump from the Sunseeker killed him outright, and we will never hear from him again." Jack shook his head, for he clearly didn't believe his own words, knowing the resilience that Horst had shown in the past. "One can only hope."

"I want you to know that we will not give up on this manhunt until we have a final resolution," said Cavendish. "You have proven to me that you two are the salt of the earth, the kind of people that would lay down your life for the other. You, Jack, had better marry her before she finds you wanting, and slips away."

"That will never happen." said Shannon defiantly. "I've sunk my hooks into him, and he's never getting away, no matter how hard he tries."

If it is possible to have a deeply worried look on your face while smiling broadly, that is the look Jack displayed as he gazed at Shannon, who displayed amusement at his consternation.

Turning back to the Inspector, Jack spoke sincerely, "Ian, in the short, troubled time I have known you, I have come to appreciate your dedication and compassion for the job you do. I want to say that it has been a pleasure to work with you and to know that you were sensitive enough to the situation, for you to work with me. Unfortunately, life calls and we have to leave. But we both wanted you to know that we appreciate the leeway you gave both of us to bring this event to a happy conclusion."

Shannon stood in a huff, "Oh, for God's sake, Jack, you sound like an insincere politician." She walked around the desk and gave Ian a hug around his neck and a kiss on his cheek, looked straight into his eyes, and said, "Thank you. For everything."

"What we really wanted to say is that we will be leaving in the morning, headed for home. We just wanted to thank you for all your help." Jack said. "And to let you know that if we come back we will be sure to look you up again."

"Thank you. I appreciate your consideration. I can only hope that it's under better conditions." Ian Cavendish, stiff upper lip and all that stuffy old school upbringing, could not help a single tear running down his face, which he made no attempt to wipe away.

Awkwardly, they made their way out of his office and the building feeling that they had just left a friend. Smart ass Jack said, "I think he's going to miss us."

"I think he's going to miss me; you, the jury is still out." She laughed at the way his face scrunched up.

They walked slowly back to the marina, and stopped by the dockmaster's office on their way to the boat. "Tommy, I want to thank you for all your help, especially in getting Shannon back to me. We couldn't have found her if it hadn't been for that GPS tracker you installed on your boats." Jack shook his hand and Shannon delivered a heartfelt kiss, and Tommy beamed at both of them. "Unfortunately, we'll have to be leaving in the morning, since we have a rendezvous at home. Can you bring the bill by the boat later?"

"Sure, and I hope you come back to us soon; we enjoy having nice people here." he said, meaning it.

As dawn broke the next morning, Jack made final preparations for their passage back to Ft. Lauderdale. A surprising number of people had shown up at the dock to see them off, and many willing hands helped slip the final lines from the bollards on the dock as Jack maneuvered the boat from its side deck with the wireless remote control. A sea of hands waved goodbye as the yacht quietly exited the marina and turned into the fairway. Jack and Shannon returned the farewell in kind.

"Despite what happened, I love this place, and I want to come back. Someday." said Shannon, wistfully.

"I know what you mean. I promise you we will come back." Jack slipped an arm around her waist, and she laid her head on his shoulder, both of them enjoying the magnificent vista opening up before them as the islands appeared one by one on the horizon from behind the encircling arms of the headlands on either side.

A security gunboat forced Jack to swing wide, away from a docking cruise ship, but it was only a minor diversion and soon they were clear of the harbor and accelerating westward toward Puerto Rico, the Turks and Caicos Islands, and, ultimately, home to Ft. Lauderdale.

Four days later, 'Final Option' and its crew cruised slowly and serenely up the New River, and as they passed the Third Avenue Bridge, Jack was pleased to see all their friends were on the dock waiting to welcome them home. Many willing hands helped to tie the boat up, and then they all swarmed aboard.

Jack and Shannon broke out the well-deserved bottles of champagne, and all night they celebrated on the flybridge. The two of them alternated turns in their telling of the tale of their narrow escape at the hands of Horst Keller. Their story was met with disbelief and much head-shaking. Since all these friends had also been present at the Christmas Eve party, it was Jack's unpleasant duty to inform them of Horst's involvement in Rain's murder. He also made a mental note to call Stephan about Rain's murder, since, despite their differences, they had both loved the woman at one point in time.

"What now?" Shannon asked, sitting together during a quiet moment in the celebrations.

Jack thought for only a second, and then said, "Since we seem to have survived the recent danger to our life and limb, I propose that, because all our friends are all together here and now, we get married right away, and then go on our honeymoon cruise of the Meditteranean."

"OK, Jack, but just one question; why all of a sudden, such short notice?"

"Because I have been thinking about what Ian said; that I had better snare you before you get away."

"You don't have to worry about that because I am not going anywhere without you, silly. You should know that by now. But, now, about the arrangements…"

If you enjoyed this book,
and I sincerely hope you did,
below is an excerpt taken from
the third book in the trilogy.

Enjoy

The
Monaco
Conspiracy

{Book 3 of the Final Option Trilogy}

A
MEDITERRANEAN
MURDER/MYSTERY

Chapter 1

May 25th, Monaco, the day before the race.

"I was only twelve years old when my older brother disappeared, simply vanished without a trace, gone. One day he was there, the next day he was not, and for ten years it was as if he were dead to me." Erin Brady paused briefly for dramatic effect, mild anger and regret blazing in her own eyes while she was simultaneously scanning the downcast eyes of the men and women who were sharing the main salon with her. She was somewhat sarcastically answering the innocent inquiry that her boss and mentor, Sam Katzman, had put to her only moments before. In an effort to keep the conversation humming along, he had asked her what the saddest moment in her life had been and was not really prepared for the answer he got. They were all seated in the main salon of Sam's 250 foot luxury yacht, 'Utopia', and Erin was a picture of understated elegance, her cream slacks and gold sandals topped with a white and red geometric patterned silk blouse specifically designed to contrast with her short dark hair and large bright eyes. Her naturally pale Irish skin had been dusted lightly with the rays of Mediterranean sunlight giving it a golden glow and she looked more like an haute couture model than the race car driver she was. Her older brother, Sean Brady, was seated in the salon next to Katie, who was his bride of just over four months. After an absence of ten years, he had been and continued to be the subject of Erin's half-hearted scorn ever since their reunion, which had occurred that past December. It had not been a happy reunion due to the unhappy and strained circumstances. Their father, a rather prominent figure in the Irish Underground, had been gunned down and left to die on a Dublin street by persons unknown, and Sean had returned to Ireland from America to find out who and why.

"I questioned everyone I could find about where he had gone, but nobody, not even my own family, could or would give me any information about where to find him." She paused to gather her thoughts. "Perhaps they thought that I was not old enough to understand, or not wise enough to keep quiet about what really occurred the night before he disappeared. All I knew was that for ten years, my brother, my confidant, my protector, my security blanket, my shoulder to cry on, was not there for me, and nobody, not my father, not my sister, nor my oldest brother, would tell me why. They all just said that Sean *had* to leave and would be back some day." Sean had, in fact, been accused of a crime committed by his cousin and, instead of staying to explain and sending his cousin to prison, he had been spirited out of Ireland by his family until such time as the statute of limitations ran out.

There was total silence in the room as they all sat shuffling their feet, looking around the lounge and out the windows unsure of what to say or do. The stewardess, who had just entered the salon bearing a fresh round of drinks, stopped suddenly as if she had run into a brick wall, and sensing the tension in the atmosphere, quietly retraced her steps, backwards. Sean looked around furtively at his wife and his friends, Jack and Shannon Elliott, and Sam Katzman, trying without success to gain their support. He finally cleared his throat noisily and, with eyes locked onto his little sister's, mumbled, "Erin, I am truly sorry about the trauma you had to go through all those years, and I promise to sit down and explain everything to you, but this is not the time or

267

place. You really should be concentrating on the job you have to do tomorrow, instead of bringing up something from the past that none of us can justify or rectify without a lot of soul searching."

She looked lovingly at him, the slight anger in her eyes already dissipating, sighed and shook her head lightly before answering, "I know, Sean, and I admit that in a lot of ways your absence has made all the difference as to who and what I am today, compared to the way I could have turned out. I really do believe that I am a much stronger person because I had to grow up without you constantly looking out and standing up for me as you did when I was young. I had to learn to make my own decisions and stand up for myself despite all the opposition I seemed to attract. I wouldn't be here today, doing the things I've come to cherish, if I hadn't had the strength you showed me that I had."

Sean, resplendent in his rented tuxedo, or 'penguin suit' as he referred to it, inclined his head in acknowledgement to the concession she had made due to the circumstances and, once again, admired the grown up woman she had become in his absence. The decisions she had made in her teen years had, indeed, led her to this moment in time, because it was her own vision and decisions as to what to do to get to where she wanted to be that had guided her to this spot. Ten years earlier, while brooding about her lost brother, Erin had retreated into a world of her own, excluding everyone including those who had tried to console or comfort her. She had learned to endure being by herself most of the time, being self sufficient and participating in solitary pastimes which, fortunately in retrospect, had included a lot of mind numbing television. It was only by chance that a local Go-kart race had been televised for the domestic market, and by the time it was over, it had captured her imagination beyond words. She had asked, demanded, cajoled, threatened, and cried her eyes out until her father, hoping to find some peace and quiet, had finally bought her a second hand kart and told her to go racing. Her oldest brother, Dylan, had been assigned by her father to look after her to ensure that she wasn't hurt doing what he considered, at first, a foolish dream.

Despite the fact that the kart was a piece of crap and probably the slowest on the track, Erin's innate driving style and her pent up aggressiveness made her a strong competitor and almost from the very beginning she was up with the leaders. Many of her competitors called her style of driving suicidal, verging on insanity, and sometimes she did seem to be overly aggressive, but several wins in the latter part of her first season allowed her to take the next step up the ladder and led to an invitation to race in Formula Ford the next season, and once again, her father had to shell out more money. This time a considerable amount of money, but after seeing the results she had managed to achieve with sub standard equipment, he didn't even argue that fiercely about how much she was costing him. As a matter of fact, although he would have denied it to her face, he even started speaking about her and her successes to his mates at the pub with undisguised pride. Bubbling over with enthusiasm, she personally went out and campaigned for sponsorship and managed to pick up a couple of local sponsors that season, in which she won several races. She surprised her sponsors, and even herself when she finished up in third place overall at the end of the season. From that moment on, she never looked back, and there was never any question about what she was going to do with her life. She was a race car driver, and she couldn't have been happier. It was at that point in time that she began her daily routine of several hours in the gym followed by track work until the slightly pudgy body that she had endured all her life had been transformed into the whip cord strong and shapely body that Jack, amongst many others, so much admired.

Her second season in Formula Ford was a charm, an unbelievable dream come true. Utilizing all the techniques she had learned from her previous seasons and all of her considerable feminine wiles, which included a lot of luck plus a little trickery, she managed to win all but two races, in both of which she placed second. This accomplishment earned her not only the first place trophy, and considerable prize money, but led to a contract to race in Formula Two the following year. It was a huge step up for her career, even if it was for one of the smaller, less financially secure teams, for it enabled her to be noticed by the people who mattered.

Her F2 rookie season was spectacular, with a second place in her first race and wins in her second, fourth and fifth races. Naturally, the disbelief of her fellow drivers that a rookie, and a girl at that, could be so dominating stung them a lot. When she was approached, surreptitiously, halfway through the season, by Sam Katzman of Midland Racing with a substantially more lucrative contract for the following season, she eagerly accepted. One of the main reasons for her decision was that the Midland Ferrari was a substantially better developed car, which featured a down-graded Formula One engine from the previous year. Besides the fact that the car's aggressive aerodynamic profile made it seem to be driving at over a hundred miles an hour whilst standing still, its black with gold pin striping, reminiscent of the John Player Special Formula One cars of a bygone era, made it one of the racing cars that the cameras always seemed to focus their lenses upon.

Taking to that remarkably faster Ferrari from Midland Racing like a fish to water, her first season with her new team was spectacular. That year she won every race but one, some by considerable margins. The only one she didn't win was the one in which she was taken completely out of the race by a fellow competitor's overly aggressive rookie mistake. Attempting to gain a position by passing Erin, he left his braking way too late for the corner and exited the track sideways, unfortunately taking Erin with him. Neither driver was hurt, but Erin learned a most valuable lesson. Sometimes shit happens, and you can't do a thing about it, except to accept it and move on. After the end of season trophy ceremony, in which she naturally walked away with first place, Sam offered Erin the choice of staying in Formula Two for the next season or accepting the Formula One test driver's spot, with the promise to allow her to race one F1 race during the year as circumstances allowed. She was completely surprised by this offer but, on the spot she gratefully accepted this unique chance to advance from the back up F2 racing program to the pinnacle of motor sport, even if it was only as a test driver, and, quitting school, she moved, lock, stock and barrel, to Silverstone in England, where the company was headquartered. She promised herself that she would not rest on her laurels and was determined to race in Formula One someday. Sam turned out to be a man of his word, and had always meant to keep his promise to Erin, regardless, but not necessarily in the way that things finally worked out.

The Monaco Grand Prix was the ultimate spectacle of Formula One race tracks, the one race every driver wanted to win, the pinnacle of achievement in many minds, and the next day, due to a fortunate or unfortunate, depending on one's point of view, evolution of circumstances, Erin Brady, little sister of Sean Brady, would be in the fifth starting spot in her first Formula One race in her Midland Ferrari F1 racing car.

"Naturally, none of us would be here today if Sam hadn't been at the Silverstone race track the very day I was debuting in Formula Two, and if he hadn't been impressed with my driving style. It does take a fortunate set of circumstances sometimes, don't you agree?" As Erin spoke, Sam Katzman's head was bobbing up and down, making him look to all those present like an oversized bobblehead. Sam was the team principal for the Midland Formula One racing team and the person responsible for courting, recruiting and training Erin in attaining her position as the number two driver on the team. He was extremely proud of his achievement in bringing this young lady to this point in her career and looked forward to working with her toward even greater heights. Unfortunately, the number one driver, Carlos Sierra, had been involved in an off track motorcycle accident and had broken his leg, elevating the number two driver, Klaus Von Schauben, to the number one spot which allowed Erin, the team's test driver, to slip into the number two spot behind him.

Much to Sam's and Klaus' surprise, and everyone else's delight, Erin had taken to the steeply climbing, twisting and extremely dangerous Monaco course like a seasoned veteran. Relying on the experience she had gained competing on the course in the much lower horse power Formula Two car, and steering her F1 race car throughout practice and qualifying with an excessive amount of nerve and precision, she cemented down the fifth starting spot on the grid, three spots ahead of Klaus. He, of course, said it was because she had the better car, forgetting that she was now driving the same car that he had been complaining about all season long as being abysmally down on power.

Carlos, still in traction in the hospital, and Klaus, who had his own special pre-race regimen, were not present on the boat. If they had been, they might have noticed the pride and attention Sam had been lavishing all evening on Erin, perhaps even wondering just who was the number one driver for the team and speculating on the question of whether or not there was something more going on besides the enthusiasm of the owner of the team for his best driver. One might have thought that something suspicious was happening behind the scenes, except for the fact that Mrs. Sam Katzman, his wife, Sonia, occupied a special place in Sam's heart.

She was an exceptionally gifted singer, a business savvy, successful and beautiful woman who doted on her husband and to whom Sam returned those feelings tenfold. She was also very confidant of her position, and regarded Erin with a sense of pride and perhaps, a little envy, but was a good friend and whole hearted supporter of Erin's budding career with her husband's racing team.

The stewardess, who had been hovering just outside the doorway to the salon sensed that the atmosphere had lightened somewhat, and appeared once again bearing the tray of drinks which she placed on the coffee table before them. With a questioning glance at Sam, who smiled at her and shook his head, she withdrew. Everyone helped themselves to their drinks, although Erin's was only ginger ale since she was racing the next day, and Sam stood and proposed a toast. "Here's to our success tomorrow, for Erin, for the team, and for a safe and exciting race. May we all get everything our hearts desire."

Everyone enthusiastically drank to that.

After the toast, they all broke up into individual groups, with Sean trying to explain to Katie the difficulties and finer points of racing Formula One cars on the Monaco road course. Although he was not an ardent fan of the sport, and despite the fact that his little sister was in fact a race car driver, he understood the intricacies of racing a little better than did Katie. Jack found himself greatly amused when he realized that much of the information that Sean was passing on was what he had heard from Jack the day before, when they had first learned that Erin would be racing. Jack and Shannon, both being diehard F1 fans, babbled on excitedly at the prospect of tomorrow's race. It was to be the first live F1 race they had attended, their enthusiasm coming from all the races they had watched either alone or together on TV. For some unfathomable reason, they had both enthusiastically followed the sport and watched the races on TV, even before they had met and married. Shannon especially was at a loss to explain why she had such an enthusiasm for F1 racing, since most sports on TV bored her to tears.

Erin and Sam sat together on the couch discussing strategies for the upcoming race, and Jack was pleased to see that Erin had as much input into the conversation as Sam did, and that she was apparently as strong a part of the planning of the race as she was of the execution. They were both extremely animated and obviously excited about their prospects in the next day's race. Erin's body language was telling Jack that she was already driving the course in her mind.

At the sound of the salon's rear doors opening, they all turned toward the aft deck where Sonia Katzman, who had been with friends at the world famous Casino de Monte Carlo, finally made a grand entrance with several of her good friends and a multitude of hangers-on trailing along behind her, all anxious to see the interior of the fabulous yacht.

Sam, upon seeing his wife, jumped up and rushed to her side, glancing surreptitiously at the Rolex Submariner positioned prominently on his wrist. "You are early, my darling. I would have thought you would be back much later than this." He gave her a peck on the cheek, so as not to spoil her make-up.

"I ran out of money," she said, her face serious.

A startled look came over the multi-billionaire's face, and he stepped back, suddenly at a total loss for words. Had he been a cartoon character, there would have been a bright red question mark above his head. Then, all of a sudden realizing he had been taken for a ride, he grinned mischievously.

"Just kidding," she said, laughing, as she grabbed his arms and pulled him in for a proper kiss. She folded into his arms in a way that left no doubt about their feelings for each other.

The salon quickly filled with the people from Sonia's entourage, and soon introductions were being made all around. It seemed that Sonia had somehow managed to gather together quite a sizeable collection of the rich and famous during her time ashore. Jack noted with amusement the contrast created by the arriving guests, who were all dressed up in their tuxedos and elaborate evening gowns from their casino visit, but who were walking around in their bare or stocking clad feet due to the bright white carpet in the luxuriously appointed main salon of Sam's yacht. There was even one gentleman wearing a top hat, who reminded Jack of a singer from Jacksonville, Florida. 'Hell,' he thought, 'it might even be him. After all, anything is possible in Monaco.' Jack surprised himself by suddenly realizing that, although he was not a fan of the gossip magazines or shows, he nevertheless recognized quite a few of the people in Sonia's entourage. Even one or two of whom he admired.

The interior crewmembers of the yacht were kept quite busy supplying the guests with their desired drinks, and soon all were finding places upon which to perch on the tanned leather lounges, numerous armchairs, club seats and bar stools situated at the ultra modern stainless steel and glass bar. Splashes of bright primary colors in the cushions and a couple of priceless artworks on the walls competed for their attention along with the muted 65 inch flatscreen TV which was currently showing Erin's Formula Two victories from the year before.

One couple in particular caught Jack's eye, suddenly realizing that they were an actor and an actress, both of whom were starring together in the latest, greatest blockbuster movie, and, glancing around, he saw that Sean had also noticed them.

The couple moved with a certain haughtiness toward Erin, who was standing alone since Sam's departure in order to greet his wife, and Jack was close enough to distinctly hear the twenty something actor sneeringly remark to Erin, "So you're that *girl* who thinks she can win a Formula One race? Really? Especially this one? Are you serious? You don't really look good enough to me. Besides, everyone knows that F1 racing is only for men."

Sean quickly started to move forward, an ugly look clouding his face, but was restrained gently by Jack and together they moved closer, trying to be unobtrusive. "Don't worry about Erin. That young woman can look after herself," whispered Jack to Sean. A quick, but shallow smile and a nod of the head from Sean acknowledged that Jack was correct in his assessment.

Erin turned to face her tormentor and just looked amused. Apparently she had heard all this before, probably ever since she had started racing. She looked the unpleasant actor right in his eyes, and said, "Hey, don't I know you. Todd something-or-other, right? Say, have you ever considered taken acting lessons? From the look of your latest effort, you definitely need to!"

People in the immediate area stopped their conversations abruptly and looked at the two antagonists, for that is what they had turned into in the first few seconds of their conversation. Todd's mouth dropped open and he stammered, "Wha ... wha ... what do mean? Haven't you seen the latest box office figures? Don't you know how much money I am making?"

Erin forced herself not to laugh out loud, but barely managed to stifle herself. "No, I don't, and I don't really care. And you know why? I'll tell you. It's because, just like serious racing, serious acting is not about the money. It's all about attempting to achieve perfection in the performance, the skills, the art, the feeling, that's what makes people appreciate what an artist does, and, unfortunately, I'm afraid your skills fall way short."

"You can't talk to me that way, you little ... bimbo!"

"Really? Seems to me I just did." The smile on Erin's face was a vision to behold, and the crowd around her acknowledged her victory with applause. Todd, in total disgust that his scheme to embarrass Erin had gone so wrong, grabbed his young costar's hand and physically hauled her out of the salon and down the passerelle to the shore, with the look on the young woman's face being one of sheer embarrassment and abject apology.

As the uproar and laughter finally died down, Erin stretched to her full height, hands together and arms stretching way above her head, and announced to all and sundry, "Well, I'm tired and I do have a race tomorrow, so I'm going to bed. I am more than pleased to have met all of you. Thank you all for a pleasant evening and please remember to cheer me on tomorrow." She then turned and headed forward to the stairs and gracefully exited below deck to her cabin, kindly provided to her by Sam and Sonia, her two biggest fans. While Klaus also had a cabin on the boat reserved for his use, he had decided to stay ashore with friends. He was barely able to suppress the feelings of displeasure that he had with Erin's unexpected success so far since it affected negatively his position on the team, and therefore he had chosen to remain at arm's length, offering neither help nor hindrance to his suddenly extremely popular teammate.

Shortly thereafter, Sean, Katie, Jack and Shannon made their round of good nights to old and new friends and retired to the 'Final Option', Jack's 70 foot Neptunus, moored Med style, stern to the wharf, right next to Sam Katzman's 250 foot Lurssen, 'Utopia'. Jack's boat looked like a tender for the 'Utopia', but, despite her size, she had easily borne her crew, consisting of Sean, Katie, Jack, Shannon and their two paid crewmembers, Paul and Tracie, safely and comfortably across the Atlantic Ocean on her own bottom, which was no small feat.

The party continued in a somewhat subdued fashion for another couple of hours until finally common sense prevailed.

When the guests came to the realization that they had a race to attend the next day, they took their leave of their hosts.

Hidden in the shadow of a portable generator, which had been set up to power one of the many jumbotron TV screens that had been located around the racetrack, a pair of malevolent eyes watched as the last of the stragglers left the 'Utopia'. Unnoticed by anyone, those same eyes had watched Sean and Jack and their wives walk from 'Utopia' to 'Final Option' a few hours earlier with a deep seated hatred of the two couples. Even then the rage had been setting in, and now it was in full bloom. The eyes watched with great interest, and not a little regret, as two hulking guards, ex-military men without a doubt, stationed themselves in front of the gangplanks leading to both boats, and within sight of one another, so those who were ensconced within the vessels were assured of a good night's sleep.

Deciding that discretion really was the better part of valor, and that nothing further could be accomplished, Horst allowed the rage to slowly subside and, slinking from his hiding spot, made his way back to his small, comfortable but way overpriced hotel room a little way inland up high upon the mountain behind the harbor.

He had already discovered that, these days, it was impossible to sabotage a race car due to the almost maniacal security measures in place. The extreme scrutiny against cheating from the F1 officials worked against his original plan to extract revenge on his avowed enemies by causing Erin's race car to crash. It was also no longer as easy to manipulate officials or mechanics as it had been in the old days in the States. The plan that his friend Hassan had laid out for him the week before had better work, for he had no idea how long his targets would remain in Monaco after the race, nor where they planned to go afterwards. In fact, it was only by a stroke of *good* luck, for a change, on top of the rest of his thoughtful planning, that he had been able to locate them in the first place.

After four stiff drinks back in his hotel room, he decided that he had better get some sleep if he was to prevail. He acknowledged that he had been burning the candle at both ends for far too long and some rest would definitely be beneficial. Maybe if Hassan had a little good luck tomorrow, and the man's plans worked out as well as they hoped, it would provide the final solution he was looking for to achieve his goal, the elimination of what he considered to be his worst enemies.

Made in the USA
Columbia, SC
25 August 2017